Assassination Education

David Witt

Fat Chance Publishing

ASSASSINATION EDUCATION

ISBN 978-1-7342023-8-0

FIRST EDITION

Cover Design by Matt Witt

Attributions:

brusheezy.com

Printed in the United States of America

To Karen, my awesome and lovely wife without who's unending support this novel would not have been possible. From reading rough drafts to suggesting ways to publicize my work, she was an important part of bringing this book to market. That's been more important than ever in 2020 and 2021! She has been a constant source of encouragement throughout our life journey together, and I can't wait for our next adventure!

Special thanks to the Thursday writer's group who welcomed me with open arms and honest feedback. You offered me an education and a sense of community for which I am grateful. I am so glad we went online and continued in a virtual format in the face of the pandemic. I'm really happy we were able to resume live meetings in the second half of 2021.

I thank Morgan Williams for his perspective and editing. I admire his ability to take a good scene and point out ways that I can make it better.

I also thank Denise Craycraft for her perspective and editing. She has an incredible eye for detail and an understanding of characters that makes my work shine.

Sincere thanks go to Matt Witt, my multitalented son, who created the cover for this book. Even as a child, he had an eye for color and design, and it was a special pleasure to see him take my input and create something far beyond what I imagined.

Assassination Education

Chapter One

The dream always begins with Julie Simmons standing from the table at Luigi's, an Italian restaurant with stone archways and red and white checked tablecloths on the upper east side of Manhattan. She's saying goodbye to friends, Tilden and Trish Rogers. "Too bad Jason's in L.A. pitching his show, he really wanted to be here. Let's do this again soon."

One year ago, Jason Simmons missed this night of conversation, pasta and wine with his wife and their closest friends. He was in California trying to sell his idea to executives of the SPLAT TV network. He wasn't part of the night of banter and camaraderie in real life, but his mind crafted a vision of the entire evening fabricated from conversations, remembrances, police reports and video recordings. Jason knows these specific details because Trish told him the story at Julie's wake. He knew exactly how the night had gone, and tonight he played this reconstructed version in his dream…again.

Trish's voice turns playfully sarcastic. "Oh, so Hollywood royalty wants to be seen slumming with us commoners?"

"It's good for our image to have some 'regular' friends." Julie makes air quotes as she replies.

They giggle and give each other a best friend hug. Julie whispers into Trish's ear. "I love you guys."

Trish answered in kind and the bestie embrace ends. The cameras of Jason's dream follow Julie as she heads for the door, pausing for an eternal final wave before she exits.

The next scene is a long shot of Julie walking toward a fixed camera. The steady mist hanging in the damp evening air deposits droplets on the lens, giving the light from the softly glowing street lamps an added eerie dimension. Carefree step after carefree step, she makes her way up the street, unknowingly closing the distance between her and the imaginary camera recording each and every footfall. Even in this nightmare he appreciates the cinematography.

She keeps her head down as she walks with her vintage red umbrella pulled low, and doesn't see the two black-clad-hooded figures now trailing behind. Their strides are longer and taken at a more determined pace. One is tall and seems athletic, with a swagger in his gait, while the other is shorter and marches like the pistons in an unstoppable machine. Jason knows this because police release grainy images captured by a security camera on a hardware store across the street. The evening news programs show the pictures along with a tip-line number. None of the calls result in a firm lead.

Every fateful step Julie takes brings her closer and closer to the lens of Jason's dream camera, and to the scene of the crime. She takes one final step, then glances up with a smile on her face, unaware of the darkness that will engulf her only seconds later. Jason wished he didn't have this dream replaying nightly like some gothic TV drama, but because he does, he can pause the playback and savor this image of Julie's angelic visage. This is the best part, and while he can rewind to this section and watch it again, he is always eventually forced to hit 'Play' and advance the film to its haunting conclusion.

The camerawork in his dream now always shifts to a jump-cut style. First, the taller of the two figures grabs Julie's arm from behind, while the smaller one rips her purse away. Julie reacts in confusion as the camera spins around with her and she comes face to face with her attackers. "What the hell?"

The editing cuts to a close-up, and her expression changes from confusion to fear. The perilousness of her situation is captured in her suddenly wide eyes. She speaks with a quiver in her voice. "Just…just take the purse. Take it all…"

Next, the camera switches perspectives, peering over Julie's shoulder into the hooded shadow obscuring her attacker's faces. The smaller of the two speaks in low, ominous tones. “Yeah, I’ll take the purse alright…and anything else I want.”

Julie is pulled closer to the void beneath the black hood. She screams. “Stop! Stop!” Her facial muscles tighten as panic seems to take control and her arms flail wildly against her attacker. For a brief moment one of her hands breaks free of the evil gripping her, and swings wildly. The sound effect of a sword slicing through the air, like in a video game, is included in Jason’s dream as her fingernails rake across the assailant’s cheek, drawing blood. Police would find skin cells under her nails, but there were no DNA matches in the database.

The taller attacker reacts to the yelp of his wounded accomplice by pulling a knife. A glint of light on the hilt is captured from a boom camera above. With deliberation, the attacker plunges the weapon down, deep into Julie’s chest. He repeats the act again and again with stabs to her neck and torso. Julie screams, “No!” over and over. Her one-word protests become a little lower and less audible each time the knife is driven into her body.

Spurts of blood gushing from severed arteries are captured by the ever-present dream camera, soaking her white silk blouse. It now zooms in for a close-up as her mouth continues to form the word ‘No’, but no sound escapes her lips. The focus of her eyes becomes a distant stare into nothingness, replacing the desperate tight look of terror.

The blade entered Julie’s body thirteen times and Jason is forced to watch each in excruciatingly clear HD, unable to move or utter anything other than grunts or groans. The medical examiner counted and measured each wound, using words like ‘deliberate’ and ‘vicious’ in his press release.

Finally, the attack stops, and the two figures release her limp body. Julie falls to the ground like a ragdoll in the spatters of blood. The final shot is at ground level, capturing her face in a vacant death stare as her oozing blood forms widening circular pools on the sidewalk. In the background, the two figures stroll away with her purse swinging lazily from the gloved hand of her shorter killer. The deadly duo gradually moves out of frame. Jason is always forced to watch the entire episode, paralyzed by the forces that replay the dream each night.

Until tonight, the nightmare ended here, as the playback fades to black. Jason is then shoved into a state of full wakefulness. His day begins and he sits on the edge of the bed alone in the final minutes of morning darkness. The horror of his dream has been numbed by countless repetitions, and increasing quantities of alcohol in the months since Julie's death, and he has had ever-increasing difficulty getting mentally prepared to face the new day. As the first shard of sunlight penetrates their dimly lit bedroom, he mentally tries to run through his schedule, pushing his visions of Julie's murder into the deepest recesses of his mind.

He's learned to accept this nightly ritual, along with his recurring headaches, as his personal hell, like Sisyphus pushing his boulder up the hill each night, only to have it roll back down each morning. But tonight, purgatory changes. Tonight, the playback doesn't fade to black. Tonight, the playback continues rolling into a new, never before witnessed scene.

This evening, Jason doesn't awaken in the final minutes of darkness before dawn. He remains locked in his mind's personal screening room as the dream rolls on. Instead of fading to black, the action continues to unfold as the camera slowly pushes in again on Julie's death stare. A few seconds elapse locked on her vacant gaze, then the corners of her mouth twitch, almost imperceptibly. A few more seconds pass, and the movements become unmistakable. Julie looks directly into the lens with dark eyes that have lost their shine.

Adrenaline enters Jason's bloodstream and his heart pounds, watching this new revelation. The camera pulls back from Julie's close-up, abruptly stopping when her waiflike body is in full frame. There's a pause for a beat, and then the very dead Julie begins to get up. As she stands, the camera rises with her. Again, the camera pushes in, focusing only on Julie's unblinking stare. Seconds pass until she speaks directly to Jason in a disconcertingly calm and sweet voice. “Don’t be afraid.”

Aware of his body tensing as he dreams, Jason remains frozen, immobilized and unable to speak…and he’s definitely afraid.

His dead wife speaks again. “I’m ready for my interview.”

Jason’s eyes fly open and he bolts upright in bed, gasping for air.

Chapter Two

Everyone has buttons and when they are pushed in certain sequences, predictable behaviors occur. Husbands and wives become skilled at decoding their spouse's closely guarded codes. In dysfunctional marriages, men and women push each other's buttons to gain an advantage when arguing over things like money. The same recognition of soft spots and vulnerabilities happens in business partnerships, and as in the best marriages, these buttons shouldn't be pushed…unless there's a really good reason.

****

"Hey, sleepyhead, you're never gonna guess who called and wants to be on our show." Anthony hinted as he leaned against a painted black steel support pillar near Jason's desk in their converted warehouse office.

Jason didn't glance up from his computer replaying a scene from their most recent episode. "I give. Who's begging to join the pantheon of celebrities that have appeared on *Ghost Stories of the Stars*? The pope?"

Anthony laughed, even though Jason seemed to be going for sarcasm. "That's setting the bar kind of high, don't you think? I may not have landed God's chosen one, but he's a pretty damned big fish. Go ahead, take another guess."

"No, Anthony, just tell me. I'm not in a joking mood today." The dark circles and new wrinkles around his blue eyes that had appeared in the last year matched that assessment.

Anthony, a big guy with a ready smile, was almost always in a joking mood. As a partner in their production company, he continued with gusto, unfazed by Jason's downner attitude. "Alright. So, you're not going to believe this, but I just got off the phone with William

Brandt's publicist. And before you ask, yeah, I'm talking about *that* William Brandt."

Jason's long gaze into the heart of his computer monitor was broken. "Don't go screwing around with me like that." His square shoulders turned to face Anthony, seeming to assess if he was being pranked. "There's no way someone like William Brandt wants to be on our show."

"Dude, I'm as serious as a turkey at Thanksgiving. Turns out he really digs us. Who knew? And again, before you ask, yes, this is for real. I didn't go trolling or nothing, he just called out of the blue! Well, technically his publicist called out of the blue, but you know what I mean."

"A premiere with a star like that would mean huge ratings and millions of new viewers for season two." Jason pulled up a calendar onscreen. "We would need at least five days for interview prep and script writing, two or three days to shoot and then at least a month in post-production. If we could trim maybe five days, we could do it! Imagine the promos for an Oscar winning billionaire!"

Silence filled the space between them, and Anthony stalled, tapping one of his well-worn Hush Puppy shoes against the other. "Well, the first part of that timeline won't be a problem…well, it will be a problem…but not that way."

Jason's momentary excitement short-circuited as his athletic frame sagged back into his black-mesh ergonomic office chair. "Just spit it out. What's the catch…and why must there always be a catch?"

Anthony's rounded shoulders shrugged. "See, he's kind of got a timeline of his own." He paused and shifted his thick frame, then looked down through his wirerimmed glasses at his faded blue jeans. "He's flying off to some economic thing in Switzerland tomorrow, so I had to agree to start the interview with him by six o'clock tonight…or not at all."

"Damn it, Anthony!" Jason flung his ink pen, then flopped back in his chair, running his hands through tousled wavy brown hair.

“We’ve been hoping for a break like this, but there’s no way in hell we can be ready to shoot by tonight. Jeez, I’m not even sure we could get a crew on location by then, much less prep for an interview for a star like him.”

Easily dodging the thrown projectile, Anthony put his hands in his pockets. “I can call back and cancel, if you want, but we’ll never get another shot like this.” He paused. “You know, a real journalist would push his mother in front of a train to land an interview with William Brandt, even if it was on short notice.”

The barb landed with the desired result. “That’s a load of crap and you know it! We spent ten bloody years ducking bullets in Iraqistan. We’ve interviewed everyone from opium growers to heads of states. Hell, we even interviewed a damned Al Qaeda commander and lived to talk about it. You know good and damned well we’re real journalists.”

Now Anthony set the hook. “True, but for the past twelve months, all we’ve done is interview Hollywood B listers babbling on about spirits and paranormal happenings in their monster mansions. I can be ready by six. How about you? You think you’ve still got big enough kahunas to go without a net? You know, no prep, no script. Just you, me, William Brandt and maybe, oh I don’t know, maybe fifteen million sets of eyeballs watching our final product?”

Jason’s steel blue eyes shot him a hard look. “So, we just need to do the interview segment tonight, right? We get full access to his house for all of our other shots after he leaves, right? Tell me you made that part of the deal and I’ll start loading the van now.”

He beamed. “Bro, you know I did. I sweet talked that publicist like I was rappin with a sous chef at a stripper convention.”

The laugh was loud. “Anthony, I have no idea what that even means.”

Anthony was glad to see a flash of the old Jason again. “Got you to laugh, though, didn’t I?”

"Yeah, yeah you did." Jason stood and grabbed his navy-blue blazer. "You know, this is going to make us famous, one way or another, right?"

His hands rubbed together in anticipation. "It'll be like old times, just us and our subject. You do your thing in front of the camera and I'll do mine from behind. We could do this in our sleep."

Chapter Three

True first impressions are the material for pop songs, you know, like *When I Saw Her Face*, by the Beatles. Or sometimes you find yourself in an unfamiliar situation and it sets your skin crawling, as in *Star Wars* when Luke Skywalker says, "I've got a bad feeling about this." Our senses are always alert to subtle clues about our environment and the people around us. But what about a celebrity, when you've already seen their image on the big screen a thousand times? Is meeting them face-to-face for the first time really a first impression?

****

"William Brandt, you've lived a charmed life. You were voted most likely to succeed in high school, and once named sexiest man alive by *People* magazine. You are a movie star, an industrialist, and listed by Forbes as one of the fifty richest men in the world. How does it feel to be you?" With his extremely limited prep time, Jason kicked off the interview with bravado and a few easy to find facts from Google. There wasn't even time to rush home and change into a suit to match his famous guest. He rolled with the khaki pants and the white collared shirt he had worn into the office, thankful he kept a blazer there for just such emergencies.

The sixty-five-year-old, who didn't look a day over forty-five laughed easily. "Sometimes even I can't believe the good fortune that's come my way. I was born a premature runt to a single mother, and luckily, I inherited a teaspoon of talent. Of course, I did put in a lot of hard work and caught more than my fair share of breaks along the way, but really, my story is the story of America. A place where the circumstances of your birth don't determine your future." He sounded a lot like former President Reagan, and with his thick mane of black hair cut in a similar style, and his resting face an almost smile. He looked a bit like a young version of him, too.

Wow, this guy is good. With his pitch perfect delivery of those few lines, William Brandt confirmed that he was either the best actor of his generation, or the humblest man in Hollywood. Most Americans considered him both, and now Jason witnessed first-hand why he was deemed a national treasure instead of a world-class prima donna. "So, take us back in time. Tell us about that premature runt's early days." The show had a tried-and-true formula, and the first ingredient of their winning recipe was for the star to talk through their biography.

With their usual team on location filming a *Housewives of Hollywood* special edition episode, they managed to wrangle a stand-in professional crew at the last minute to film their hoped-for big break. Jason always wore a miniature earpiece to hear Anthony's direction to the crew in the background, but usually tuned it out to better focus on the interview subject. He knew his producer was smiling when he spoke softly through his headset to the cameramen, his lifelong obsession with food coloring his word choice. "Easy as pie."

"My first memories are happy ones, actually right here in this very house. You see, my mother worked here as a maid for the Irvington family. I had the run of the place when they were away, and they were away a lot. It seems like only yesterday I was sliding down that banister." Brandt, wearing a black Italian cut suit, flashed a smile that was simultaneously innocent and mischievous as he and Jason sat in heavy oxblood red leather club chairs in the domed grand foyer of the home. The Italian black and white checkerboard style marble and original dark paneling gave the massive entrance a formal, yet classic feel, as if it would never go out of style.

Anthony directed the crew with whispered commands. "Camera one to the staircase. Follow the curved banister to the top, then back down to Jason." He was getting a shot for the final edit. In post-production they would cut to exterior shots of the enormous

Connecticut Greek Revival style mansion, as well as this clip of the banister.

Continuing, Jason effortlessly guided the conversation through his guest's bio. "Sounds idyllic, but things changed, didn't they?"

Brandt answered, sounding reflective. "They sure did. You know, I lost my mother when I was eight. She was a real saint, the sweetest person in the world, and I loved her very much." He paused for a moment. "I just wish…I just wish we had more time together."

Without thinking, Jason replied. "I know how it feels to lose someone too soon. Things like that can really haunt you, can't they?"

In the silent seconds that followed, Anthony dropped his head and whispered into his mic. "People, Jason's not making pie anymore, looks like he's mixing a fruitcake." The season one disaster with one of the Antonio sisters taught them not to use words like 'haunt' or 'ghost' too early in an interview. While this didn't seem as bad, he looked up and wiped a bead of sweat from his forehead with the sleeve of his flannel shirt. "Camera two, push in slowly on Brandt. If he's going to go postal, let's at least capture it for eternity."

Unlike last season's incident, William Brandt didn't storm off set. Instead, he nodded, but now the sentimentality in his voice was replaced by a hopeful tone. "Oh, I missed her alright, but I got on with it."

Projecting his own feelings at losing his wife too soon, Jason tugged the lapels of his blazer. "That must have been a pretty rough time for you, right?"

Anthony tensed and whispered. "Slow down, Jason. Stir gently. Camera one, push in on Jason."

With another head-bob, Brandt continued with an optimistic calmness coating his words. "I'll admit, the first few days after she died were really rough, and I cried a lot. I mean a whole lot." He stopped his recollection for a moment, the black pupils of his gray eyes seeming to stare into the past. "I suppose any little boy would be shaken. My mother had just died, and on top of that I was sent to live with strangers. But, after a few days, things got better. Luckily, my foster parents were good people and I just knew everything would work out the way it was supposed to."

Jason's fingers gripped the arms of his leather chair. A mixture of jealousy at how easily the young William Brandt shook off the emotional turmoil of his loss, combined with a sense that there was more to the story. The blend didn't sit well in his gut. "So, you lose your mother when you're eight, and after a few days you just get on with your life? It was that easy?"

Brandt laughed softly. "Well, an eight-year-old mind can be a powerful thing. See, one night, soon after her death, I had a dream. A dream that changed everything."

"Go on." Jason nudged. *Now we're getting somewhere.*

It didn't take much of a bump to get Brandt to continue. "The dream started out scary." He pointed to the landing at the top of the stairs. "I was standing up there and I saw my mother's murder, here, where you and I sit today. The police say she walked in on a couple of men robbing the place."

Anthony spoke in hushed tones. "Did he just say what I think he said? Hell's bells! We're not having fruitcake after all. We're having double fudge chocolate cake! Camera two, tighter on Brandt."

"You saw your mother's murder? That must have been traumatic." Jason's eyes widened, and his broad face turned ashen.

"No, no, no. Not in real life, I was in school when it happened. As I said, I just dreamed I saw it, that's all."

Swallowing hard, Jason stalled for a moment to gather his thoughts. As the interview progressed, he became more and more uncomfortable with the parallels between his own recent experiences of his dreams with Julie, and what Brandt was describing. Clearing his throat, he unsteadily plowed ahead. "Still, that must have been…difficult."

Brandt continued his upbeat recollection. "I guess it would have been if that's the way the dream ended, but you see, it didn't. I dreamed my mother spoke to me and told me what I needed to hear. She gave me hope."

Anthony shared his excitement in a whispered voice with the crew. "I love chocolate…and look at Jason. Who knew he could act so well?" Cameraman two snorted.

Jason's eyes flashed a look of uncertainty toward camera one as he could now hear his heart beating in his ears. "What…what could a dead woman say that would comfort a young boy?"

Brandt seemed to practically leap to give an answer. "I was in mourning and needed comfort. I needed to know that everything would be okay, and she reassured me that it would. She told me, 'Don't be afraid.'"

Barely keeping his volume contained, Anthony gave commentary to the team. "Lick the bowl and bake at three-fifty."

Those are the very words Julie said to me! Jason's mouth watered, tasting of stomach acid. "If I'm being honest, that would have totally freaked me out."

Anthony bounced, seeming to sense how well this awkward exchange would later play on televisions around the nation. "We get frosting, too!"

Blushing, Brandt seemed to brush off Jason's concern. "It was just the opposite for me, it was very reassuring."

Jason answered in disbelief, knowing how those same words had affected him less than twenty-four hours ago. "So, one dream with your mother telling you everything is going to be okay, and you're good? Just like that? No more tears, no more fears, no more anxiety? Just like that, everything's all better?"

"Well…it wasn't just one dream." For the first time, Brandt looked the slightest bit uncomfortable, his smile not as natural as moments before. "You see, I've had more dreams over the years…and I've told other people about them…even sometimes said the ghost of my mother visited me."

This revelation was why they were here, why their show existed in the first place. But with his own very similar experience, it no longer seemed like a gimmick to Jason. He knew he was staring too hard, but couldn't stop, as he tried to push away the unwanted thought that their experiences were too similar. "Your mother's ghost kept coming to you?"

Anthony, on the other hand, was ecstatic. "Candles too!"

Sounding as if he had found his cheerful rhythm again, Brandt continued. "You see, I've figured it out. Whenever I've had hard times or a tough decision, my mind projects the image of my mother in my dreams to help me sort things out. It helped me so much as a child that I guess it sometimes still works that way." His relaxed posture indicated he seemed pleased with his answer.

"Sounds to me like you thought you were haunted by her ghost."

William Brandt didn't hesitate. "That's what I thought when I was eight, but no, I don't see ghosts. I was just a scared kid who made it through some rough times and came out okay. And, like most people, I've had a few bizarre dreams in my lifetime." He shrugged. "But that's all they are…dreams." With that answer Brandt smiled his billion-dollar smile directly into camera two.

Anthony stepped onto the well-lit set. "Cut! That was terrific everyone, now let's set up in the library for the movie highlight segment. By the way, who else is hungry?"

Chapter Four

Almost everyone has an inner monologue, it's how we're built. Ideally, it helps us think through problems. *My car is almost out of gas, but I'm running late for my dentist appointment. Maybe I have enough to get me there, then I'll get gas. I'll risk it.* That inner conversation happens all the time, but sometimes it's just nice to talk things through with someone else.

****

Three hours after wrapping the shoot, Jason was back in his snug New York apartment pouring a double shot of bourbon over ice, before collapsing into his favorite chair. He hadn't changed a single thing in the year since Julie's death. A large window in the living area was the most prominent feature, but in typical New York fashion, the view was of a brick wall. The kitchen partially opened to the den, home to appliances Jason rarely used anymore. Several framed pictures of the couple rested on a credenza near the door, and he looked at them often, thinking of their years together, now cut short.

His body was exhausted, but his brain buzzed. The interview with Brandt kept replaying in his head. He poured more golden-brown liquid over gradually melting ice, trying to bring his mind and body into equilibrium. Each tip of the bottle produced a tumbler with less ice and more bourbon and soon his old overstuffed leather recliner felt like a warm cocoon. He turned the TV to his preferred sports channel.

The hope was for distraction, but a baseball game between two teams he didn't care about couldn't keep his attention. The announcer droned on as he sipped and drifted.

"Jason, over here. I'm ready for my interview." Julie's voice drew his focus toward the same set he had just left.

A chill ran down his spine as his eyes darted, trying to get his bearings. *Where am I?* After a few seconds, he realized what had happened. *Damn it. I fell asleep in front of the television again.* While he dreaded his nightly dream of Julie's death, he had become accustomed to the identical ritual every night, but *this* was unfamiliar.

Tonight's dream was already off to a very different start than all others involving her, and his entire body tensed. Instead of beginning in Luigi's, he found himself standing in a sea of darkness, a participant in the experience, not simply an observer. A short distance away he saw a duplicate of the foyer of Brandt's home, but now it floated like a bright mystical island in a black ocean. The cameras and lighting were all the same, but there was no Anthony or crew, just a very different looking Julie sitting alone in one of the two blood-red club chairs. *I have got to stop drinking on an empty stomach.*

"Come on over…talk to me…don't be afraid." She beckoned him in the same way she used to when asking him to get seldom used dishes from the top shelves of their cabinets. Her tone expectant, but short of a direct order.

Caution slowed his steps toward the light. He waded in blackness that roiled around him like fog, and he felt like he was walking through a boggy swamp with muck sucking on his shoes. After a few more steps he was close enough to see how different she looked. Gone were the black leggings and white blouse that in his prior dreams always ended covered in blood. In their place was an off-the-shoulder, full-length, form-fitting white sequined dress that sparkled in the bright lights. Diamond chandelier earrings sent sharp bolts of light flickering into the darkness. "Julie, is that really you?"

Her answer came accompanied by the wave of her hand. "Of course it's me. Who else would it be? Now hurry up and get over here. We only have nine minutes before this segment ends."

He covered the distance from where he started to the fringe of the glowing set and stopped, unsure of his next words, or steps. Curiosity and caution wrestled drunkenly to a draw in his mind as he stood at the boundary delineating light from dark. "You look so…so different. What…" He paused, then started over. "What the hell is...?" He stopped again, his thoughts jumbled.

She answered the incomplete question making perfect sense, while at the same time making no sense at all. "Things have changed, Jason, there are new rules now. These new rules require I come to see you whenever *I* want, but dressed exactly the way *you* wish to see me. It's a little twist that keeps things interesting, don't you think? Thanks for choosing this outfit, it was always one of my favorites. I was getting bloody tired of wearing the same thing every night. Pardon the pun."

He remembered that less than an hour ago he picked up the framed picture of her wearing this very dress, and staring at it, wished she were still alive. *It's just a dream. Play along and it will be over soon.* "You always did hog all the space in our closet."

"Now there's the sense of humor that I know and love. As for the wardrobe selection, you really outdid yourself. Do you think it looks as good on me now as it did two years ago when I wore it to the correspondents' ball?"

I remember that night...we were so happy... She looked a little thinner than he remembered, and her skin was a purer shade of pale, but nonetheless, she was beautiful. He took a half step into the bright lights of the set and the absurdity of the moment hit him. "Oh my God. It's over isn't it? I've really gone crazy." He kept his distance as he nervously pushed both hands through his thick brown hair.

Her words came quickly. "No, no, not at all, sweetheart. We're just taking our relationship to the next logical phase. You're not going crazy, in fact, you're making progress. Think of it as making it to the next level on one of those video games you love to play."

Laughing uneasily with his fingers locked behind his head, he stood on the precipice. “Anthony’s been telling me to get help, professional help. I need to remember that in the morning.”

She touched the matching chair. “Oh, quit being such a baby and get over here and start this interview before the break. I’m telling you, we don’t have a lot of time.” Her sequins dazzled as she shifted in her seat and fluffed her coal black tresses.

He took his next steps hesitantly toward her on the well-lit set and noticed the lighting was perfect, as always. *Even in my dreams, Anthony does a great job.* Julie looked divine, and the closer he got to her, the harder his heart pounded. He warily took his place in the matching chair. “Okay, we’re both here. Now what?”

She demurred. “It’s like any other interview you’ve ever done. You ask me a question and I answer, and you know, we’ll see where things go. Just like you did in that interview with William Brandt a few hours ago.” She patted his hand. “That’s what I want to talk about. Ask me my thoughts on your Brandt interview. Go ahead, I promise I won’t bite.”

The touch of her hand felt cool, but strangely reassuring. Jason gave a weak laugh as he slyly glanced around the set, searching for the nearest exit, the way he used to do when he was about to start an interview with the Taliban. But tonight, there were no exits in sight, just him and his dead wife. *At least I understood the Taliban.* “Okay then…this is so weird…one more time, what are we doing here?”

“Focus, dear. Focus. It’s an interview.” She spoke slowly, loudly and deliberately in her New York brashness. “You ask questions, and I answer. That’s the way interviews work. Just do what you always do, like you’ve done a thousand times before.”

He reminded himself, *this is only a dream. It will be over soon.*

She touched his hand yet again. “I can hear your thoughts too, just so you know. And that Taliban comment…really?”

“Hey, that’s not fair.”

“More rules. You’ll get used to them. Now, ask me about Brandt, come on, the commercial break will be here before you know it.”

Instinctively, Jason glanced to the right of camera one, expecting to see Anthony in his usual position, but he was nowhere to be found. Finally, he turned to Julie and asked the first question of the night. “Okay…what did you think of the interview? Anthony thinks it will get a bigger Nielson rating than the Beatles on Ed Sullivan back in the day. You know how he talks.”

Smiling, she looked squarely into camera two. “Oh, Jason, it’s going to make fabulous television, certainly. But it wasn’t *your* best work, now was it?”

“Whoa! Remember, you’re the one who wanted to talk about this subject. Did you bring it up just to give me a hard time?” *She’s more critical than I remember.*

Julie gazed sweetly into camera two again, playing to…who? “I just call it the way I see it. The truth is, you got played, right from the get-go. Don’t you agree? And by the way, I’m not being bitchy on purpose. We just have a lot to accomplish in a short amount of time.”

With jaw set, he stared at her. “Do you always have to be right? That interview, the whole thing, it was just too damned…too damned…hell, it was too damned something. I’m not even sure what really happened. All I know is that I almost blew it in the first thirty seconds, Brandt gave me an eerie vibe, and Anthony, well Anthony was his usual brilliant off-the-wall self. I’ve never been part of anything like it.” He paused for a moment and stole a glance toward her. “You think I got played?”

“Jason, the world-famous William Brandt calls out of the blue and says you can have this interview, but only if you get to his house by six o’clock. Come on. Does that sound like he was being spontaneous or manipulative? He was pulling strings and you and Anthony were dancing like mad marionettes.” She flailed her arms as if they were attached to invisible wires.

Lowering his head, Jason admitted what he already knew in his gut. "That deadline was stupid crazy."

Julie clasped her hands in her lap, her alabaster skin resting on ivory sequins. "That's right. He's a control freak, dear. Always has been, and always will be."

"Control…right. Then why be on our show in the first place? Hell, he's got an Oscar on his mantle and billions in the bank. America already loves him." He shook his head. "Why do it at all?"

Her pale skin radiated like an angel in a ball gown. "Excellent question, Jason. It gets right to the heart of the matter. Why *did* William Brandt want to be on your show?"

Leaning back, he rubbed the spot between his eyes, as he did when his headaches were especially bad. He felt the beginning of a migraine. "Think, Jason, think. What was really going on tonight?"

Smiling almost exactly as she used to and slowly twitching her bare shoulders, she seemed to taunt him the way a matador baits a bull. "Seems pretty obvious to me. Come on, Jason, spit it out or ask me for help. The clock's ticking." She pushed him for an answer in the same way camera two pushed in for a close-up of her.

Tired of stubbornly stalling as he struggled to come up with an answer, he let his guard down. After all, she was his wife, not just any random visitor from the morgue. Her teasing smile, which she reserved just for him, was exactly as he remembered, and her pouty lips were impossible to ignore when painted with her favorite lipstick, Signal Red. But tonight, there was a sharpness, an edge that was not there when she was alive. He brushed the difference away as just being another facet of his dream, and he reflexively smiled back, same as he always did. "Okay, smarty pants. Give it up. Why did William Brandt want to do our show?"

"Brandt doesn't do anything without a plan. He wanted to tell that story exactly that way, and do it on a show like yours because lots of people watch, but no one takes it too seriously."

A sideways glance flew her way. "It's not like we're reporting on firefights in Kandahar like we used to, but Anthony and me, we still do good work."

"Just calling it like I see it. He brushed away this potentially embarrassing story about seeing ghosts and endeared himself to the public even more with that touching remembrance of his mother. You got played by a master."

Stewing in Julie's scorned silence, Jason sighed and surrendered. "I still don't get it. B-Lister celebrities come on our show for publicity and they say all kinds of crazy stuff. It's part of the gig. Brandt doesn't need that. He owns a mega corporation and he's got a blockbuster due out in three months. None of it makes any sense."

Her head lowered and she pointedly shot back, "Think bigger. The man is one of the most recognized people on the planet and has more gold than Midas. He's not thinking about his next role or his next billion. He's playing a completely different game. As they say in acting class, 'What's his motivation?' Listen to your gut, Jason, what's it telling you?"

Camera one pushed in for the closest of close-ups. Jason's creased face filled the screen, deep in thought. He was determined to break this riddle without her help. *What could the man want if not money or fame?* He went through the list of other usual motivations. *Women? Married to a model for a while and once dated a Playboy centerfold. He can get a date. Respect? Got that when they gave him the Oscar for his portrayal of Stanley Livingston in 'One Long Trip.' Besides, you don't come on my show to build your serious acting cred. Think, think. What's left?*

Jason's spine stiffened and the camera pulled back to capture his physical transformation. From thin air, an answer flashed in his mind fully formed. "The only thing left for a guy who has everything money can buy is power…real power. Not regular super-rich-guy power either. If I'm right, he's interested in history book kind of power."

"Now you're getting somewhere."

He beamed. “William Brandt rarely settles for anything less than the best. Would he really aim for the very top?” He rolled the idea around in his mind like rosary beads and found no fault in it, at least not at this hour of the night. “He wouldn’t be the first president to have a celebrity background. Holy crap, he used our show to get that one little secret out in the open. Now it’s out there with his perfectly normal explanation. It’ll be a non-issue four years from now.”

Perfect red lips parted in a dazzling smile. “You’ve always been so good at figuring out puzzles.”

Blushing, he smiled at the compliment, the way he did when she was alive and complimenting his brains or, as she described, his ‘ruggedly handsome’ looks. He did consider himself smart, and thought of ‘ruggedly handsome’ as shorthand for a fit guy with a strong chin, but a slightly crooked nose broken a couple of times on the football fields of his youth. “We’ll see how it sounds tomorrow, but right now it makes perfect sense.”

Then he gazed into her eyes, just like he used to. But tonight, only a dull reflection stared back. This woman looked almost like his wife, but she wasn’t. Julie was dead. He lowered his head as his momentary happiness deflated like a day-old balloon. “I guess I must have known that all along, right? You’re just a figment of my imagination, helping me see what I already know, aren’t you?”

A shy glance went first to camera two, then to him. “That’s the easy explanation, isn’t it? Everything fits in a nice tidy box, just like good old William Brandt told everyone. Except…except what if I’m really here? What if Brandt really does talk to the dead? What if it’s all real?”

He slumped all the way back in his chair. “He seems like an odd bird to me, but he obviously comes across as a pretty normal guy to everybody else. Tonight, he looked straight into the camera and told the truth. Him seeing his mother, me seeing you, we’re both just trying to deal with our pain. And just like he did, I’ve got to move on.”

Laughing, she placed the back of her hand against her forehead, like a swooning Southern belle. "Oh, my dear beautiful, Jason. You are so naïve. You and I? We're just getting started. We have so much more to talk about."

The muscles in his jawline twitched again as he raised his voice and punctuated his words with repeated stabs of his index finger. "I mean it, Julie. I'm tired. I'm tired and I can't take it anymore. I've beaten myself up for not being there when you died. I'm sorry. I'm so sorry that I wasn't there to stop it, but you're dead! *You've* got to accept that fact! You…are…dead!" Following two deep breaths, Jason continued with only a bit more control. "But now, thanks to a little help from my new friend, William Brandt, I finally understand what's happening to me."

His anger appeared to have no effect as she coyly ran one finger up and down the seam atop the arm of her chair. "It's good for you to let go of that anger, truly. But what if I could tell you about things you don't know? Hmm. Things you couldn't possibly know. What if I could tell you the future?" She held up her finger. "Think about it for a moment before you answer." She resumed running it endlessly up and down the seam again. "Now that…that would make things really interesting, wouldn't it?"

With his venting complete, a new calm manifested. "It's time for me to go. I've got to pull myself together." He gripped the arms of his chair, preparing to stand and walk back into the surrounding darkness.

She leaned forward and grabbed his hand, her icy touch paralyzing him. "You're right, you're absolutely right. It is time for you to move on, and that's why I'm here. Let's say we get started with the next phase of your life, oh I don't know, maybe tomorrow? Would that be soon enough? Shall I tell you about the twister headed your way, or would you like it to be a complete surprise?"

Unable to move, he answered. "Go ahead and tell me, if it will make you shut up and go away." Convinced this was all just a bad dream he wanted to end, his delivery was stone cold, devoid of any warmth, spousal or otherwise.

"Now that wasn't a nice thing to say, was it?" She kept one hand on his and pointed a pale skinny finger with the other. "You and I, we have a lot to accomplish together, so you better get used to seeing me. I know you'll come to appreciate me more as you get used to this new arrangement, just you wait and see."

She stopped pointing and an enigmatic smile replaced her chilly expression. "In the spirit of our new arrangement I'm going to tell you about tomorrow. You're going to meet someone new, and she's a real bat out of hell. Trust me. We'll talk more about her later, but right now I've got to go. We're up against the break."

She removed her hand from his and he jerked awake in his recliner, as if hit by a bucket of cold water. He shivered as a movie trailer promoting the soon to be released, *Dracula – A Time to Reap*, starring William Brandt, illuminated the pixels of his HD television.

Chapter Five

Prophecy is a key component in almost every religion. We all want to know what secrets the future holds and those who claim the gift become saints, or more often, are revealed as frauds. But we've all heard stories of people who cancel their flights because of a premonition, then see on the news that the plane they were supposed to be on crashed. Precognition can't be real, can it?

****

The compressed timeline to get this episode of *Ghost Stories of the Stars* ready to air forced Jason and Anthony into a divide and conquer strategy. The day after the Brandt interview, Anthony was back at the mansion getting additional footage while Jason's long fingers melded with his keyboard writing the voiceover scripts which would be added to the video. He stopped for only a few minutes to refill his coffee cup and stretch, then rolled up the sleeves of his blue Oxford shirt and got back to work. Concentration and clarity were needed to accomplish this mission, any distraction was to be avoided at all cost.

The receptionist buzzing his desk phone broke Jason's train of thought. "Mr. Simmons, there's a reporter here to see you. A Ms. Nicole Broussard."

He rubbed his tired eyes with his palms and contemplated this development, trying to decide if it was unexpected or not. *Damn you, Julie Simmons.* "Ella, tell her I'm busy. Tell her to come back after the twenty-fifth."

Ella's disembodied voice soon returned. "Mr. Simmons, she says it's urgent."

It's just a coincidence, that's all. I'll see this woman, then get her out of here. I'll be back on task in no time. I'll show Julie. He realized he was actually considering that the dream Julie was real, and he knew that couldn't be the case. Pushing the button on the intercom again he spoke firmly, "Alright, tell her she has two minutes, but that's it. After all, who am I to stand in the way of the First Amendment?" He mumbled to himself after releasing the button. "Dreams won't run my life."

A whirlwind of color and energy blew through his office door. She extended her hand with acrylic French nails tipping each finger. "Nicole Broussard, but everybody calls me Nikki."

He stammered. "Please…uh…Nikki. Have a seat." As he pointed to the plain wooden chair on the other side of his desk, he was caught off guard by the sight of the younger woman sporting a strange updated Bride of Frankenstein hairdo. The cut was a hybrid between a bird's nest and haute couture, while the color was at the crossroads of pink and red. On the whole, the 'do' had a theatrical, whimsical effect. *Interesting.* He composed himself and addressed the cute woman with strange taste. "What have we done that's newsworthy enough to bring a member of the press to our little shop?"

He lowered his tall frame into his swivel chair as she spoke. "I'll get right to the point. I'm doing a story on William Brandt, and a source tells me that you interviewed him last night. I was hoping we could do a little horse trading. You know, see if he said anything of interest, compare notes on what I've already discovered. I'm sure we can help each other out here." She punctuated her request by crossing her legs. Thigh-high yellow leather boots that almost reached the hem of her short black mini-skirt made the gesture impossible to ignore.

Jason questioned with a shrug and outstretched hand. "I'm sorry. I was told this was urgent, and who did you say you were with?" He tried to keep his eyes fixed on hers as he now noticed she went braless under her sheer leopard print blouse.

"Believe me, this is a matter of national security. You can trust me on that. Oh, and I'm with the *National Conversation*, digital division."

“Ohhh…” Jason cleared his throat and relaxed. *She’s not a real journalist. I’ll have her out of here in no time.* “Now I understand.” *Who does Julie Simmons think she’s dealing with anyway, an amateur?* “I’m sorry, Ms. Br…I mean Nikki. I don’t have anything to tell you.”

She chomped on her wad of gum. “I get it. Just because we’ve predicted the end of the world twice in the past five years, you think we don’t do hard news. Well, we do. Who do you think broke that nuclear ground water contamination story in Florida a few months ago? Huh? I did, that’s who.” Her eyeliner pencil worked overtime accentuating emerald green eyes that flashed with fierceness.

He played along for a minute more, chiding the woman as he recalled the story. “Didn’t your paper also say that aliens were making the townspeople glow?”

A wicked smile flashing neon purple lipstick should have been a signal to Jason. “Sure. That’s the way the story started, but once the mainstream media got involved it brought down the governor, now didn’t it?” Then her expression changed, seeming to get more serious, like a sleek cat playing with its prey. “You should know I always get my man. Always.”

Jason smiled defensively at the aggressively attractive woman. “I’ve enjoyed meeting you, really. You’ve been an unexpected break in a very long day, I mean that. But I’ve got a killer deadline.” He stood and extended his hand to end the conversation. “Good luck with your story.”

She stayed seated with crossed arms under firm breasts. “You’re not at all like I thought you’d be.”

He continued, standing awkwardly with an outstretched hand while she sat firmly anchored to the chair. The longer the standoff lasted, the more he became intrigued by her attitude, so he lowered his arm. “Oh really, and what did you think I would be like?”

She wasted no time, with words as direct and audacious as her hair. “I thought that you, of all people, would understand what it’s like to be judged. Look at you, for ten years you covered the most important stories of both war and peace. And now? Now you talk to celebrities about seeing dead people. Sure, you're the star and the producer and probably make a lot more money, but people judge you, don't they? Are you telling me you can't spare a minute for someone who knows exactly how you feel?"

Jason sat down, stunned by her boldness and fascinated by her insight. She had struck a chord, because he knew precisely what she was talking about. Old friends still working in the mainstream media didn't return his calls, or if they did, they seemed to want to limit their exposure to him, like trying to avoid catching the flu from someone they now considered infected by fluff journalism. "Maybe I can spare a minute…for a fellow journalist that is. So, what angle are you working anyway?"

Her energy filled the room with lively hands choreographed to unexpected words. "Picture this streaming from the device of your choice: 'US Government Targeted by Occult.' Under that we run a picture of William Brandt. What do you think?"

He rubbed the bridge of his nose for a moment. His raised expectations crashed into his worst preconceptions. She really was just another schlock tabloid reporter. *Be nice. Just humor her for another minute and get her out of here.* "That would grab eyeballs alright, but there's just one problem. Brandt's not in the government."

Her wicked smile turned conspiratorial. "You want to know a big secret? I have a source that says Brandt's going to run for president. What do you think of that?"

He was glad that his eyes were closed again so she couldn't see his reaction. *How could she say that? Maybe there is something more here than meets the eye, but stay focused and get her out of here. You don't have time for this, you've got tons of work to do.* He smiled nervously and his mouth felt dry. "That's an interesting theory you've got there. But really, Nikki, I'm under a very tight deadline and I need to get back to the grindstone. I'm sure you understand. Maybe some other time?"

Standing, Nikki leaned over his desk, her hands placed halfway across, with her plunging neckline level with his eyes. "I understand, you've got your deadline, but even a busy man like you has to eat sometime." Her smile widened and her voice lowered to a sexy register. "Let me buy you dinner and I'll show you mine if you show me yours…notes that is."

Did she just say what I think she said? His cheeks flushed and his tongue was tied. "Uh…maybe we could see if the pieces fit together…you know…our stories."

Green eyes sparkled mischievously as she winked. "Then it's a date. I'll see you at the Blind Bat in Hell's Kitchen, say nine o'clock?"

Chapter Six

"Addiction: a strong and harmful need to regularly have something (such as a drug) or do something (such as gamble)." *Webster's* definition is short and sweet but fails to fully capture the powerful pull exerted on the addict. To what lengths would someone go to scratch the itch? How low does a person have to go before they turn away? It's difficult to answer that question for yourself, but impossible to answer for someone else.

****

Jason sipped his bourbon as he watched Nikki stir her martini. "What's a Harvard educated journalist like you doing working for a rag outfit like the *National Conversation?*" Jason avoided the mistake he made before interviewing William Brandt, even if his research on Nicole Broussard did take precious time away from his work on the season two premiere.

"Will you at least let a girl finish her first drink before you interrogate her?" She winked at him mischievously. "Besides, my resume is shorter than yours, so you go first. Why don't you tell me how someone goes from winning a Bayeux-Calvados award as a war correspondent to producing and starring in a show about celebrities and their ghost stories? That's got to be a long road."

It seemed to him a not-so-subtle dig at both his show and their ten-year age difference. His initial uncertainty about meeting her turned to physical queasiness. "This was a mistake. I'm sorry I've taken up your time tonight." He started sliding out of the high-backed black leather upholstered booth, now regretting taking even more time out of his packed schedule to go home and change into a suit, sans the tie. *Why was I trying to impress her?* He knew the answer and felt ashamed of his clumsy attempt at a date.

Nikki's laugh was reassuring in this bar filled with what seemed to be aspiring actresses from the neighboring Theater district, and young businessmen in suits who were offering to buy them a drink. She grabbed his hand with a warm, but firm grip. "Nonsense, we're just getting started. Now tell that nice serving wench to bring us another round and we'll get to know each other a little better. We'll talk shop later." She released his hand and finished her dirty martini in one gulp. "Ah, the first one always goes down so easy."

I do want another drink, and who knows, maybe the night won't be a total loss. He stopped his slide and laughed nervously. "Well, we're both here, and you've gone to the trouble of dressing up and everything. I guess another wouldn't hurt. Besides, I don't have anywhere else I need to be right now." That was a lie. He needed to be back in the shop. He signaled the waitress for another round and stole a glance at Nikki's curves. She wore a short, tight black evening dress that fit as if made of spandex. His eyes lingered a bit longer as she went back to her empty glass for the olives on the toothpick.

She talked while chewing. "So, really, how did you end up in the celebrity business? You had such a straight-laced TV news thing going."

"Not much to tell, really." He tried to stay focused as she looked vivacious in basic black, which served as a more than suitable backdrop for her soft bronze metallic eyeshadow and pastel pink lipstick. The hair however, still threw him. "Anthony and I went to Afghanistan early in the war and got addicted to the life of foreign correspondents. Working in a combat zone was simultaneously petrifying and amazing."

Stopping for a second, he reflected on those black and white days. "That's how the war was for us. I remember being pinned down for an hour with a platoon of battle-hardened marines, fearing for my life, yet never feeling more alive. I lived for the next fix and felt invincible…or at least I did until our car was blown up." Pausing, he thought about Ahmed, their driver killed in the blast.

While he was reflective in the moment, Nikki was impatient. "Obviously you didn't die, so what happened next? How did you go from there to the trash TV business?'

Her direct question caught him off guard, which caused him to laugh. "For your information, that's called a dramatic pause. Most people wait for the speaker to continue at their own pace. I guess print reporters aren't trained to think that way."

He continued with a flourish for her amusement. "Now, where was I? Oh yeah, so after we recovered from our injuries, we took stock and decided to change our lives. We worked stateside for a while with a network, but that was *sooo* boring, so we decided to do something different. We came up with this *Ghost Stories of the Stars* idea and I've been interviewing people as strange and foreign as anyone I ever met on the battlefield. The main difference is that they usually don't have guards packing machine guns."

The bleach blond waitress with the nose ring set their second round on the table and Nikki drank it like it was chilled lemonade on a hot summer day. "These are *sooo* good. They make'em just the way I like'em. Must be some kind of special gin or something." She slid the already half empty martini glass between them on the heavy wooden table, then looked both ways as if to see if someone was watching. She lowered her voice to a conspiratorial level. "Have you ever been to rehab?"

As if on reflex, he glanced at the remaining dregs of her second drink, then back at her, trying to decide if she was serious or not. "Can't say I have."

Catching his expression, she laughed loudly, seeming pleased she had surprised him. "Well, let me tell you, Mr. Adrenaline, while you were in Afghanistan on your battlefield high, I was in college working on a major in journalism and a minor in heroin. Somehow I made it out of Harvard *and* a twelve-step program by the time I was twenty-one." She drained the remainder of her drink. "Not sure which was more impressive, but I'm nine years clean." She winked at him and held her glass aloft as her loud whistle signaled their waitress to fetch another round.

Shaking his head, Jason laughed lightly. "Then I'm in the presence of greatness."

"Yes. As a matter of fact, you are. But I couldn't have done it on my own, oh no. I had lots of help becoming the professional you see before you today. See, everything I needed to know, I learned in boarding school, long before I graced Harvard with my presence."

Using a toothpick as a pointer, she continued. "Look, the bad girls taught me to party like a rock star, and I did it well. The mean girls taught me all about bullies, and I learned to be one when needed. And the smart girls, well, they taught me to finish what I start. A job's not done until it's done right. That's how I made it through Harvard, and in case you're interested, it's also a damn good recipe for how to derail your life, if you take it too far."

She stopped for a moment, then continued in a more somber tone. "I applied to the *National Conversation* on the break between semesters of my senior year. It was just a lark, really. Then three months later my phone rings while I'm on spring break in Vegas. The ringing woke me up in a cheap motel off the strip with my Morals in Journalism Professor in bed beside me and a gram of black tar heroin on the nightstand. I had no recollection of how I got there. They offered me a job, and from where I was in that moment, it seemed like a step up. I got clean and graduated and haven't looked back."

He still wasn't sure if she was telling the truth or not, but she was certainly a good story teller. "How about the good girls? You didn't mention them. What did they teach you?"

"Good girls? Ha, there are *no* good girls." Nikki looked up at the tin squares that paneled the ceiling and shook her head. After several seconds, she lowered her gaze and cast a naughty glance. "You ever been to Heaven?"

The abrupt change of subjects left him confused. “Heaven? Not sure what you mean.”

“Well, finish that drink and let’s get out of here. We could both use a little hallelujah tonight.”

Chapter Seven

Former Secretary of State, Donald Rumsfeld, said it best: "As we know, there are known knowns. There are things we know we know. We also know there are known unknowns. That is to say we know there are some things we do not know. But there are also unknown unknowns, the ones we don't know we don't know."

****

An electronica beat pulsed inside Heaven, the aptly named club located in an otherwise non-descript high-rise in the trendy SoHo neighborhood. Jason leaned on the stainless steel framed, tempered glass railing of the fortieth-floor balcony, steadying himself as the glowing light of a coming new day slowly lit the city. "I haven't danced like that in years."

Standing behind him, Nikki massaged his shoulders. "Then you need to hang out with me more often, old man."

The fresh air helped clear his head. "Funny, real funny. Is full throttle your only speed?"

"Hey, baby, that's the way I'm wired. Work all day, play all night. And speaking of work, the sun's coming up so let's swap tips on this William Brandt thing before you sober up."

It was only somewhat intentional that he slurred his words. "So, you plied me with liquor and a night on the town just to pump me for information? I thought I was special."

Removing her hands from his shoulders, she wrapped them around his waist. "I needed information and I like to dance. I kind of look at it as a twofer. Not sure if you've noticed, but I have no problem mixing business with pleasure." She drew closer, pressing her sweaty body against his, whispering. "So, what did that sly old fox have to say?"

Gripping the cool railing, her heat transferred to him and he did his best to steady his balance, and his libido. In front of him the Statue of Liberty stood in the hazy light between evening serenity and morning vibrancy. He summoned his clearest thought as it was time to get down to brass tacks. "You waltzed into my office, so you go first. You said something about a source?"

"Fair enough, but this goes both ways, right?"

"Both ways."

Nikki released her hold and slid beside him on the rail, where they faced the coming dawn. "My informant is a consultant to the NYPD. She has intel that Brandt will soon announce he's running for president. And he's running this year, not four years from now."

"Bullshit." His reaction was immediate and unfiltered. "The election's two months away. It's between Wellington, who has never met a war he didn't want us to enter, and tax and spender Carver, who might bankrupt the country. I'm not crazy about either of them and wish there was another choice, but it's way too late for a third-party candidate."

"Then you're really going to get a kick out of this." Her dark-brown eyebrows arched. "She says he's already picked a Cabinet and all of them were raised by single mothers, just like him. A couple even went into foster care, same as he did. How weird is that?"

Jason shook his head. "Sounds like your consultant's been smoking something recently made legal in New York."

"She usually works kidnappings, missing persons, that sort of thing. This isn't her usual beat."

The sun rose from its watery grave and the light of realization hit Jason's face like one of the klieg lights on a set, suddenly turned to its brightest setting. "She's a goddamned psychic, isn't she?"

The protest was immediate and loud. “Gifted. The word is ‘gifted.’ And I’ll have you know she found three of the Brooklyn Basher’s victims last summer, so I don’t want to hear any shit about my sources. She says she knows things about Brandt, and I believe her.”

With his head cocked skyward, Jason laughed the laugh of the clinically insane. “So, it’s official. I’ve gone over to the dark side. All I need is some heavy breathing and Darth Vader claiming to be my father.”

Joining him in laughter, Nikki did her best Vader impression, which wasn’t very good, making it all the more funny. “The force is strong in this one.”

After a good laugh they stood quietly as a heavy backbeat filtered through the suddenly opened double doors of the club. A woman carrying her shoes by the straps walked beside her date, a guy with a snake tattoo slithering up his neck. They had come outside to smoke.

Nikki gently brushed Jason’s cheek. “What’s going on in that battle-battered brain of yours?”

He hesitated, unsure how vulnerable he should be, but a night of drinking gave him courage. “It’s just that lately I’ve heard some crazy things, things that can’t possibly be real, and I’m beginning to wonder about my…” His words trailed off, not wanting to say the word, ‘sanity’ aloud. “Now you tell me that a psychic gave you a tip that I know to be impossible. I would describe it as coming out of left field, but that would be an insult to left fields. It’s preposterous and yet…the more I think about it…this can’t be good.”

Putting her arm around him, she pulled him close. “It’s okay, Jason. Go toward the light. Don’t be afraid. Just take a little peak at the other side.” She laughed again and looked him in the eye. “Seriously, this kind of stuff is normal in my line of work and I’ll attribute anything you say to an anonymous source. No matter what he said, it can’t make better headlines than Elvis caught shoplifting at the Tupelo Wal-Mart last week, now can it?”

"Yeah, I think it can." He felt warm inside and didn't want the feeling to go away, but he knew it would. It had been a fun night, but in the light of morning he could sense that like all good things, it was time to end. It was time for him to deliver on his end of the bargain. *Here's your story, girl. Take it and go.*

Taking a deep breath, he stepped across to the other side. "Last night, good old William Brandt admitted to talking to the ghost of his mother in his dreams. Says it started when he was a kid. Now his story is it was just his mind's way of working out his anxiety, of dealing with her death. Better than Elvis, huh?"

"Better than Elvis' missing twin. I'll get my twenty-fifth front page with this one." Her eyes widened mischievously and instead of suggesting they call it a night, she surprised him. "You up for breakfast, old man?"

"Depends. You still buying?"

She kissed his cheek, then playfully nipped his ear. "Only if it's breakfast in bed at the Ritz."

Chapter Eight

New beginnings are fraught with a myriad of feelings and emotions. New is exhilarating, and sometimes scary. The anticipated future has been altered and now unforeseen avenues open. The architecture of the brain builds additional synapses to incorporate this altered reality, and that intensifies the experience. Most of all, though, new beginnings bring hope.

****

The blaring foghorn ringtone finally penetrated the haze of sleep and hangover enveloping Jason's brain. He reached over the side of the bed, fumbling with his pants to retrieve his phone, then saw Anthony's name showing on the screen. "Hey. What's up?" Jason's greeting was thick and mumbled.

"Tie one on again, buddy?"

Glancing at the clock, he saw it was almost two in the afternoon. "Sort of. It's kind of a long story. Whatcha got?"

Nikki called from the bathroom of their suite at the Ritz Carlton. "You talking to me?"

Anthony's snicker preceded his words. "Who's that bro? You having a sleep over?"

Jason knew that if a thought came into Anthony's mind, nanoseconds later it came out of his mouth. He put his hand over half the phone, answering Nikki. "No. Work call." He turned his attention back to his business partner. "Dude, not now. Sorry about leaving all the work to you today. I'll be in soon, and I'll stay late to make it up."

"Don't even think this is the end of this conversation, but right now you need to turn on the TV. Check out CNN 'cause our boy Brandt is holding a press conference from Switzerland."

Jason scanned the floor looking for the remote that had somehow gotten knocked from the nightstand. "CNN? Give me a sec, I've got to find the channel here."

"Here? So, you're not at your place?" There was a pregnant pause before Anthony continued. "You had hotel sex, didn't you? You dog!"

Finding the button, he flipped past the menu screen giving guests the opportunity to order pay-per-view movies. "Shut up, man. I found CNN. What am I looking at?"

"So far, Brandt's been talking about poverty and pestilence. I'll hang up so you can watch. I'll see you in a couple of hours, then you've got some explaining to do."

Hanging up, Jason called out. "Hey, Nikki. Our guy's on TV."

She came out of the elegant chrome and marble appointed bathroom wearing only a lacy black bra and matching panties as she worked at getting the back on her left earring. "Quick, turn it up. Let's see what the Dark Prince is up to."

For the first time, Jason was seeing Nikki, all of Nikki, in the full light of day. Her legs were long, her tush firm and her abs ripped, but what stood out was the large tattoo running the length of her left ribcage. It was a gnarled crucifix hewn from rough timber, to which an image of Christ's battered and bloody body was nailed. It seemed incongruous with what little he knew of her. *There has got to be a story there.* His unobstructed view was blocked when she finally got the back on the stubborn earring. Her chiseled arm lowered, partially covering her elaborate inkwork.

William Brandt's voice broke his concentration as he spoke to reporters from an outdoor stage in Geneva, the famous Jet d'Eau fountain shooting water hundreds of feet in the air as his backdrop. "There is an insidious scourge sweeping across the face of our planet. It's more powerful than the world's mightiest armies and does not respect the lines on any map. It's a threat to each and every person's health and even to the long-term survival of our species. Climate change may be the biggest problem humans have confronted, and the prognosis isn't good. Each of us living today will be held responsible for leaving future generations burdened with a sick planet, one that's getting sicker by the day. With no simple solutions in sight, a sword of Damocles hangs over us all, compelling men and women of conscience to act. That's why I'm directing my company, BrandtCo Enterprises, to release at no cost the specifications for a new technology that can effectively and cheaply remove up to twenty percent of greenhouse gasses from automobile and factory emissions. We no longer have to live in fear. We no longer have to live under the threat of destruction. Together, we can make the world a better place and heal the wounds of our shared planet. Together we can change the future."

Cheers erupted from the gathered crowd as the headline runner under the image of a triumphant William Brandt scrolled with the text of his message on a ten second delay. Nikki turned away from the TV and headed back to the bathroom to finish dressing. "Told you he was a politician."

Jason picked his red boxers off the floor, pulled them up, then followed her. He spoke as he filled a glass with water. "We'll see. It's a big leap from a press conference in Switzerland to the White House in two months, even if he did just promise to save the world like some kind of Superman." He admired her reflection in the mirror and compared it to his blurry eyes and day-old stubble. "You're looking chipper today. Does anything slow you down?"

She winked at his reflected image as she ran her fingers through her hair, restoring the edgy look from yesterday. "Pure dedication to my craft. I can whip you in shape when I get back from Ireland, if you're interested in an intensive training regime, that is."

He put his arm around her waist. "Ireland, huh. Next story on the other side of the pond?"

"Personal business, but my flight doesn't leave for five hours." She turned to face him, then bit her lower lip as she looked up. "We can get the first lesson in before we check out, if you're an eager student."

Chapter Nine

The Road Not Taken is a poem by Robert Frost, published in 1916. It begins, 'Two roads diverged in a yellow wood, and sorry I could not travel both.' While there are several interpretations of the entire work, there is one inescapable idea contained in this first line. Some decisions can't be avoided if we are to move forward. A choice must be made, knowing our lives would be different had we taken the other path.

****

"Sorry I'm so late." Jason returned to the office wearing the same suit as last night, only now it was wrinkled from laying in a heap on the hotel room floor all night. Adding to his bedraggled appearance was a ring around the collar of his shirt from working up a sweat on the dance floor. His stubbled face completed the unkempt look as together he and Anthony resumed work on the Brandt episode.

The razzing from Anthony that started on the phone intensified in person. "A hotel on the first date? When you're ready to get back into the swing of things you jump right into the deep end, bro."

Trying his best to ignore his friend's jabs, Jason pulled open the left bottom drawer of his desk. "I'm having a drink. Want one?"

Anthony's good-natured kidding ended abruptly. "No, dude. We don't mix alcohol and work…ever. You know that."

"I'm making an exception today." The reply from Jason broke their longstanding agreement. "We'll still get everything done."

Alcohol destroyed Anthony's family, the final act when his father drove his car into a tree, killing himself. These days he rarely drank, and in the year since Julie's murder, he had offered numerous times to help Jason deal with his increased consumption. Holding up his hands, Anthony protested. "That idea sounds like Brussels sprouts to me, but I'm not your mother…just your business partner."

While not putting the bottle away, he somewhat heeded Anthony's advice and sipped slower than usual.

Every hour or so Anthony checked in with Jason. "Whatcha workin on?"

He knew this was his partner's way of attempting to gauge the bourbon's effect on his work output without sounding too obvious. Jason always answered without slurring his words. Six hours later it was Jason who was making a point, but being as blunt as possible. "See, nursemaid. We got everything on our checklist done and I didn't even get a DUI."

"Ha-ha, very funny. That doesn't change the fact that drinking on the job is a bad idea, a very bad idea, and I don't want to work this way. We agreed on that, so don't do it again. Please? Anyway, I'm going home to crash. You need a ride?"

"Nah, I'm going to spend the night here. Not much reason to go home."

Jason locked the main door behind Anthony and poured another bourbon over ice before slowly sinking into the comfy leather sofa in the common area of their warehouse office space. He sipped his drink and thought about the night before with Nikki. It had been a long time since…

Her voice seemed to float from…where? "I told you she was a bat out of hell, didn't I? And I like her too, but that doesn't mean I want to dress like her."

Rubbing his eyes, he saw Julie standing in the vacant lobby of an old-time cinema, the scent of buttered popcorn piled behind the glass of a concession stand added mood to the space. She was dressed just like Nikki when he first met her, wearing a leopard print blouse, black mini-skirt and thigh high yellow leather boots. She stomped her foot. "Please, don't do this to me again."

Looking around at his surroundings he realized he was dreaming once more, but this time he knew what to expect, and his belly laugh was almost uncontrollable. "It's a good look for you, really. You should dress like that more often."

"Come on, you bastard. White sequins were a good look for me, but I'm too short and too old to pull this off. You should treat your wife better, if you know what's good for you."

"Or what?" His laughter continued. "You'll stop showing up in my dreams? If you won't go away, I might as well be entertained. I need to start thinking about tomorrow night, maybe a bikini? Rules are rules, you know."

Putting her hands on her hips, she smirked. "I'm glad you're amused. And speaking of being amused, I guess you liked my little surprise? Nikki makes quite the impression, doesn't she?"

Jason's face morphed from delight to seriousness, and his laughter stopped. "It's kind of weird talking about another woman with my wife, even if you are, you know, dead and all."

"Relax, sweetie. I'll always be your wife, but our relationship has changed. Now I can do things for you that she can't." Then she grinned naughtily. "But by the same measure, she can do things for you that I can't anymore. You know…physical things." She winked. "So, you liked her?"

Looking down, still wearing his brown dress shoes from the night of dancing, he remained unsure if she was even real, and if she was, whether he should be talking about this with her. Tonight, she seemed nicer, more like when she was alive, so he answered. "Yeah, we had fun. I felt alive for the first time since…"

"It's okay, dear. I'm happy for you." Julie clasped his hand with her cold grip. "You deserve a good time after all you've been through. The good news is that we haven't seen the last of her, either. But until she returns, we have some entertainment of a different sort. The movie is about to start, so let's go find a seat."

As Jason and Julie sat alone in burgundy crushed velvet theater seats, the screen flickered with black and white images. A hand-held camera followed a young man dressed in boxy khaki pants held up by suspenders. He was wearing an oversized shirt with a striped pattern, his right hand shoved firmly in his front trouser pocket, as he walked past stores with signage written in what appeared to be German. Unable to read the language, Jason whispered. “What are we watching?”

“Think of this as a director’s cut of a scene from a much longer feature. Tonight, we’re following Ari Salzman along the streets of Vienna. It’s 1908.”

Jason teased. “I didn’t know they had hand cams back then.”

“Shh. It’s *your* dream, just go with it. Now, here comes the good part. Be quiet and observe.”

Onscreen, young Ari entered a café and found a seat along the wall. He spoke to the waitress and she delivered coffee in a white china cup as he kept his right hand shoved in his pocket. He fumbled awkwardly as he added a cube of sugar to his drink with his left hand. Three minutes passed as they watched Ari sip coffee. He began to perspire as he fixed his stare on a dark-haired young man sketching on a notepad on the other side of the room. Jason fidgeted. “This is the good part? Not exactly a thriller, is it?”

“Shh. Here it comes.”

Ari’s trembling hand pulled a revolver from his trouser pocket. Looking to his left, then right, he was careful to keep it below the table, out of sight from anyone else, as he aimed it at the aspiring artist. The camera captured a drop of perspiration falling from Ari’s chin onto the gingham print tablecloth.

The camera then switched perspectives, focusing on his hand gripping the pistol. He pulled the hammer back and took aim. Seconds passed as he stared, then he removed his finger from the trigger and returned the hammer into place. Slipping the gun back into his pocket, he continued sipping coffee with his unsteady left hand until the youthful adult across the room folded up his sketchpad and departed. The screen went black and the house lights came up.

Julie released her cold grip on his hand. “Amazing story telling, wasn’t it? You could cut the tension with a knife.”

“Really? I didn’t think it was a Sundance nominee or anything. What was the point, anyway? Nothing happened.”

“Very perceptive, Jason.” She smiled. “The film’s called, *The Day Adolf Hitler Wasn’t Assassinated.*”

His brow furrowed. “You mean the young man that Ari followed was Hitler? That really happened? Did some guy almost kill him before…before he became a monster?”

“You could ask him yourself, but he and his entire family were shipped to the Mauthausen concentration camp in 1939.”

“You’re making this up. That really didn’t happen…did it?”

Julie uncrossed her oversized yellow boots and turned toward Jason. “What if it did, exactly like you saw it? What if Ari was told that he needed to kill that young man to save his family as well as millions of others, and he didn’t? What would you think of him?”

Without hesitation, he fired back. “Then he missed the opportunity of a lifetime. He could have saved at least six million lives that day.”

She challenged his assuredness. “Even if it meant sacrificing his own? You saw what he had to do. He would have been charged with first degree murder and surely convicted. He would have swung from the gallows for gunning down an innocent nineteen-year-old art student.”

Feeling righteous in his judgment, he pushed back. “Six million spared in exchange for one sounds like a pretty good bargain to me. I think most reasonable people would take that deal.”

A cold hand touched his again. “Would you feel the same way if the evidence Ari saw came to him in a dream, maybe in an old theater like this? What if Ari saw visions of concentration camps and gas chambers on this very screen? He sat in that café weighing the evidence on the scales of his mind. He sifted and measured, over and over as his coffee cooled. 'Do I trust my dreams or do I trust my eyes?' You saw his struggle. He didn't make the decision hastily, but in the end, he made a choice. In the end he ultimately decided he couldn't trust his dreams."

Sitting in silence, Jason stared at the blank screen in his own dream. "Are you going to ask me to make a choice like that?"

The house lights flickered. "That's our sign that we need to leave. They have a business to run, and so do you. Now, think about what you saw tonight. Think about what you would do if you were put in a place like that, a position where you were asked to decide between your visions or your eyes."

"Is William Brandt a monster? Are you going to ask me to kill him before he becomes president?"

Julie stood and looked down at Jason. "When the time comes, someone will die, that's certain. The only question is, will it be the right person?" Jason's mouth opened upon hearing her evasive answer, but she interrupted. "Speaking of killers, these boots are murdering my feet. No more Nikki clothes!"

Chapter Ten

Guy talk is usually confined to a few safe topics. If they work together, then business is always on the top of the list, it just is. Sports are one of the safest areas, seldom venturing to vulnerable subjects. It's the rare guy conversation that veers very far from these kinds of innocuous themes into riskier ones, like feelings. Trust is the catalyst for that discussion, and even then, it's often a brief, contained event. Guys…

****

Jason was already hard at work and greeted Anthony when he arrived. "Morning."

"Twitter's blowing up over Brandt. It's mostly that #climatepolitician thing, but your girl Nikki's story adds to the mix. You couldn't have picked a better time to do a little pillow talk with a *National Conversation* reporter." Anthony continued razzing Jason three weeks after Nikki's departure.

"How long are you going to keep it up? I mean, we've exchanged a few texts since then, but it was just a one-night thing." Jason smiled when talking about her, even as he protested his friend's needling. "But seriously, this multimedia buzz around Brandt is going to make our show a must-see event. Maybe you're right. Maybe it will be bigger than The Beatles."

Anthony appeared to be in a terrific mood. "We should work under these kinds of deadlines more often. The show has come together beautifully. I think it's our best episode ever."

A sideways glance went Anthony's way, as Jason recalled his conversation with Julie on the interview's merits. "Really, best ever? I kind of thought it lacked something."

"Are you kidding? Maybe it wasn't your best work from a technical standpoint, but the energy between you two popped. It was different alright, like peanut butter and papaya. It was onscreen magic."

"I'll have to trust you on that, because that's not how it felt. Speaking of trust, what do you think of Brandt, now that we've profiled him?"

Anthony leaned back from the monitor, headphones draped around his neck. "Honestly, I like him. He's eccentric, no doubt about it, but I admire his pure optimism about the future and his out of this world good luck. Good things happen for that guy, he must have terrific karma."

"You mean like investing every dollar he made from the movies into tech stocks in the early nineties, then getting out before the dot-com bubble burst? He used that fortune to start BrandtCo Enterprises."

Leaning further back in his chair, Anthony propped his size fourteen shoes up on his workstation. "Doing it once was impressive, but he did it again with real estate and banking. He got out in '07, ahead of the crash. You gotta admit that the guy is super smart, super lucky, or both. And besides, I really liked him in *Days of Montana*."

Jason shot a rubber band at his friend, his chunky bulk almost causing Anthony to fall backward in his chair. "A chick-flick? Of all his movies, that was your favorite? Really?"

Anthony steadied himself. "Damn it, Jason, that wasn't funny. Well, it was kind of funny, but don't do it again. And yeah, I did like him as Elliott Saunders, misunderstood cowboy. I thought he showed how completely he could immerse himself in a character. He carried that movie because the supporting cast sucked. The man can act his ass off."

"Yeah, the man can act. We all know that." The lightness of the moment drained from Jason's voice. "Do you think… there's another side to him? You know, a dark side?"

"Dark side? What are you talking about? He's given away more money to charity than you and I will ever make in our lives…combined…by a factor of at least ten thousand. Then he tops that by giving away that carbon trapping technology, which nobody can even put a price on. So, yeah, that puts him right up there with Charlie Manson in my book."

"When you put it like that it makes him sound like a damned saint, and I don't believe that. I mean, he talked that crazy stuff about his dead mother in our interview, and I've got this feeling in my gut that his acting abilities might cover for something bad. It all seems strange to me."

Anthony shot the rubber band back at Jason. "Dude, how many of these shows have we done? I'll tell you. Twenty-six aired and another sixteen already in the can. How many of those stories do you think were true? Huh? The man had it rough growing up and he got through it the best way he could, that's all."

Jason sighed. "Yeah, you're probably right. It's just that *something's* bothering me and I can't put my finger on it." He stopped talking for a moment and sat straighter in his chair. He had a confession to share with his best friend. "Maybe it's just me. I haven't been sleeping that well and I've been having more of those dreams…you know, with Julie."

Anthony answered in what passed as his serious voice. "Bro, I'm telling you, you need to ease off the bottle and get some professional help. Our noggins got bounced around like dice at a Vegas craps table, and well, there's what happened to Julie. You've been in the blender lately, and I worry about you."

Opening up was uncomfortable. *I should have kept my mouth shut. I sound crazy.* Jason also didn't want to hear any more complaints about his drinking. It was a mistake to talk of addiction, or Julie and his dreams. *Change the subject.* "I'm sure it will pass after we get this season opener stuff behind us. Hey, I've got an idea. Let's throw a party here at the shop, for the premiere next week, you know, to celebrate. We can have the telecast showing on multiple monitors all around the place and a huge projection screen on the back wall. Nothing like party therapy, right?"

"You know I love a good party, but only if you invite that Nikki chick. I've got to thank her for all of the free publicity. And when you talk to her, ask if she has a single friend she might want to bring along."

Chapter Eleven

At every football game, twenty-two players are on the field at any given time. Intricate plays are drawn up for the eleven men on offense and defense. In their planning for the game, everyone watches film to learn the tendencies of their opponent and how to attack or defend. But once the ball is snapped, preparation becomes execution. Each play is alive with almost infinite possibilities. Every player must rely on others to perform their assigned duties as they try to do the same. The coach yells. "Do your job!"

****

Jason became a regular at the Blind Bat. The place held one of the few truly happy memories from the past year that a couple shots of bourbon could activate on demand. It was a light night in the place, and the hum of the crowd was subdued. He usually sat in the same booth as he had on that first night with Nikki, and on more than one occasion, nodded off with the noise of the bar providing his drunken sound track.

"Twenty-six point six seconds. That's how long this will take, so pay attention." Julie stood in a neon green halter top and Daisy Duke cutoffs, pointing at the large screen in Times Square. Jason's dream had transported him from the Blind Bat Bar and Grill to the center of the city. "And enough with your teenage fantasies. I want real clothes next time, not a copy of what the underage girl with the fake ID back at the bar is wearing."

Rubbing his eyes, Jason teased. "I can't say that I'm exactly glad to see you again, but you do look good with a little cheek showing." Still unsure if her appearances were anything more than drunken dreams, they weren't as jarring, and humor infused them more often.

"Real clothes, damn it! I want real clothes when I see you next." She breathed in what seemed to be a calming breath, then exhaled slowly. "Are you ready for tonight's feature?"

"What the hell, why not. What's on the bill, a little light comedy?"

Tourists flowed around the pair standing at the crossroads of the world, oblivious to their presence.

One of the giant digital screens that assaults the senses in this most garish venue lit with the clickety-clack imagery of an eight-millimeter film. The grill of an old Lincoln Continental limousine rolled into view, and Jason recognized it immediately. "The Zapruder film. What's a home movie of the Kennedy assassination doing playing in Times Square?"

"Shut up and watch. It's only four-hundred-and-eighty-six frames."

The crowd around them was unaware of the historic images on the multistory screen. This was a private viewing for the two of them.

"Whatever." He rolled his eyes and shrugged. "I've probably seen it a hundred times."

The playback continued as the car turned onto Elm Street in Dealey Plaza. President John Fitzgerald Kennedy, his young wife, and their entourage waved to the crowds lining the sidewalk as their motorcade passed. It was a beautiful sunlit autumn day in Texas. Then, at frame three-hundred-thirteen, the president's head exploded in brilliant Kodachrome color. A bullet from Lee Harvey Oswald's gun, fired from the sixth floor of the Texas School Book Depository, found its mark.

Looking down on his dead wife, Jason spoke somberly. "Even on the hundred-and-first viewing, it still makes me sick, so let's cut to the chase. You're going to tell me that Oswald had a dream that caused him to kill President Kennedy, right?"

"You're a quick study, but that's the obvious part. Yes, he saw his part in history in his dreams leading up to that day, and he embraced it. Would you like to learn a couple of things you don't already know, Mr. Smart Ass?"

Neon lights and gigantic billboards advertising shows on Broadway gave their gloomy discussion a 'Day of the Dead' feel. "I'm sure you'll tell me even if I don't want to hear it, so go ahead. Enlighten me."

Julie slapped his face hard. "I'm not here for my health, I'm here for your education. It may someday save your life, so pay attention."

"Ouch! That hurt." His eyes widened as he rubbed his cheek. "And what do you mean by that?"

Composing herself, Julie went on. "Where was I? Oh yeah, we're here in Times Square. Did you know that Abraham Zapruder, the guy that filmed Kennedy's assassination, also had a dream?"

Casting a wary eye, Jason brushed his stinging cheek. "He dreamed that he should capture the images of a president being killed? I think I would have heard about that."

"No. His dream was the conventional kind, a nightmare after witnessing a horrific event. He dreamed that frame three-hundred-thirteen was shown here in Times Square with the caption, *See the President's Head Explode!* After his dream he refused to allow that frame to be published for several years.

"So, if we're not here to talk about Oswald or Zapruder, what are we doing here?"

"Let's watch it again and this time we'll stop at frame seventeen, well before the fatal shot." The home movie started, this time in slow motion. It stopped automatically, freezing an image in place mere seconds into the replay. The limousine was not yet even in view, only the police motorcycles leading the caravan of vehicles.

Julie pointed. "Right there under the sign. See him? The African American man under the storefront sign. See him?"

"I see a couple of guys. Which one are you talking about?"

"The one in the white shirt, there, just to the left of the cop's helmet. His name is Jerome Jordan. He had a dream, too. Bet you haven't heard of him, have you?"

Jason shrugged. "You've got me. I've never heard of Jerome Jordan. Was he part of some deep, dark conspiracy to kill the president? One that no one else knows about except you? I can't wait to hear this one."

Suddenly, a cold breeze rushed through the square as Julie stared relentlessly, speaking with barbed words. "Jason, I'm your wife and I'm trying to help you. This is important, so do you want me to tell you Jerome's story, or not?"

Closing his eyes, Jason took in a deep breath and questioned his mental state, and knew from recent experience that the best way to get through this was to let his dream play out. "I'm in this far, might as well finish it. Go ahead. Tell me the story of the mysterious Jerome Jordan."

"Remember, I'm doing all of this for you, so pay attention." The brisk wind subsided and warm late-summer air again filled the space as she continued the lesson. "Keep in mind that none of this is in the history books, but let me give you a little background on Mr. Jordan. He started having dreams in the spring of 1963. In his dreams the famous civil rights leader, Medgar Evers, who had been assassinated just a few months before, came to him and told him that he was important to the cause. Told him that he would change the future for all people of color in America. He just needed to make a small sacrifice."

"I have no idea what you're talking about. Was he supposed to kill someone too, like Salzman in Vienna, or Oswald in Dallas?"

"It's not always as dramatic as that. Sometimes your part in history is defined by what you don't do. Take Jerome, for instance. All that was asked of him was that he quit his job. That's it. Fifteen months later the Civil Rights Act of 1964 passed. The landmark legislation changed America forever, especially for people of color, and it was all because Jerome Jordan quit his job."

"I don't understand. I've never heard of any of this…this Jerome Jordan story. I think this is just another one of your made-up poppycock stories designed to…well, I'm not sure what you're trying to do. I just wish you would stop."

Grabbing his hand, she squeezed tight. "Jason, you have lessons to learn. You can get this on the first go-round, or you can repeat the class. It's your choice."

"That's like a choice between drowning in a puddle or drowning in the middle of the ocean. I'm going to die either way, it's just a decision about how wet I'm going to get in the process."

Laughing, she punched him in the shoulder. "You are so funny! Finally, you understand! That's exactly how this works. Shall I proceed?"

He rubbed his shoulder, thinking, *she never acted this way when she was alive*. "Go ahead, Daisy Duke."

She looked up and punched him again, this time lightly. "As I was saying, Jerome worked as a watchman at the Texas School Book Depository. He was dependable and competent in his job, and if he had stayed, there is a good chance that he would have questioned Oswald about why he was going to the sixth floor the morning that Kennedy was killed. He would have thwarted the assassination. Instead, he quit his job, and the rest, as they say, is history."

"I get the assassination part, but how does that get the Civil Rights Act passed?"

"Here's the deal. Kennedy was in favor of the legislation. In fact, he had sent it to congress earlier in 1963, but Southern senators were determined to block it. If Kennedy had lived it's likely the bill would have been delayed by years, or perhaps never passed."

A mounted policeman rode past Jason as he and Julie stood discussing killing a president, and like the rest of the crowd, he was oblivious to their presence. "Kennedy's assassination helped get the law passed?"

“The new president, Lyndon Johnson, rode a wave of sympathy following Kennedy’s death to drive the bill through a stubborn senate. Jerome eventually wound up owning a string of convenience stores in suburban Dallas, and Barrack Obama was elected as the first black president less than fifty years later. It all happened because Jerome believed what he saw and heard in his dreams.”

Jason’s faith in her version of history was less than full. “Is that story true? Did it all happen that way?”

She answered coyly. “Much of it is, but that’s really not the point, is it? Did you learn tonight’s lesson? That’s the only thing that matters.”

Putting his hands on her shoulders, he looked directly into her dull, dark eyes. “What’s going on, Julie? For nearly a year I watched you die, night after night, powerless to stop your murder. Nothing ever changed. Night after night it was always the same.”

Glancing skyward for a moment, as if subconsciously seeking divine guidance, he quickly turned his gaze back to her. “Then I cross paths with William Brandt a few weeks ago and everything changes. Now I’m dreaming of you in all of these different locations and you’re telling me all this crazy shit, all the while wearing outfits from my imagination. You tip me off about Nikki showing up, and you’re giving me these alternate history lessons. Either I’m going crazy, or you’re setting me up for something. I deserve to know. Which is it?”

Signal Red lipstick accentuated her wicked smile as she answered while being held in his tight grip. “You’re on a roll. What do you think? What’s your gut telling you? Are you nuts or destined for history? This is your dream, not mine.”

Frustration and annoyance found their voice. “Urrr…Why is this happening to me? I’m not crazy, at least I don’t think so, but I also don’t believe in spirits coming from beyond the grave. Yet here you are. Anthony tells me I’m drinking too much and that I need professional help. Maybe I do.”

"Just because you don't believe in something doesn't mean it's not true, and I don't think you're crazy or need professional help. How about I tell you about the future again? How about I tell you about tomorrow, you know, as another sign? If it doesn't come true, then by all means, do what Anthony says and get some counseling. That sounds reasonable, doesn't it?"

He dropped his hands and looked again to the black sky above. "If it doesn't come true then I'll definitely get some help." He paused and hoped he was making the right decision. "I can't go on living this way, but I guess I can see how tomorrow plays out. What will one more day matter?"

She raised her chin and smiled victoriously. "That's the spirit! Now, remember the lesson from tonight. You don't have to see the whole picture to know you need to do your part. So, let's talk about our party tomorrow night. It's going to be memorable. Nikki will be there and she's still smoking hot. Your office will be packed and everyone will leave saying they'll never forget the evening. It will be mind-blowing. Trust me on that. Oh, and when you give Nikki a call tomorrow, drop a hint that she needs to be ready to write her next big story. It will get the wheels in her pretty little head spinning with some ideas."

"What kind of story? This premiere is a big deal for me and Anthony, but it's just a season-kickoff for a smalltime show on a third-rate cable network."

"Rules. I have to follow rules, remember? I can only tell you what I'm allowed, when I'm allowed. But I can assure you that doing as I say will only help you see more of Nikki. You've just told me that you're going to trust me on this, so step up and be a man."

"This is stupid. I'm supposed to call her and out of the blue tell her to be ready to write a big story, but I can't tell her what it's about? She'll think I'm an idiot."

Julie put a finger on her chin. "Listen to me and listen closely. You like her and want her to like you, too. Right? Well, she's in the news business, so if you give her leads on big stories, she will appreciate it and want to see you again. That's the way the world works."

Rubbing his forehead, he felt another headache coming on. "Even if this premiere were to turn into some kind of big event, which I can't imagine, I don't want her to like me just because I'm a good source."

Replying in a mock sultry voice, Julie used air quotes. "You want her to like the, 'real you', just like I always have. But at the same time, you want her to answer when you call while she's getting to know the 'real you.'" The blunt version of his dead wife resurfaced. "Trust me on this, give the girl a little notice to be ready to write. She'll appreciate it. And, oh, she will bring a friend to meet Anthony, if you ask. I can't wait to talk about your night after it's over, and come on, would it kill you to let me wear something a little more appropriate next time?"

Chapter Twelve

The ear hears, and the mind interprets. Context often aids in understanding, as when a teacher scolds a rowdy first-grader. "You've been a naughty boy." The child feels scorned, and understands the words to mean his behavior is unacceptable. In another setting, the same words have a different meaning. A whip cracking dominatrix repeating, "You've been a naughty boy," elicits a completely different reaction from a willing adult male. If all situations were black and white, we probably wouldn't have the word misunderstanding in our vocabulary. But we do, because we live in a world filled with shades of gray.

****

In a good mood, Jason finished his third drink. He eavesdropped as Anthony, who was dressed in a suit, talked to the blind date Nikki arranged. It was the first time in recent memory he had seen Anthony in something besides a flannel shirt, jeans and his ubiquitous Hush Puppies shoes. But something was off. *Is he wearing Spanx? Just wait until tomorrow. He'll never hear the end of this.*

He chuckled at the whole thing as his friend chatted in his own unique way of using language. "The buffet was delicious, and the open bar is fun, but it's almost time for dessert."

He translated Anthony's off the wall comments for Nikki and her friend, Aleka, a tall blond ski instructor from Vermont. "Just in case you didn't catch it, I think he's saying it's only ten minutes until show time."

The foursome stood around a bar table near the large screen suspended from the ceiling of their warehouse office. The party to celebrate the season two premiere of *Ghost Stories of the Stars* was in full-blown event mode. Jason surveyed the room seeing only happy people, and all seemed right.

With Anthony turning his full attention to Aleka, it gave Jason his first chance of the evening to talk to Nikki alone in this room full of well-wishers. Pop music played in the background as he whispered in her ear. “You look amazing.”

She winked. “Like my new ‘do?’ It’s the latest from Paris, it’s called ‘explosion.’ My stylist says it’s original, just like me.” Gone was the pink and red infused bird’s nest, and in its place was a wedge cut with highlights of various shades of red, yellow, purple and brown. The fall foliage theme highlighted her green eyes which stood out even more when complimented by her spectacular emerald party dress.

“I love it, and I also love your stories on Brandt. They really bumped the hype for our show tonight. The network is expecting our best ratings ever.” Jason felt on top of the world.

Nikki teased. “That shouldn’t be too hard for something called SPLAT TV.”

“You know what they say, people who live in glass houses…” He laughed easily. “Now, excuse me for a minute while I thank all of these people for their hard work and support.”

He fastened the top button of his black pinstriped suit, then positioned himself directly in front of the large screen, grabbing a spoon and rapping the side of his nearly empty glass three times. The milling crowd silenced as the engineers at the sound and video control board lowered the music volume. “Twenty-five days, that’s what we had. Twenty-five days to film and twenty-five days to write. Twenty-five days to score and twenty-five days to edit. Anthony and I had twenty-five days to get this episode ready to air.”

Smiling, he scanned the crowd. “The fact of the matter is we wouldn’t have even come close to doing it without the talents and support of so many of you gathered here tonight. Together we accomplished something we can be proud of. Together we tell a new story. We give the world a new image of William Brandt, one of the most public figures in the world. In the process, we will give our show the boost we all know it deserves. I've been told this will be a memorable night, and I believe it. So, to all of those who contributed and to all others who are just here for the party, grab a glass and join me in a toast."

As everyone raised their drinks, feelings of warmth and expectation filled the room. Their office had never hosted an event like this, and Jason was excited. In his brief pause, he wondered if this was what Julie meant about a night they would never forget. "To all the ghosts and ghost stories in America. May they always entertain us and our fans." Glasses clinked around the room as Jason smiled a host's confident smile, feeling that the event was truly special, but had not yet risen to the level of unforgettable, as he had been promised. *Is this it, Julie Simmons? Is this all there is?* The music resumed playing in the final few minutes leading up to the broadcast.

As soon as he returned to his spot with Nikki, his phone buzzed in his pocket. In fact, there was a collective buzzing of digital devices throughout the space. Everyone checked their glowing screens, then one gasp was added to another as a hush fell over the place, punctuated by scattered moans and muffled voices.

Aleka's voice trembled. "Oh, no."

The music felt much too loud as the background cacophony of people talking was now muted. Jason looked around, then finally pulled his phone from his pocket as he heard a woman behind him begin to cry. He read, then re-read the first few texts and tweets all containing the same words in various combinations. *Presidential Candidate Prescott Carver Assassinated.* He steadied himself and addressed those at his table with a look Anthony would later describe as 'Like a fallen soufflé.' Jason's words were simple and to the point. "Carver's been killed."

A couple of small monitors placed around the room to watch the premiere in places with obstructed views of the main screen, were switched to breaking news coverage from one of the major networks.

People crowded around them to see and hear the most up-to-the-moment news. Suddenly, a story about a celebrity, even one as big as William Brandt, didn't seem so important. The festive mood from minutes ago vanished like an ice cube in a hot cup of coffee.

In a daze, Jason walked over to the crew at the control panel, waving his hands over the boards. "Stop the music…now. Change all the screens to the news. Change them all." His stomach felt queasy as the realization of what was happening settled over him like a black cloud. Just as Julie promised, it had become a night everyone would remember.

Chapter Thirteen

Magma chambers below the earth's surface roil with super-heated lava. Pressure builds as it pushes against the crust of the planet, probing the weakest points. Most often these are found where tectonic plates grind against one another, each marching to their own eons old beat. Eventually, a fault is discovered and a volcano explodes, releasing molten lava and hot gases. Once the pressure is released, equilibrium returns. The city of Pompeii, with its residents frozen in their last moments, is a silent reminder of the power and destructive force of one of these eruptions.

****

Jason sent everyone away from the party and went home to drink alone. Nikki gave him a kiss on the cheek and dashed off to file a story. She said she already had a few ideas in mind thanks to his cryptic advanced warning. Even in his unsettled state, sleep came quickly…as did a visit from his dead wife.

"Was I right or what? Everyone there will be able to tell their grandchildren where they were when they heard the news of Prescott Carver's assassination." Tonight, Julie sat cross-legged on the leather sofa in the apartment she shared with Jason. She wore thick, white cotton pajamas with little pink hearts, holding the TV remote as the news coverage of the presidential candidate's murder droned on relentlessly.

Even in his dream Jason drank. In his cozy living room, his whiskey glass formed a thick watermark on the narrow-by-necessity side table. A coaster set they purchased on a vacation in Ireland, sat conspicuously beside the tumbler. Not using anything to protect this antique piece of furniture was one of Julie's pet peeves, and he hoped it would piss her off, even in death. He spoke words he would never have to Julie when she was alive, but the living Julie would never have set him up for a fall. "You bitch. How could you do that to me?"

"Whoa, Bucko. I didn't make that man shoot Carver. He controlled his own destiny. Give me some credit here, I did tell you something big was going to happen."

"Damn it, Julie. You know what I'm talking about. You let me invite all those guests with all that hype when you knew what was going to happen. You could have warned me, and you didn't. You led me to believe that something good was going to happen. I hate you."

The harsh comment seemed to have no effect on her. "That's the way the rules work. You and I don't write them, but we do have to follow them. I told you what I was allowed to tell you. That's the deal."

"Then I want out of this arrangement. I'm going to make an appointment to see someone tomorrow, some kind of therapist. I can't take this anymore." He took a big sip of his dream beverage and closed his eyes, hoping she would just go away.

Julie didn't move a muscle, acting as if she hadn't heard a thing he said. Pointing the remote at the TV, she turned up the volume. "Let's watch him die again. They're showing it in slow motion this time."

"Are you deaf? I'm finished with you." He leaned back and closed his eyes again as the commentator started his description of the deadly encounter between assassin and victim.

Leaning over, she punched him in the arm. "Watch this. It will be important, trust me."

Grudgingly, Jason opened his eyes as the announcer continued. "At this time, it's being reported that the gunman acted alone. As we isolate him with our spot shadow, we can see him raise his arm and fire three shots, just after Senator Carver repeats his campaign pledge."

They watched the candidate deliver his trademark lines as the narrator went silent. "In just over a month, the American people will speak with one voice, declaring they want a better life for themselves, for their children and for their grandchildren. My promise is that I will work day and night to have that voice heard. The people will be heard! The people will be heard!" The crowd cheered the oft repeated phrase.

The first of three flashes appeared in the spot shadow micro-seconds before any sound. Three holes appeared on Carver's starched white shirt and for an instant, silence reigned, like the moment before a priest says amen when ending a prayer. Pandemonium erupted as the men closest to the killer reach desperately with outstretched hands to pull him down. Secret Service Agents raced to whisk away the crumpling and now blood-soaked senator. Screams of panic became the primary vocabulary of this particular chaos in the packed auditorium in upstate New York.

The camera is jerked as some rush toward the location of the gunfire, while most flee. In a few seconds the man who fired the shot is taken down, and after a few more seconds is snatched to his feet and dragged toward one of the exits. The whole incident took less than one minute from start to finish.

Julie turned the sound down as the non-stop coverage continued. "Fascinating, isn't it? Seeing history unfold like that in our lifetime…I mean in your lifetime."

He was in a sour mood, but answered her question. "I don't see any humor at all. Something terrible has happened to our country, and to that man and his family." He sighed. "And it didn't exactly help me either." Jason folded his arms, his gaze directed at the TV instead of Julie.

"Oh, Jason. Come on. After all you've seen these past few weeks, you can't possibly think this didn't happen without being part of something bigger. Can you?"

He hesitated, aware that just moments ago he tried to cast her out of his dreams, but he couldn't resist answering. "Let me guess, that guy, the one who shot Carver had dreams telling him to kill him so he wouldn't become president. He was led to believe that murdering

Carver was actually for the greater good. Right? That's what you're telling me?"

"I don't need to tell you anything." She looked at him coyly. "You're figuring things out all on your own, aren't you?"

His gaze turned toward her, focusing his emotion through his eyes like twin lasers. "You know, everything isn't always about some grand conspiracy. Sometimes crazy people do cruel things and the universe doesn't give a crap. I mean, look at you." He spoke aloud the truth he had come to accept since she died. "You were killed for sixty-seven dollars in cash, and the police still haven't found your killers. Your murder was just one more random act of violence in a world that just doesn't give a damn."

"Aw, that's about the sweetest thing you've said to me since I died. I mean, you really do miss me. It hurts to hear your pain, even if you are wrong. It's so…touching."

Jason rose from his chair in a full rage, angry about an uncaring world that had taken away his wife and his happiness. His hand reflexively grabbed the first thing he could find, and it happened to be the hand-blown glass vase they purchased in Murano, Italy on their honeymoon, six years ago. He flung it with all his might against the wall at the end of his living room. "God damn it, Julie. You were murdered and don't even seem to care!" He spat the words like fire as dead brown flowers lay on the floor among scattered pieces of broken blue glass.

She flinched when the vase hit the wall, but remained seated. "That's right, take deep breaths. Let the anger out. That's it, now take another breath. Just let it go, let the anger flow out of you."

Sitting on the edge of his chair, he put his head in his hands with his elbows on his knees. He sobbed and his body convulsed in rhythmic waves as his emotions swelled and searched for release.

Approaching, to comfort him, she stood beside his crumpled body, with cool fingers running through his sweaty curls. "That's right, honey. Let it out, just let it all out. Cry all you want and let go of that anger." She pulled his tall, sobbing frame against her fuzzy pajamas. "Of course I miss you too, sweetie, but you've got to let go of our old relationship and embrace our new one, like I have. I know it's not easy, but it's what you have to do, you'll see. We still have a future together, it's just different than the one we planned."

Speaking between gasps, he held on to her. "I know…it's just been so hard for me…losing you was so hard." Leaning back, Jason looked up, wishing her black eyes were blue again. "We had plans…we were going to work together, you were going to leave *Rare Air*, and become the guest booker for our show." His voice choked as he brought up a deeper wound, his words crying out from the depths of his soul. "We were going to start a family!"

She responded evenly and calm. "And you would have made a great father, Jason, but history has other plans for us. I know it hurts, but you *have* to let go of all that rage. Just release it and embrace our new future."

"I know that you're gone and never coming back, but…talking to you these last few weeks has made me miss you, the living version of you, even more." His body shook. "I loved you so much."

Falling back into her embrace, she stroked his dark brown locks. "I'll always be here for you, Jason. Not even death can keep me away."

When his crying eased, she squatted to look him in the eye. "Would it help if the police made some progress in my case? Would that make you feel better?"

Wiping tears with the back of his hand, he answered. "Maybe. I don't know. The only thing I know for sure is that I really miss you."

"Well, let's see if it will help. You have to promise me that you will act surprised when they come tomorrow. Can you do that?"

"I guess so. Is there really a lead in your case?"

"Yes dear. I guarantee it. Trust me on this. Now remember, act surprised tomorrow."

Chapter Fourteen

'Fool me once, shame on you. Fool me twice, shame on me.' It's an old saying that has ancient origins. It's staying power to contemporary times means its truth is linked to basic human nature. The question is, why do we forgive someone after they deceive us once? Why do we give others the chance to fool us a second time? There is no single answer, but when it's between a man and a woman, the answer more often than not… is love.

****

Jason dressed a little nicer than usual for an office day, taking Julie at her word that he would be visited by the police. He wore pressed black slacks and one of his favorite intentionally untucked dress shirts. Looking across the open space, he addressed Anthony. "That was some kind of night."

Anthony reverted to form, wearing one of his dozens of flannel shirts over jeans. The events of the prior evening must have hit him hard as for once he didn't use a food analogy. "We had snow on the beach last night, didn't we?" He leaned back in his chair and flipped a toy football in the air in a perfect spiral toward the ceiling. Gravity then did its part, pulling it back toward him like a missile falling from the sky. He repeated the action again and again. Even the ever-ebullient Anthony was bummed out today.

Last night he intended to give his partner a hard time about wearing elastic shapewear to make him appear slimmer, but the way things turned out, it just didn't feel right. Jason shared his glum mood. "Yeah, a perfect night ruined. How did things turn out with you and Aleka? You seemed pretty into her." He was leaning back in his chair as well, feet up on a credenza as a team of people in white overall uniforms worked. They were sent by the catering company to clean up the mess in the open space.

"Did you know she's a ski instructor in Vermont? Cool chick, but we got buried by the avalanche of news about Craver, like everyone else. We exchanged numbers and called it a night. I'd like to see her again, but who knows? How about you, how did your night with Nikki turn out?"

Softly, Jason answered. "Mostly like yours. She headed upstate to get an angle on the assassination, and I fell asleep in my chair at home and had the weirdest nightmare. Ended up smashing a vase against the wall."

"Whoa, dude. I'm telling you, you need to get some help before you do something you regret. Let me hook you up with the shrink who helped me. My headaches are so much better now."

Last night's crying spell had washed away much of his anger at his dead wife. And Jason didn't answer immediately. When he did, he surprised himself. "I think I'm beginning to get a handle on things. When I woke up this morning, I felt a lot better, like everything's coming into focus. I feel like I'm beginning to get more perspective on life. You ever feel that way?"

"Man, every day that I wake up is special, but right now my brain is frozen. We crammed that entire William Brandt episode into such a tight timeline that I'm thinking about as clearly as a snowman." He tossed the toy football in the air again and waited for it to fall back into his hands. "How about we take a few days off and clear our minds? Maybe do some hiking in the mountains to scout winter ski slopes or something. Maybe head up to Stowe?"

He caught his friend's not-so-subtle hint about wanting to see Aleka again, and laughed. "Yeah. A few days off sounds like a good idea to me, too. The network is going to rerun the Brandt interview next week and we've already got sixteen episodes in the can. We're ahead of the game. Why don't you head to the hills and see who you run into? I think I'll stay here in the city. Who knows what could happen?"

As if on cue, Ella buzzed from the front desk. "Mr. Simmons, there are two men here to see you. They're from the FBI."

Jason quickly masked his smile before feigning surprise.

Anthony, on the other hand, was truly shocked. “Dude, the feds?”

He used his best stunned voice. “I have no idea why they’re here, but I told you I had a feeling things were going to get interesting. I’ve got to start playing the lottery.” Jason replied to Ella. “Send them in.”

Two beefy forty-somethings in nearly matching black suits and thin black ties marched out of the reception area and across the open warehouse space toward Anthony and Jason. They made a straight line past the cleaning crew and couldn’t have looked more stereotypical if they tried. The heavier of the two spoke. “Jason Simmons?”

“Yeah, that’s me. What’s this about?”

“Is there someplace we can talk, somewhere private?” They both glanced simultaneously at Anthony, then the cleaning crew.

“Sure, Anthony, you mind giving us some space?”

“No problem.” He looked nervously at the cops and Jason was sure it was related to the night they first met. There was still disagreement on whose idea it was to crash popstar Gwen Blaze’s wedding, then getting tossed in jail for a night. Anthony rose from his chair. “I’m heading for the mountains.” With that, he turned and beat a quick path to the exit.

Jason now addressed the workers. “Hey guys. Take ten, we need a few minutes.”

“Sure, boss.” The foreman responded and one by one the team filed out.

His attention now returned to the agents. “How about we have a seat and talk over there?” He motioned to a conference table a few feet away.

The stockier of the two agents again spoke as his partner secured the door, as everyone except the three of them exited. “We’ll stand.”

When his colleague returned, the thick man resumed speaking. "I'm Agent Kevin O'Reilly and this is Agent Keen Adams. We're from the New York office and we've got some questions for you…questions about your wife's murder."

"Sure. Do you have a new lead?" *It's all playing out the way she said it would.*

Agent O'Reilly led the interrogation. "Mr. Simmons, was your wife involved with any religious organizations?"

"What?" *That's an unusual question to ask about a mugging victim.* "No. I mean we went to Mass a few times a year, but that was about it. What does religion have to do with Julie's murder?"

"Do you know a man named Powell Moberly?" The agent pressed on without acknowledging Jason's inquiry.

Jason thought for a moment. "That name's not ringing a bell. Should I know him?" *Where's he going with this?*

"Think hard, Mr. Simmons, this is very important. Do you or your wife have any connection to an organization called Original Friends of Fatima?"

"Fati what?" *What the hell's going on? She didn't warn me about this!* "I thought she was killed in a mugging gone wrong. What do you know?"

Agent O'Reilly pressed harder. "We're getting a warrant to search your home and your office as we speak. Do we have your permission to start now? Your cooperation will be noted and appreciated."

Feeling his chest tightening, Jason questioned. "Search warrant? Wait just a minute. Will one of you tell me what's going on here? Maybe start with why the FBI is here instead of the New York City police? Tell me what's going on."

The agent's expression didn't change, seeming to drive home his point. "We're the ones asking questions here, Mr. Simmons. Do we have permission to start our search, or not?"

The smug feeling from a few minutes ago was completely gone. *Julie! You could have warned me this was coming!* His eyes darted from one agent to the other, then back again. He had faced scarier men than this in his war reporting and he wasn't about to give up his constitutional rights without a good reason. "Guys, you've got to give me something before I let you search my home and business without a warrant. This is still America."

Agent O'Reilly delivered his reply like an actor in his hundredth performance of the same play. "With all due respect to our constitution, we don't have to tell you anything, we just have to get a judge to sign the papers. That's going to happen in the next thirty minutes. So, do we have your permission to start? You're slowing down our investigation into the murder of a patriot."

"A patriot? I don't understand." Jason felt his face warming, and struggled to get a full breath.

Agent Adams eyes widened as he spoke for the first time. "Mr. Simmons, are you okay? You don't look so good." He shot a quick glance with a furrowed brow to his partner, then back to Jason. "Can I get you a glass of water, or something?"

Reaching for his collar to loosen it, Jason found the top button wasn't fastened. He spoke between gasps. "I just need some air." He glanced around, then decided to head toward the closest window and open it, but after taking one step in that direction, things blurred and the room spun. His words slurred. "I don't feel well." His field of vision narrowed, and darkness closed in as he tried in vain to push it away. *Julie…help me!*

"Mr. Simmons. Mr. Simmons, can you hear m…"

Chapter Fifteen

There comes a time in every relationship when the couple transitions from dating to going steady. They become exclusive. It often happens after the first argument, when they realize there is enough substance to the relationship that they can withstand some bumps along the way. Things get easier, and little quirks and habits are tolerated. They are part of the package, for better or worse.

****

Julie looks good in a uniform. That was Jason's first thought as he opened his eyes and saw her in the back of the ambulance with him, wearing a navy-blue paramedic outfit.

She placed her stethoscope on his chest as the wail of the siren echoed off of the city's lifeless concrete walls. "The last time I was in an ambulance, things didn't turn out so well for me. I died!"

He spoke through the oxygen mask that had been placed on his face by the real EMTs. "Am I dead, too?"

Listening intently to his heartbeat, she answered. "Let's hope not. That would really ruin my day."

"It wouldn't do much for mine either." He looked around and got his bearings. "These straps are really tight. Could you loosen them a little?"

"Honey, this is your dream. You can drive this meat wagon through the thunderstorm, if you want, but why don't you just lay there and rest while we talk?"

"That's probably a good idea. What happened to me, anyway?"

"Best I can figure, you had a little panic attack when those nice agents came to see you. You are such a better actor than I give you credit for. You totally pulled off that 'look surprised' act. It's no wonder you and Brandt work so well together. You two make a good team."

"Imagine if you hadn't told me they were coming." He chuckled. "I might have had a heart attack!" Now they both laughed until he fully recalled his conversation with the G-Men. "You know, you could have been a little clearer when you told me there was a break in your case. A search warrant from the FBI…seriously?"

The ambulance turned a corner and hit the brakes hard. He could hear the driver cursing, apparently barely avoiding a jaywalking pedestrian more absorbed with saving her flexed umbrella, which was being ripped apart by the storm, than with traffic. The real paramedic on the other side of him steadied the IV bag that swung on the fixed hook. Jason noticed his name badge identifying him as one Charles Little, then ignored him and continued his conversation with his wife. "The FBI's involved in your murder? What's up with that?"

"The newsmen did a wonderful job spotlighting Mr. Moberly last night. If you looked closely when I told you to, you would have seen the three faint scars on his cheek."

"I don't understand…" He stopped, as it became clear. Wonder coated his next words. "He's one of the guys that killed you?"

"Yep. This morning they matched his DNA to the sample they took from under my fingernails. I told you to trust me, that there would be a break in the case." She looked up and down his prone body on the stretcher. "Last night I asked if a break in my case would make you feel better. Do you feel better?"

"Very funny." The ambulance hit a pothole and water splashed the underside of the vehicle. Julie braced herself while Charles placed his hand on Jason, making sure he was secure. His gloved touch was warmer than Julie's bare hand. Jason spoke in bewilderment. "Your murderer is also Carver's assassin. Who knew?"

Biting her bottom lip, she averted her eyes. "Well…I guess it would be fair to say that I did." Her rationalization continued. "I didn't hide it from you, you just never asked."

The pure oxygen had its intended effect and Jason began to understand his relationship with Julie more clearly. "This is the way it's going to be, right? More surprises behind every turn?"

She nodded. "You're alive, and as they say, life is full of surprises."

He shook his head back and forth across the vinyl surface of the stretcher. "That is wrong on so many levels." His anger that had ebbed with last night's tears rose again. "How about sparing me the heart attack next time and just tell me where all of this is going?"

A wicked laugh met his request. "You're forgetting the rules. I come to you when I want, and that means I tell you what you need to know, when you need to know it. And by the way, next time you put me in a uniform, can I have a gun?"

He was not amused. "You and your damned rules can go straight to hell."

"These aren't *my* rules, they are *the* rules. How many times do I have to tell you that?"

"Then tell whoever sets them I want a re-write of mine."

Julie grabbed both ends of the stethoscope draped around her neck. "Argh…There is no one person writing the rules, and there are no do-overs. They are simply what they are. When are you going to get that through your thick skull?"

The portable ECG machine began to beep more rapidly as Jason's pulse quickened. "What if I just quit playing along? What if I just die or something?"

Shaking her head, she took a deep breath. "It's not your time, we both know that. But I can tell you a little bit more about your future, if you want to know." He lay on the stretcher in silence, unwilling to play her game. She finally ended the stalemate. "Fine. I'll just tell you anyway because it's time for you to know. Do you want to take a guess who's going to take Carver's spot on the ticket?"

Jason rolled his eyes at how obvious the answer was. "This is how Brandt gets into the presidential race with just a few weeks to go. He takes Carver's place."

"He won't announce until after the funeral, but take it from me, it's a done deal. I bet your long-legged friend is already writing the story and she probably just needs an anonymous source to quote."

The speaker above Charles Little's head informed them that they were in sight of the hospital. "I guess this visit from beyond is almost over. Can you tell me if I'm supposed to be her unnamed source?"

"Either that, or she will make one up. Lack of facts don't seem to stand in the way of a story with that chick, regardless of her other…attributes."

Jason blushed again at his wife's suggestive mention of Nikki. "Even if you are dead, it's still uncomfortable hearing you talk about her like that."

She answered in a matter-of-fact manner. "Just calling it like I see it. I've always been a little like this, and being dead only magnifies it."

The ambulance came to a complete stop. "I guess this is where my role in the William Brandt story ends. Will you still come to see me?"

"Like I told you before, we're just getting started. Don't be so confident you're done with William Brandt."

The back doors flew open and a gust of wind from the storm swirled around the rear compartment of the vehicle. She leaned down and kissed him lightly on the cheek, and like a reverse fairy tale, Sleeping Beauty's kiss awoke Prince Charming. His eyes opened and the organized chaos of the emergency department surrounded him for the next six hours. He was jabbed, poked and scanned, then left alone in a room with the two agents outside the door…until the process repeated itself.

The attending physician finally discharged him into the custody of Agents O'Reilly and Adams with some advice. "You took a pretty good bump on the head, Mr. Simmons. We didn't see much difference between this CT and the prior ones from your war injuries, but you should follow up with your neurologist for a more detailed exam. You ended up here today because you were dehydrated, so drink plenty of fluids, and try to eat a little better. And a little less alcohol and some rest wouldn't hurt either."

"Yeah, doc. I'll do that." Jason's non-committal tone seemed to be noted by his two shadows.

By the time they walked out of the hospital, the searches of his home and office had been completed, and like the CT, nothing out of the ordinary was immediately found. O'Reilly handed him a card as they dropped him off in front of his building. Without an ounce of sympathy, and perhaps a tinge of suspicion, he addressed Jason. "We still have your computer, so we'll be back in touch. If you think of anything between now and then, give us a call at this number."

"Thanks for the excitement, guys." Jason stood in front of his building getting soaked in the storm's final surge as the government issued sedan drove away. He pulled his phone from his pocket in the gathering darkness of a damp evening and scrolled to the B's, then touched the entry labeled Broussard. "Hey, Nikki. Need a source for your next Brandt story?"

Chapter Sixteen

In 49 BC, Julius Caesar led his army over a small river north of Rome. By that act he signaled he had reached a point of no return. His intention was to take power, using armed conflict if necessary. Many Roman Senators fled in a bid to save themselves in the imminent civil war. History records he uttered the words, "The die is cast," as he crossed the Rubicon.

****

"Sorry about the way your party ended last night. I liked your friends." Nikki downed her first dirty martini of the evening at the Blind Bat and caught the waitress's eye, already signaling for another. "Seriously, I've really got to figure out what they put in these things, they're terrific."

"Well, I did promise a night to remember." Not totally ignoring the doctor's advice, Jason chased his shot of bourbon with water.

"Yes, you did, and you delivered. Now, speaking of delivering, my editor tells me they want to run my story in both the print and digital versions. The deadline to hit the morning edition is midnight. On the phone you promised to be a source for my next Brandt story, so out with it. What do you have?"

With clothes still a little damp from standing in the rain, he slowed the conversation. "Chill. I'm going to deliver alright, but tell me what you've got. I want to make sure I'm not way off base before we go too far."

With a smirk and head tilt, she seemed to question his motives. "Too far? I thought we already crossed that line a few weeks ago. Are you going to do a mainstream story too, or are you just helping me out of the goodness of your heart?"

The waitress with the nose ring placed their fresh drinks between them and inquired about a food order. They both answered, 'no,' at the same time, dismissing her.

"You don't have to worry about information sharing on this one. I'm just your anonymous source, so treat me any way you want." His pulse quickened as he thought about the sparks they created on their last full night together. In a nanosecond, he flashed back to the image of her standing in their suite at the Ritz in her black panties and bra. He began to wonder what she might be wearing tonight under her breezy summer floral print dress. His suddenly focused eyes spotted a hint of a bra strap. *Pink. Nice.* He picked up the short glass that the waitress placed on the table and finished his second drink in one gulp, skipping the water this time. *To hell with that doctor and his advice. I know what I'm doing.*

She winked and took another sip. "Just want to establish the ground rules before we start. I always like to know where the boundaries are before I break them." Setting down her martini, Nikki switched to reporter mode, giving him the low down on what she had uncovered. "Most of what I have, so far, is from the public record. Some schmuck named Powell Moberly has been identified as the shooter, and he's quite the nut job. Been in and out of treatment facilities his whole life."

Jason further fact checked her investigation of Moberly. "Did you know he has ties to a secret religious organization called The Original Friends of Fatima?"

"Yeah. He posted some pretty crazy things on the internet. Stuff about the Vatican hiding the true prophecy about the events leading up to the end of the world. The Three Secrets of Fatima is a real thing with the Catholic Church, but that group Moberly's affiliated with seems to be a dangerous off-the-rails conspiracy group. They've inspired other nut jobs to commit acts of terror around the world."

The waitress stopped by and asked if they wanted another round. This time her interruption was greeted much more warmly. Again, they answered in unison, but this time both saying 'yes.'

Jason chuckled. "Those boys at the networks will be working your side of the street for a few days, you know, reporting on the pending end of the world."

She raised her glass in acknowledgment. "It's about time that story caught up to my writing. So, what do you have that's new, Mr. Anonymous? What do you have that's going to make my night?"

Now it was Jason's turn to look both ways to see if anyone was eavesdropping. "Did you know this is not the first time that Powell Moberly has killed?"

Nikki's head cocked and eyebrows rose. "I've checked both state and federal databases, his record is clean." She leaned forward, elbows on the table, then shifted from matter-of-fact reporting to a conspiratorial tone. "Unless my deep-throat source knows something different?"

Looking at her for a long few seconds before deciding how to proceed, Jason again wondered how much to tell her. He figured that tonight was not the right time to disclose his current arrangement with his dead wife. There might never be a right time to bring that up. *I'll stick to the facts. That's the safe play here.* Taking in a deep breath, he released it quickly. He was ready to start talking, hoping to extend the evening, as on their first night together.
"Sooo…Moberly also killed my wife."

Sitting motionless, it seemed Nikki was processing what she had just been told, trying to determine if it could be true. She took his hand and squeezed. "Bullshit." She used the exact word he used at Heaven when he questioned her psychic lead. "Before I came to see you the first time, I read about her murder. It was a random and tragic death. Horrible, yes, but I don't recall anything about her killers being identified or arrested. Did I miss something?"

He felt the warmth of her touch and the kick of the bourbon, and he liked the combination. Being near Nikki, he felt energized. "You're right. The police couldn't connect the evidence to a suspect at the time, but they did earlier today." He paused to take another look at this beautifully fierce woman as she intently followed his story. Seeing her sufficiently piqued, he delivered on his promise. "I had a visit from the FBI this morning."

Green eyes bore into him. "The FBI? Did they come right out and tell you Moberly killed your wife?" Nikki squeezed harder and one of her acrylic nails pressed sharply into his flesh almost to the point of bringing blood.

Pleasure and pain sensors were going off like alarms in his brain, and he liked that too. He felt alive. "They didn't say it in so many words, but between their questions and seeing the faded scars on Moberly's face in the assassination video replays, I put two and two together. He did it."

She winked at him and released her grip. Then she put her hand in the air and simulated writing her signature, the universal signal for 'check please.' "That's close enough to an official statement for me. I've got two hours before my deadline. How about we continue this discussion at my place while I file my story? By the way, what's your safe word? Mine's 'Emerald.'"

"Safe word?"

She signed the credit card receipt with a flourish, then gave a playful giggle. "After I file my story…you know, if things get a little…a little…just use your imagination." Her eyelashes flashed naughtiness.

He felt like he just went from splashing in a bathtub to being dropped in the middle of an ocean. He was way out of his depth with no coastline in sight. "Oooh." He was simultaneously excited and alarmed. He and Julie had an active sex life, but they never… "Uhh…" He scrambled to come up with a word that would spring to mind if something made him feel he needed to call a timeout. Vivid images flashed in his head of their entwined bodies but he couldn't summon a single one that would make him beg her to stop. Obviously, she had the better imagination. Then, out of nowhere a word popped into his mind. "How about, Ruby." Only later did he realize that was the last name of the man who killed Lee Harvey Oswald, assassin of President Kennedy.

Chapter Seventeen

Binary code. Ones and zeroes. All computer programs, from the most basic that can add one plus one, to the most advanced that can simulate human speech, are based on those two numbers. There is no two, or three or any other number, letter or symbol. In the digital world there are only two options: a one or a zero. That's essentially what separates human thinking from the most advanced machines…at least for now.

****

Jason woke with a tingling in his arm. He pried his eyes open and adjusted to the blacklight glow that bathed the room in an ethereal hue. The psychedelic colors of an abstract art mural radiated above the headboard. Turning his head, he saw Nikki laying naked and glistening on the other side of the king-sized bed. Her tattoo of Jesus looked 3-D in the ultraviolet world of her bedroom.

He tried to take it all in and remember the details of their night. The strong scent of coconut reminded him of the liberal amount of oil they slathered on each other, and he smiled. Memories of stroking her body, and her caresses of his, sent new charges through the circuits of his brain. They were equally intense whether he was remembering the tender touches, or the rough ones.

Turning his head to the other side, a different kind of jolt ran down his arm again, and he located the source of his discomfort. His left wrist was shackled in a fur-lined cuff, secured halfway up one of the pillars of her four-poster bed. His memory of getting chained was a little fuzzy, but one thing on which he was crystal clear, was neither of them uttered the safe words, 'Emerald,' or 'Ruby.'

"Jason Simmons. I've learned more about your turn-ons now that I'm dead than I ever did while I was alive." Julie suddenly appeared on his side of the bed dressed like Annie Oakley in a cowgirl outfit, straight from a 1950's western. She wore fringed leather pants and matching blouse, with a holstered piston strapped to her waist. The holster's turquoise inlays glowed.

"What are you doing here!" His lips tightened and eyes sprang wide. "You'll wake her, or worse, shoot one of us!" He spoke in his loudest whisper.

"She drank at least a dozen martinis, so she's not waking up until it's time. Besides, I promise not to kill anyone for sleeping with you, it's part of our deal." Then he detected sarcasm creeping into her voice. "Then again, I guess sleeping doesn't exactly cover everything that happened tonight, does it?"

He rubbed his face with his free hand, trying to wake up. "That's like asking a politician when they stopped beating their wife. Any answer given will be used against them."

Julie touched her chin. "Interesting choice of words. Hmm. And speaking of interesting choices, nice job following your doctor's advice about getting some rest and drinking less."

Jason answered her criticism with the oldest excuse in the book. "I'll start tomorrow."

"Yeah, right. But speaking of tomorrow, that's why I'm here. Just let me get comfortable while we chat." She walked to the end of the bed and crawled in the space between him and Nikki.

He struggled to keep her out, but found it impossible with one arm chained. He protested as loud as he thought he could. "What the hell do you think you're doing?"

"Oh, shut up. You've got two women in bed with you, and one of them has a gun. I wouldn't complain too much, if you know what's good for you."

"Really? You think this is funny?"

Lying on her back between them, she looked at the ceiling. "I don't just think it's funny, I think it's hilarious. I'm immensely enjoying watching you squirm. That alone is worth the trip to see you, but that's not why I'm here." She paused. "What's up with my outfit tonight?"

He could feel the immediate blush of his cheeks. *Might as well tell her, she can read my mind.* His voice was shy. "The whip on the hook over there." His head motioned to the far wall. "It has an Old West look."

Giggling, she fired a reply. "Maybe we should have experimented more…but that would have lessened the shock value for you a few hours ago."

"Can we just move on?" He was embarrassed having this conversation with her, even if she was probably a figment of his imagination. "Why are you here?"

"We're going to watch a little classic cinema. You ready?"

Peeking over his lounging wife, he glimpsed Nikki. Other than her rhythmic breathing, she was as still as a stone. Jesus looked back at him sympathetically. "This is going to happen whether I like it or not, isn't it?"

"It's the rules, Jason. You should know that by now. Just relax and let it happen. Oh, and feel free to use your safe word if this gets too intense."

He yanked on his chain one more time, then resigned himself to the inevitable, resting his head on the pillow beside her. "Roll the damn tape."

Nikki's bedroom ceiling became tonight's screen as they stared upward with the start of the film. Column after column of Nazi soldiers marched into a packed stadium as Julie added commentary. "Nuremberg, 1934. I wish I had some popcorn or something. That coconut smell is making me hungry."

Jerking his arm like a trapped animal proved futile. "You're too much, you know that?" He grabbed the sheet with his free hand and covered himself.

"Just watch for a few minutes, admire the craftwork of the film."

He settled into the pillow again and watched the slick camerawork as well as the dramatic use of scoring to gradually build toward a climax. "The subject is repugnant, but technically, it's brilliant. Directed by a woman, right?"

"Glad that IED didn't scramble everything in your brain. Leni Riefenstahl was the mastermind behind this famous bit of propaganda. Hitler personally requested that she direct *Triumph of the Will.*"

Thinking back on their conversation from an earlier encounter, Jason posed a question. "Wonder how things would have turned out if Ari Salzman had pulled the trigger when he had the chance to kill Hitler. Would any of this have even happened?"

Dispassionately, she answered. "We'll never know. That ship sailed when he chickened out, and there are no do-overs in this world. That's why tomorrow's decision is so important."

He rubbed his forehead with his free hand. "Here we go again. Can you at least be a little more specific so I don't have a heart attack or something, like I almost did with the FBI yesterday?"

Even when she was alive, Julie's hands were often chilly in bed, so, giggling again, she put her deadly cold ones on him, like she used to. He flinched, and she teased. "Why so jumpy?"

Sighing in resignation, he resorted to begging. "Come on, Julie. Quit messing with me like this. Please?"

"Oh, okay. Sleeping Beauty's phone is about to ring anyway. So, what did you think of Leni Riefenstahl's decision to make the movie?" Julie stood up in the bed as she waited for his answer, pulling the pistol from its holster and aiming at the lamp on the other side of the room.

What the hell is she doing now? "Are you serious? Put that away before you hurt someone!"

"Quit whining. I know what I'm doing, and besides, this is only real in your dream…maybe. Now, answer my question. What did you think of her choice?"

Taking his armed wife's query seriously, he thought for a moment. It was not a simple question. "Well, she showed the whole world how skilled she was, that's for sure. I admire her work, she knows her craft. But here's the crux of it. She made a feature length commercial for a madman and his ideology. The fact that she did it with such proficiency and artistry just makes it all the more sickening."

Julie pulled the trigger and a loud percussive boom echoed around the room. The lamp exploded into tiny pieces of florescent green ceramic. The smell of ignited gunpowder overpowered the coconut aroma. She whooped. "One down and two to go."

Flinching, Jason's next instinct was to check on Nikki. To his relief, she remained perfectly still. *Thank God I'm dreaming and that really didn't happen.* "Damn it, Julie! Why do we have to play these games? Why don't you just tell me what you want me to hear?"

She laughed knowingly and glanced at the sleeping Nikki. "I thought you liked the unexpected. It keeps things interesting, right?" Her dull eyes appeared deep purple in the blacklight and they now stared straight into his. She blew away the smoke lingering at the end of the barrel, then lowered her voice to a sultry level. "I like to keep things interesting, too."

Turning, she seemed to lock her gaze on a new target and aimed at the TV in the corner. "So, she should have turned down the job? Is that what you're saying? She should have just turned Hitler down and not made the movie?"

This time he answered without reservation. "Absolutely."

Two shots rang out in quick succession. *Boom, boom.* Slivers of the flat screen flew across the room, with some landing on the bed. Jason was glad that he had covered himself, and again looked at Nikki. She lay peacefully asleep, oblivious to this Second Amendment exhibition of the right to bear arms.

Sharp shooting Julie seemed on a roll reveling in her accuracy. "Two down and one to go. Wahoo!"

Spinning around, she took aim at the reflected image of Jason in the mirror across the room, then continued toying with the gun, and him. "What if she took the job, but made a different film, one that laid bare the anti-Semitism and hatred of the Nazi movement? What would you think of her then?"

He fumed. He was both chained and backed into a corner, with nowhere to run. Julie was out of control and he was being forced to participate in her antics. His choice was to answer her question or argue with someone who might not even exist.

She prodded. "Come on, Jason. Show *me* some excitement in the bedroom. What's your answer? Huh? How would the world see Leni today if she had made that kind of movie?"

He answered as if a hostage in his own dream. "She would probably be hailed as a hero."

Three shots rang out. *Boom, boom, boom.* Shards of glass exploded from the shattered mirror, and her voice bellowed. "Ms. Riefenstahl had three options. She was not limited to an either-or decision, of making the movie or not. She had a third option, and didn't take it."

Puffy blacklight clouds of smoke filled the room, surrounding the fanatical Julie. He mumbled a reply, tired of her theatrics. "I don't really see the point here. Like you've said, she made her choice and that ship has sailed. There are no do-overs in this world."

With a twirl, she put the gun away. "That's exactly right. You're getting really good at this game, my handsome hunk of a husband. Her choice has been made, but yours, yours has not. The real question of the evening is what would you do if you had those choices? Answer me, Jason. What would you do?"

Just play along. It's the fastest way to get her out of my head. He raised his voice to match hers. "I'm not sure, but I know I wouldn't make a commercial for a tyrant."

She looked down on him as he lay chained. “Just play along? Really? That’s what you’re thinking? Good God! I’m trying to help you and you’re not listening. I’m trying to give you some advanced warning about tomorrow, like you asked. This is the highest stakes game you’ll ever play, so you better get it right. Like we’ve said, there are no do-overs in this big bad world.”

Walking to the end of the bed, she hopped down, then turned to face him again. Standing tall like a sheriff before a showdown in an old west movie, two warnings were issued. “I need you to think about what you would do if you had the same choice as Leni Riefenstahl. Think about it hard, because history will record your answer.”

Turning her gaze toward Nikki, a smirk inched across her face as she spoke her second notice. “And you better make sure she unlocks your cuff before she bolts out of here.” Her stare lingered for a moment. “It’s time for me to go.”

On cue, Nikki’s phone rang. Jason awoke for real and gently nudged her as the caller on the other end redialed every time her cell went to voicemail. She was out cold and it took a couple of minutes to wake her. Between gentle prods he looked around the room and everything was as it had been before he closed his eyes for sleep. The smell of coconut remained, but he could swear he also smelled a tiny hint of gunpowder.

The combination of prods and the nonstop ring finally woke her enough to answer on the fifth set of rings. She groggily put the phone to her ear and muttered a few words before springing up and throwing a suitcase on the bed. She shouted to him. “I’ve got to go. I’ve got to get there now!”

Jason heeded Julie’s advice. “Hey, hey. Give me the keys before you leave!”

Chapter Eighteen

'Just say no.' It was an anti-drug slogan launched during the Reagan presidency, and its champion was First Lady, Nancy Reagan. The slogan was aimed at countering peer pressure on young people to try drugs. Her method was simple and easy to remember. 'Just say no.' Nancy was always open to try new things. In fact, she was the first occupant of the White House to openly use an astrologer. This practice began after John Hinkley's attempted assassination of her husband. She believed in control of all aspects of life, and what's easier than just saying no?

****

Jason and his hangover went home and slept in late the next day. All of his clothes were piled on his bed as a result of the FBI search, so he crashed in his recliner before heading to the office around two that afternoon. Ella greeted him with a message: Call William Brandt as soon as possible. He shook his head. *Damn you, Julie Simmons.* By three o'clock a car was in front of his office and he was whisked downtown to BrandtCo Enterprises headquarters, where he was shown to a large corner office on the fiftieth floor.

As Jason walked into the elegantly appointed room, Brandt turned away from the floor length window trimmed in a wide dark wooden frame, with an impressive city view. He greeted Jason with the most recognizable smile in the world, wearing a tailored light-gray suit and bright-blue tie. His steel gray eyes seeming especially bright today. "Sorry about the unfortunate timing of the broadcast of our show."

Seeing Brandt dressed so sharp, Jason wished he had grabbed something nicer from the heap of clothes in his apartment than a vintage Rolling Stones concert tee-shirt and distressed jeans. Sighing, Jason answered as Brandt motioned for him to have a seat on the opposite side of the massive desk. "Yeah, I didn't know Nielson counted numbers that small. Hopefully, the rebroadcast will do better."

"I have a feeling it might get huge numbers…just a hunch."

"Oh?" Jason's thick eyebrows arched. "It would be awfully hard to recapture the buzz we had going. You know how difficult it is to seize the public's imagination once, let alone twice."

"You're right, of course, but it is possible." Brandt paused and drum rolled his fingers on the huge mahogany desk with hand carvings of lions on the side facing Jason. "The public is fickle, always interested in the next big thing. They want a spectacle." He paused for a brief second. "So, what if we gave them what they want? What if we gave them a spectacle? What do you think it would do for the rebroadcast ratings if I stepped into the presidential race in replacement of Prescott Carver?"

I knew it! Jason inhaled slowly, making sure he heard Brandt correctly before answering. *I was right, Nikki's psychic friend was right. This is really happening.* "Yes…that would capture the public's attention again. Definitely." The full weight of what Brandt just said sank in, and once again his little show was put into a bigger, national spotlight. "That's a big decision, for you and the country. Have you made up your mind?"

Brandt stared, seeming to evaluate Jason's take on what he said.

Jason met his gaze, knowing in his gut that regardless of how Brandt answered the question, he had decided. He was going to run.

The movie star turned industrialist finally continued. "I've had a couple of restless nights thinking it over, weighing the pros and cons, so to speak. His funeral is tomorrow, so I've got a couple more days before I have to publicly declare my intentions. After all, it would be inappropriate to announce anything before I pay my respects. That's why I called. I have an idea I want to run by you."

"Me? You want to run something by me?" Jason's brain went into overdrive. *I'll bet you've had a couple restless nights. I'm sure mama's been giving you her opinion. And what do you want me to do? Make a movie, like Leni Riefenstahl?*

The inner turmoil Jason was experiencing must have shown on his face because Brandt chuckled. "Let me explain. No other politician in the party can step in now because they would need to raise a massive campaign war chest through donations, and that takes time they don't have. And even if they could, there's only thirty or so days until the election. They would almost surely lose. Most would rather wait until next cycle than have the stigma of losing attached to their name." He shook his head in disgust. "And word on the street is that even Carver's VP choice wants to step aside because he performed so poorly in the primaries. They're all chickens worried about their personal futures instead of thinking of our country."

"I hadn't thought about it that way, but it makes sense." Jason nodded.

Brandt continued his pitch. "I have more than enough money to self-fund, but whoever enters the race as a replacement for Carver is facing long odds, even someone as well-known as me. That much is certain, and where you come in."

"Me?" *I can't make a movie in just a few weeks.*

Brandt spoke as calmly as if discussing the merits of a bottle of Merlot versus Shiraz. "If I do step in, I intend to win, and it's too late to do that with a conventional campaign. I've thought about it long and hard, and I've come up with a strategy that can work. That's where your skills will be needed. See, the mainstream media is going to vet me on my knowledge of everything from the economy to the Middle East, and I'm ready for that. I do pretty well in front of the camera, in case you haven't noticed."

Jason laughed softly at that remark. "Everyone says you're the best actor of your generation."

Brandt's cheeks reddened a bit, as if to prove the point. "History will be the judge of that."

History. Jason stiffened at the mention of the word. *This was what Julie was talking about last night. Brandt is going to ask me a question and history will judge my response.* His mind went to full red-alert.

Brandt kept talking and Jason leaned in, trying to hear the nuance of every word, of each syllable. Everything could hang in the balance. "The base of the other party will never vote for me, even if I was the reincarnation of Jesus Christ himself, that's a given. And the base of my party would vote for me even if I was the devil incarnate, that's the way every presidential election goes."

Those lines distracted Jason. *Why does he talk like that - About Jesus and the devil?*

The actor continued explaining his plan. "What's different this time is the people in the middle. Those people have to make up their minds in just a few weeks instead of a few months. They have to decide if they can trust me as president."

Jason re-engaged. "Everyone knows you and most of them like you, but that's not the same as believing you're the right man to safeguard nuclear launch codes."

"Precisely. My job is to convince them I'm a better man for that responsibility than Governor Seymour Wellington, the man who has never met a war he didn't want to join."

There was silence as both men paused. For Jason it was a moment to try and figure out Brandt's angle and where this conversation was heading next. He couldn't, so he asked a journalistic question, assuming Brandt wanted him to know. "How do you plan to accomplish that?"

"If I accept this challenge, I'm going to be in two debates and make the rounds of about a hundred political shows in the next four weeks. I'll be on Fox News and CNN touting my concerns for the environment and my company's contribution to clean it up. Politics is all they will want to discuss."

A sigh followed Brandt's assessment of what lay ahead. "Don't get me wrong, I need people to know my views, but I will have to run a two-year campaign in a matter of weeks. If all I talk about are my views on things like reforming entitlement programs, I'll lose. It's that simple… and I don't like to lose."

As closely as he listened to Brandt, Jason still had no clue what he might ask of him. "You want to run an unconventional campaign, I got it. What I don't have is a reason for why you invited me to your office this afternoon."

Standing, Brandt walked around to Jason's side of the aircraft-carrier-sized desk. He leaned against it and stretched his right arm toward Jason with his upturned hand and fingers cupped, as if he were holding some invisible, yet real container of truth. "You mentioned my fans earlier, the people who feel they know me, and like me. They feel that way because they've seen me in films, and read about me in tabloids. That's how they know me. I've got to keep my entertainer public persona front and center, right up until Election Day."

Jason hung on his words, beginning to understand where he was heading.

"They need to see me talk about how excited I am about the upcoming release of *Dracula – A Time to Reap*, which coincidentally opens the weekend before the election. They need to hear me talk about who I last dated and which celebrity I dine with when I swing through LA. I've got to reassure my fans that I'm more than just another suit promising to protect social security, or fund the military. They've got to remember *why* they like me. If I do that well, I can ask them to vote for me, and I have every expectation they will. That's how I can win and where you come in."

Jason leaned forward in his seat, drawn in by the passion and conviction of Brandt. "Makes sense. Play to your strengths." His body tensed. "And me, what do you want from me?"

On a roll, Brandt spread his arms wide as he explained his vision. "I see us sitting down every few days on the campaign trail. We'll talk celebrity gossip, fashion trends, and you can throw in a few hardball news questions every now and then. Hell, I'll even toss in a ghost story from time to time, if you think it's a good idea. We'll upload it to the internet in hopes the episodes will go viral, and maybe even run a couple of network specials, if we have time. I want you to help me speak directly with my fans on a regular basis, right up until the election."

Brandt's body moved toward him, and Jason almost felt a kind of gravity, causing him to lean closer as well. He tried to close the deal. "What do you think? Can you see the vision? Will you join me?"

Despite the tension of the moment, or maybe because of it, Jason laughed. "You want me to do a running entertainment gig with you on the campaign trail?" He shook his head. "I don't think I'm your man." His brain replayed Julie's summary of Leni Riefenstahl's choices. 'Do the job, don't do the job, or do it differently.' He had just said no.

Brandt pulled back and Jason physically felt the man's invisible tug, bringing him to the edge of his seat. He didn't give up easy. "Nonsense. You're the most qualified person on the planet. You've got hard news experience from the war, so people respect you. You've been doing celebrity interviews for more than a year, and you're good at that too. Just look at our episode, it's television magic. I've been interviewed thousands of times and I've never encountered anything like what we experienced. No one else has the total package. What'll you say? Would you like to get back in the fast lane? Be back in the thrilling business of real reporting?"

Moving back in his seat, Jason created physical space between himself and Brandt as he felt his chest tightening. He took in a deep breath to avoid passing out like he had when the FBI came to his office. *Real reporting...* "I'm flattered, of course, but I'm not sure this gig is for me. Besides, I would need to clear it with Anthony, we're a package deal. And then there are the obligations to our current show."

Brandt pressed. "Of course you would need to clear it with your partner. He seems like a free spirit, so I'm guessing he's game for about anything. As for your network, I think we can get that squared away. I'm going to ask the CEO to join my campaign as an advisor. We go back a long way."

Clearing his throat, Jason realized that yet again, he was unprepared for a meeting with William Brandt. He needed a way to get out quick before he said something he would regret, when inspiration hit. "I should let you know that I'm somehow connected to the man who assassinated Prescott Carver. It probably wouldn't be a good look to have me around the campaign." Jason smiled. *That should give me a free pass.* His confidence in that assessment faded almost immediately as a slow smile widened on Brandt's face, like a poker player drawing to a full house.

"I'm glad you brought that up, I was hoping you would. My security team has researched your connection and believes it's purely coincidental, and my publicity team thinks it might get us a couple of headlines. Remember, I want to run an unconventional campaign, and that connection could generate even more publicity. More importantly, I just have a gut feeling you would be a kind of good luck charm. Call it a hunch."

The burn that he had in the pit of his stomach the first time he interviewed Brandt, returned. *I'll bet you have a hunch. It's your dead mother telling you that, isn't it?* "Looks like you've thought of everything, but I'm still not convinced this would be the right move for me, or your campaign." *There's no way in hell I'm joining you on the campaign trail.*

"I can assure you I think it would be a brilliant idea for you to team up with me, and before you decide, there are a couple of other things you might want to consider. First, we'll be talking about a few million dollars to pull you away from your current project. After all, a man's got to eat."

He felt his eyes widening, and try as he might, he couldn't stop the physical reaction. This was what Nikki said to him on her first visit to his office. *How could he know her EXACT words?*

Brandt continued. "And then there is the matter of your friend over at the *National Conversation.* I believe her name is Nicole Broussard?"

Now Jason was having real trouble catching his breath. *How does he know about Nikki? We've only been seen together in public a couple of times.* He forced another deep breath to keep himself from hitting the floor again. With a quiver, he answered. "What about her?"

"I just want you to know she would be welcome everywhere you go. She can even ride on my plane with you and Anthony, if she wants. She would be granted a press pass at every event, and I might even give her a couple of exclusive interviews. The *National Conversation* has kept my name in the headlines for years, so inviting her along for the ride fits perfectly with my strategy. Hope that's okay with you?"

He wiped his damp hands on his jeans. "You make some interesting points, a lot to think over." The thought of spending so much time with Nikki changed the equation, and he was tempted to say yes, to agree to everything. Then Julie's lesson came to him again. Leni Riefenstahl could have chosen a third answer. His disparate thoughts gelled and became a demand. "If I agree to this, I would have to have total editorial control, the final decision on every piece. Would you accept those terms?" Jason would join the campaign, but only if free to do it his way. He would tell Brandt's story how he wanted. The good, bad or ghostly.

Brandt smiled his famous smile, then firmly reached for Jason's hand to seal the deal. "This is our time, Jason. Together, we will make history."

Chapter Nineteen

Trust can be given or earned, strengthened or broken. It is the fundamental feature in most long-term relationships. But how do you build trust where none exists? One way is the 'trust fall.' That's where an individual falls blindly backwards into the arms of others. The tried-and-true method rests on the theory that you give trust until you have evidence you shouldn't. After all, nothing ventured, nothing gained.

****

The first stop on candidate William Brandt's campaign was set for New Orleans. Louisiana was billed as a swing state by political pundits, so it made as good of a first foray outside of New York as any for this hastily assembled run for office. Jason sat next to Anthony on the chartered plane, nicknamed the *Hollywood Express* in reference to Brandt's stardom. It seemed like any other flight Jason had been on except everyone onboard was there with a singular point of focus- William Brandt and his candidacy. The hundred and fifty or so people on the plane were divided. Low-level staffers and reporters, like Jason and Anthony, occupied the economy seats while Brandt and his senior advisors sat in the first-class area at the front of the Boeing 737.

Jason yawned as the cabin pressurized, while his production partner looked out the window at the receding New York City skyline. The small screen on the back of the seat in front of him afforded the opportunity to watch movies, sitcom reruns, or keep track of the plane's progress on a simulated map of the United States. He chose the map, then drifted off to sleep before they even crossed over New Jersey airspace.

Julie came down the aisle swinging her hips in a naughty short-skirted version of a flight attendant uniform. Her navy pillbox hat over her shoulder length silky-black hair matched her two-piece outfit that featured white, low-cut lapels over a skimpy skirt. The black spiked heels were more appropriate for a sexy Halloween costume than for a real working flight attendant. She stopped her beverage cart only when she reached his row. "Coffee, tea or me?" She laughed as she tossed out the title of a fictious flight attendant memoir from years ago.

He grinned, amused by the entire situation. "How about a couple of those little bottles of bourbon? Oh, and *two* glasses of water. Doctor's orders, you know."

"Well, aren't we in a good mood today, Mr. Simmons? I assume you're at peace with your decision to sign on as William Brandt's social media lackey?"

"I have more than a few reservations, but I'm here." He glanced around the plane full of aides and members of the media. "Another minion serving the rich and powerful. How about you? What are you doing here?"

"Oh, Jason. I'll always follow you wherever you go. Besides, it would be awfully boring to stay in the city alone, and I want to give you a few pointers before your next interview with Brandt. You've kind of struggled in your encounters with him to this point."

Glancing over, he saw his business partner, who was oblivious to his conversation with Julie, confirming this was definitely another dream. "Anthony and I talked about that at length. The post-production research from our show helped, and we've done nothing but prep for the past few days. We're ready for this."

She poured him two glasses of water, then addressed the infamous *Ghost Stories of the Stars* interview that re-ran last night. "Congratulations on finally getting the Neilson ratings you deserved. You were so upset when it ran the first time, but I told you it would work out for the best. You've got to start trusting me on these things." Setting his cups down on his tray, she was careful not to spill a drop. "Now that you've joined the circus, what's your approach? Are you going to be a modern-day Leni Riefenstahl?"

The pilot's voice interrupted their conversation. "We've reached our cruising altitude of thirty-five thousand feet and you are now free to move about the cabin. You are also free to explain all decisions related to why you are joining this campaign."

Jason chuckled. "I like the Flight Attendant Julie a lot better than the gun-toting version, but I'm glad we had that talk the other night. It helped me understand I wasn't limited to a yes or no answer. There is a third option. By the way, that gunfire was really disturbing."

"As long as you got the point. That's all that matters." She pointed her index finger like a gun, then pretended to blow smoke from her fingertip. "I thought it was a blast."

He waved her comment away. "If you say so. All I know is I'm going into this with the goal of showing America the real William Brandt, whatever that might be."

When she bent over, searching for two airplane sized bottles of bourbon, he couldn't keep his eyes from checking out her derrière.

She caught his stolen peek. "It's very flattering you still think I'm attractive, but as we've established, that's outside the rules of our current arrangement. You will, however, be glad to know that Ms. Whips-and-Chains will be joining the caravan in Las Vegas later this week. I'm not sure if she's packing any toys in her carry-on bag."

Blushing, both from getting caught looking at her like that and because he was glad to hear that he would see Nikki soon, he cleared his throat. "Uh, thanks for the update."

She sat two miniature bottles of spirits beside his cups of water. "What I can do for you is give you one suggestion about a question to ask Brandt during your first interview tomorrow. Ask him why we're coming to New Orleans as the first official stop of his campaign. Save that question until the very end to get maximum effect."

"We're way ahead of you on that one." Feeling smug, he continued. "The state is up for grabs and the Electoral College map is driving our itinerary. He needs Louisiana if he's to have any shot at winning."

A self-satisfied look of her own reflected back. "I'm sure that's true, sweetheart, but like I said, you've got to trust me on these things. When I ask you to do something it's for a reason." Julie bent down and put her cold hand on his, staring at him directly with her empty, dark eyes. "I need your word that you'll do this. For your last question tomorrow, ask him why he chose to come to New Orleans first. Will you trust me?" She went from playful ghost to serious spirit, yet again.

He looked into her dim eyes and answered warily. "I'm learning to trust you."

Her smile spread from cheek to cheek. "That's the plan."

With that, she released his hand and he awoke with a start, splashing water from the two cups on his tray. He rubbed his eyes and turned to Anthony. "How long have I been out?"

Anthony eyes were wide. "Long enough to order two bourbon and waters in your sleep."

Chapter Twenty

First dates are tricky. You really want to know if you've met your soulmate. The thing is, if you go too fast by asking too many personal questions, it's a turnoff. You might miss out on something special by trying too hard. It's best to keep things simple, maybe enjoy dinner at a nice restaurant. Okay, maybe it's acceptable to ask one of those deep questions, but only one, and only if the timing feels right.

****

Anthony and Jason had their crew set up in the flagship restaurant of famed chef Henri Landry, located a few blocks away from Lafayette square. It was a classic, old New Orleans building with a small wrought iron balcony on the second floor running the length of the building. Perfect for watching Mardi Gras parades. Inside, black square posts supported aged wooden barreled ceilings. Crisp white tablecloths completed the high-end feel of the place.

The agenda called for Brandt to arrive at six o'clock after a rally in the convention center. As Jason and Anthony were quickly learning, running behind schedule was par for most political campaigns, and today was no exception. A large crowd gathered outside, hoping to catch a glimpse of the star, turned politician. They were informed that Brandt wouldn't arrive until half past seven.

Only those with political connections were allowed inside and only the most influential of this select group dined at adjacent tables. Part of the setup was that they would be served at the same time as their party's nominee, and having smelled hints of paprika, cayenne, and garlic wafting from the kitchen for more than an hour, they were hungry.

Other than hunger, the common denominator shared by everyone, from the lowliest busboy to the most generous donor, was each had been screened and searched in the hyper-secure environment following Prescott Carver's assassination. Jason paced anxiously and ordered a shot of bourbon to calm his nerves, knowing it would upset his partner. *What does he know? I've got my drinking under control. This just helps me relax a little. Maybe even do my job better.*

Anthony shook his head.

When Brandt entered the dining area, he stopped to shake hands with several tables of supporters, lingering with the most prominent of all, the governor and first lady of the state. He chatted for a moment with the politician, then turned his charm toward the man's wife. "Louisiana is fortunate to have a woman as intelligent and beautiful as you representing this state." He kissed her hand and most of the women in attendance clapped approval of the gesture, then Brandt was shown to his seat.

The action continued as Secret service agents positioned themselves just off camera. As a major party nominee for the office of president, Brandt was being guarded by the same special protection afforded presidents since 1901. Anthony nudged one of the agents, a beefy man with dark skin and hints of gray in his clipped sideburns, aside to assume his regular position beside camera one. He started the countdown to officially begin the interview. "In three…two…one. Action!"

The audience applauded as the candidate waved to them as if riding on a float in a parade.

Jason was more nervous than he expected, unsure if that was because of the restive live audience, or all the drama with Julie leading up to his decision to take this job in the first place. He addressed the onlookers. "Welcome to the first in a series of real-world talks with the newest candidate for the highest office in the land. Over the next few weeks, we'll be inviting the world to join as I sit down with Mr. Brandt in locations across our great country. Don't expect another boring news show with talking heads. We'll be joined by some of the most interesting people in the world, most of whom would never be invited to the set of a Sunday morning news show. Sit back and tune in as we start our journey."

The tightly packed crowd clapped appreciatively and he started the interview with a softball question to allow both him and Brandt to get their footing in this new kind of arena. "How does it feel to be on the campaign trail?"

"It's gratifying to see all of my fans here today. It reaffirms my decision to enter the race." Other than using the word 'fans' instead of supporters, he sounded like any other candidate. This would be the end of traditional campaign interview questions.

Speaking into his headset, Anthony directed the crew. "Alright people, tonight we're making a roux, so let's keep things simple. Camera one, on Jason and camera two, on Mr. Brandt."

As every cook in Louisiana knows, the most basic roux has only three components. Oil, heat and all-purpose flour gradually whisked in. When prepared properly, this serves as the base stock for Cajun recipes such as Étouffée. Tonight, it would be Jason's job to be the heat to Brandt's oil. The guests represented the flour, the texture so to speak. If all went well it would signal the start of something bigger, better, bolder.

Now that Jason and Brandt had gotten started it was time for the first pinch of celebrity flour. Jason knew a little audience participation would warm things up and play to Brandt's natural abilities. "Let's welcome our first guest of the evening, the man who opened his restaurant for us tonight. Let's give a hearty welcome to the one and only, Henri Landry."

The diverse crowd, some dressed in the bright purple and flashy gold of LSU, the state university, cheered loudly as the celebrity chef appeared from the kitchen. Servers followed, carrying bowls of steaming hot gumbo for the hungry guests. Anthony captured the action as the smell of celery, bell peppers, and onions filled the room. “Camera one, follow the head honcho wearing the white hat. He’s our first meal ticket of the season.”

Jason had researched the connections between Brandt and the chef, and their warmth toward one another was palpable. “I believe you two have met.”

The portly and effervescent Henri elaborated in his hearty Cajun accent. “This is my star pupil. I taught him everything he knows about competitive cooking.”

Brandt’s gray eyes reflected light like a Damascus steel knife blade rapidly dicing an onion. “With this master chef’s tutoring I kicked ass on season one of *Celebrity Cook-off*. My succulent sea scallops crushed that housewife from Beverly Hills.”

Henri beamed. “I always back a winner!” He added his exuberant catch phrase. “Booyah!” The partisan audience applauded even louder.

The two talkative men swapped stories from their prior encounters with Jason adding a gentle prompt from time to time to keep the action moving. After five good minutes he interjected. “Chef, there are a lot of hungry people here, and I know you need to get back to the kitchen. Before you go, would you introduce our next guest?”

Anthony whispered into his headset. “Push in on the booyah guy.”

Henri stood and looked directly into camera one, his bushy black mustache bouncing as he spoke excitedly. “New Orleans is one of the most unique cities in the world. We’ve always been known for great food and as a place to let loose and have some fun. Since 2005 we’ve also been known as the place that faced the headwinds of hurricane Katrina.”

He paused for a moment as the rustling audience stilled. Most of them were local and the reminder of that cataclysm, even all these years later, quieted the raucous crowd. Landry was also a television professional and he let the emotion simmer for a moment. “Since those dark days, we’ve battled back to become the vibrant city you see today. Local can-do spirit was aided by the generosity of people from around the world, like Mr. Brandt. Another of our most visible supporters is also a friend and peer of his. Please join me in welcoming the irrepressible Twila!"

Directing, Anthony spoke. "Camera one, on the star." The audience erupted in their largest response yet, as the actress who was so famous she only needed a one-name intro, strolled into the room.

She gave them both a hug and kiss on the cheek and Brandt flashed his famous smile. He was totally at ease rubbing elbows with Hollywood royalty, and doing it live with a restaurant full of fans seemed almost second nature. As the applause finally subsided, Henri excused himself as Brandt and Twila took their seats.

Jason stirred the rich movie star mixture. "Twila, let's talk about your passion for the people of this city and your ongoing contributions to make it an even better place." Her dark skin popped against her canary yellow A-line dress with the front zipper pulled down low, revealing her ample cleavage.

The discussion of her efforts to help rebuild the Lower Ninth Ward naturally led to talk of climate change and how BrandtCo Enterprises' carbon emission technology could lessen the chances of another killer hurricane in the future. This was the hard news segment of the show that had been promised when Brandt made his pitch to Jason. After a couple minutes of deep climate discussion, Jason steered the conversation back to the star angle. Like any good celebrity host, he gave Twila the chance to plug her upcoming movie. "I hear you've been filming in Thailand."

"Yes! The beaches were stunning, and the jungle lush. It made the ideal backdrop for the movie. It's titled *Love, Sex and Murder in Paradise!*"

This was the celebrity angle Brandt asked for, so Jason kept it going, aiming to broaden the demographic appeal. "Tell us, Twila. Who else is in the cast?"

Twila turned toward camera one with a seductive stare. "Well, ladies. You simply have to see this movie when it's released. It's the debut film for Todd Helmsley." She paused and licked her lips. "You've known him for his previous work as 'Todd the Bod' of the Chippendales." She fanned herself with her hand. "Let me tell you, he's even hotter on the big screen."

As the women in the audience oohed and ahhed, Jason cut a glance at Brandt and saw a satisfied grin. This seemed exactly the way he wanted these interviews to go. "Twila, I understand you have a fundraiser you need to get to, so any last words?"

Her broad smile, framed by her pouty lips, radiated sincerity. "New Orleans has seen first-hand the devastating effects of monster storms worsened by climate change, and it's only going to get worse. The world is at a crossroads, but there is still time to change the path we're on. So, this is my challenge. America, if you give a damn about the future of this planet, vote for William Brandt."

She struck a chord with the partisan crowd who had lived the experience she described, and they responded by standing and cheering wildly. Jason stood and clapped. *So, this is Brandt's campaign.*

Anthony rubbed his hands together. "Camera one, follow her off the set, then back to Jason. We're in the homestretch and I can almost taste dinner. Time to get the takeout box ready."

Jason took his seat and waited for everyone to settle. He and Anthony had talked about turning it over to Brandt at this point so he could make a political pitch to his fans. The interview had gone fantastic and this would give him the opportunity to segue from his Hollywood persona to a political one. Tonight, he was mixing those sides of his personality into something new. This was his recipe, his big plan, his roux, so to speak to win the election.

As he waited for the last few audience members to quiet, Jason thought about Julie's request. He had mulled it over all day and now felt his heart beating faster as he reconsidered his decision. It had been a lot easier to make that promise when there wasn't a live audience hanging on every word. With everyone set, he saw an expectant look on Brandt's face, waiting for the next question.

Anthony noticed Jason's hesitation. "People, he's going off recipe again. Camera one, push in for a close up on Jason. I think he's about to turn up the heat."

With his heart in his throat, Jason spoke. "New Orleans has been a terrific first stop on what promises to be an exciting campaign. I'm glad we could share your personal connections to the city, and with your fans across the country. Before you speak directly to them, I have a final question." He thought he detected a millisecond of an uncertainty in the actor's face.

Like the consummate professional that he is, Brandt leaned back in his seat, relaxing. "Ask away, I'm an open book."

Damn, he's smooth. Jason tried to think of ways to bridge into the question, but couldn't, so he decided to fire away. *Here you go, Mrs. Julie Simmons. I hope you know what you're getting us into.* "Why did you choose to come to New Orleans as the first stop in your campaign?"

A slow smile crept across his face. It wasn't the brilliant trademark flash, but more gradual, resembling an expanding sunrise over a bayou. "Thanks for asking that question. You've really done your homework."

As if. This is all Julie's doing. I just hope it doesn't explode in my face.

William Brandt lowered his voice and the audience leaned closer. He pulled them in the way a storyteller draws campers when telling a scary tale around a fire on a moonless night. "I was born in Connecticut and it remains my home to this day." He paused a beat, then continued. "But one side of my family has roots here in the Crescent City. Ancient roots, long ago severed."

Jason had no idea where this was going, so he used the best all-purpose question in the interviewer's handbook. "Oh?"

Brandt stole a glance at the closest of the crowded tables before returning his gaze to Jason. "Family is forever…until it's not."

Expectant murmurs from fans nearest Brandt and Jason added to the ambiance of the old building. Everyone in the room was now in the orbit of the master as he leaned forward. "Here's the story as told to me. You see, my mother was born into a poor family here in New Orleans during hard times, and the family struggled to make ends meet. My maternal grandmother was a proud woman who vowed the same fate would not befall her newborn daughter. She swore the curse of poverty would end with her generation."

The word 'curse' echoed in Jason's brain, demanding action. "Fate…curses…vows…in New Orleans. It all sounds so Voodoo."

Brandt laughed off the Voodoo comment as easily as he had the ghost remarks about his mother in their first interview. "That would make a better story, but the truth is my grandmother was a conniving, manipulative busybody. I'll bet a lot of my fans could say the same about some people in their families."

Laughs were scattered throughout the crowd as Brandt, yet again, seemed to have as much in common with the everyday problems of his supporters than with either the movie star or business tycoon set. Even Jason chuckled, thinking of the reputation in his family of one of his aunts. "What happened?"

Turning, Brandt looked directly into camera two. The live audience was spellbound and he was now staring into the eyes of the digital fans that would see this clip tomorrow. "My grandmother had a master plan. By the time my mother was of marrying age, by hook and crook she had arranged a chance encounter between her daughter and a rich young man from one of the wealthiest families in the city. It was a bit like Cinderella at the ball, except money was the motive, not true love."

"Your grandmother must have been pleased."

"She was, and as she hoped, he fell helplessly in love with the beguiling beauty from the wrong side of the canal. A wedding date was set and preparations progressed according to her plan. But, unbeknownst to my grandmother, my mother met a suave sailor who swept her off her feet."

Jason could now see where the tale of true love was headed. "And that was definitely not part of the plan."

Nodding, Brandt continued recounting his family lore. "That's putting it mildly. She was so furious my mother had gone against her wishes, she threw her out of the house, telling her never to return. She believed my mother had ruined the best chance the family would ever have to change its fortunes." Brandt shrugged. "Everyone knows the rest. My mother moved to Connecticut with my father, then he was killed when a storm swept him overboard in the middle of the Atlantic. She eventually found work as a maid in the mansion I now own."

Jason put the final touches on the story of true love overcoming all. "Now you are one of the richest men in the world. Looks like your grandmother got her wish, just not the way she expected."

Making his final camera adjustment, Anthony whispered. "Camera two, push in tight on Brandt. This roux is righteous."

On cue, Brandt flashed his smile. "She should have known not to mess with fate."

Chapter Twenty-One

'Denial is not just a river in Egypt.' That pun pokes fun at the human capacity of self-delusion. Everyone else around us can see the problem, but as we're in the business of fooling ourselves, it doesn't matter. No one else can make us change our behaviors, but sometimes they can at least get our attention.

****

Jason and Anthony worked all night editing the footage of the New Orleans interview with Brandt into a seamless version suitable for uploading onto YouTube and Facebook. They traded network quality for immediacy, and almost instantaneously the ten-minute clip began trending faster than a cute cat video. By the time the flight attendant asked everyone to turn off all electronic devices for their ten o'clock takeoff, they received over one-hundred-thousand hits.

Anthony reclined his seat as soon as allowed. "I guess Brandt really knows what he's doing with this unconventional campaign. Eighteen-to-thirty-four-year-olds are going to be all over this Hollywood angle."

Jason stared sleepily out the window as they climbed through overcast skies on a commercial airliner headed toward Las Vegas. Brandt and the rest of his entourage flew out the night before to prepare for the first presidential debate, leaving him and Anthony to finish their work in the Big Easy. "He said he's in it to win it. Looks like he knows what he's doing."

The plane broke through the cloud deck into bright sunshine and Jason pulled the shade down on the window. "Do you still like the guy? I mean, do you think he would make a good president?"

Without hesitation, Anthony answered. "I've liked him from the beginning, and every time we interview him, we learn a little more about his background. He wasn't born with a silver spoon in his mouth, that's for sure. I've got more in common with him than Governor Seymour Wellington." He said the governor's name with a snobbish northeastern accent.

"Yeah, I know what you mean. What do they have, three - no four congressmen in that family?"

Anthony pulled a black sleep mask from his carry-on bag, preparing to get some shut eye on the long flight. "Besides, that man is stiffer than a body in the morgue. I'd rather see the country take a chance with someone to whom I can at least relate."

"We've tried that before with mixed results. Remember that guy?"

He shrugged. "Totally different vibe." He yawned and drew the black eye patches of the mask down. "That's enough talk about politics for me today. Wake me if I snore too loud."

"Will do." Within a few minutes Anthony was breathing with a slight whistling from his nose, arms crossed over his plump stomach covered in one of his ubiquitous flannel shirts. Jason pulled out his earbuds and passed the time watching re-runs of sitcoms- and by drinking. By the time the credits for the second show finished rolling, Jason was on his fourth bourbon. Up next was an old period comedy set on a Southern plantation, and it happened to star one Julie Simmons.

On the small screen, she stood looking into a three-sided dressing mirror. "I love the hoop skirt, but the corset is too tight, even for someone as thin as me." She tugged at the fabric of the dress with ruffled sleeves and tiered lace layers, trying to give herself a millimeter more breathing room.

The costume caused him to laugh again, like he had for several of her outfits. "You couldn't get down the aisle of this plane with that thing on. Are you sure that dress came from my imagination?"

She turned away from the mirror to face him. "Those are the rules. Maybe you're in the mood to have one of those dramatic scenes where we're like Rhett and Scarlett." Julie winked. "I'll steal Rhett's famous line and tell you I don't give a damn."

Anthony snorted beside him and Jason knew for sure he had fallen asleep as well. *At least this will make the flight seem shorter.* "The fact of the matter is you do give a damn, and this is my life we're talking about. Not yours." Lately, his mood swung as wildly as an unmanned fire hose, his drinking taking a steeper toll on his mental health by the day. Now it went sour. "I think it's time we talked about these damned rules again."

She played the role of coy antebellum belle, exaggerating a thick Southern accent. "I told you back when we first started that the rules were the rules, and that hasn't changed. Surely someone as intelligent as you can grasp that simple fact, especially after I've explained it over and over."

Frustration with her continued evasiveness bubbled in his gut. "Maybe we *should* have one of those overacted blow-ups, because you're being as hard-headed as Scarlett. You fill my head with talk about William Brandt one night, Hitler the next, and then mix in a little Nikki nookie for good measure. You tell me you're here for me, but I'm in worse shape than ever. The fact is, you're probably just a figment of my imagination anyway."

Julie put her hands on her corseted hips, and the antebellum accent disappeared. She lashed at him in her New York City directness. "Don't go blaming me for what you've done to yourself. Do you have any idea how much you've drank in the past year, the past month, hell, the past hour? Huh? Take a look in the mirror before blaming me for your sorry state of existence." She was on a roll and spun the big dress for emphasis. "We've got work to do, and here you are, drunk before noon. I can only do so much from beyond the grave, Jason. You're the one in the land of the living. You've got to get a grip and do your part!"

He was surprised by the blowback. "Just wait a damn minute, I've been…" His next word was whispered. "…trying."

"You'd better start trying harder, dream boy. Who's been feeding you info to have better interviews? Me, that's who! And who has been nothing but supportive of the new woman in your life? Me again, and that's not the easiest job for a dead spouse, I'll tell you that. I am here to help, but I expect a little more effort on your end from now on."

The verbal slap in the face got his attention. "I just thought that…I don't know what I thought. I feel like a pinball being flipped from one bumper to the next."

Her hands fell to her sides as she dropped her confrontational stance and frowned. "Aw…my poor baby. I know it's been tough for you, but know that everything that's going on is happening exactly the way it's supposed to. Trust me."

His drunken anger morphed into inebriated self-pity, and his eyes filled to the brim. "I'm trying to trust you, but can't you tell me what it all means? I feel so lost and alone, and I can't even tell anyone about you."

"I know, honey. But the rules are that I can only tell you what you need to know, when you need to know. And that's what I'm going to do right now. I have good news for you. Your friend, the one with the handcuffs, she's waiting for you in Vegas. You won't be alone tonight. I bet you'll be glad to see her, right?"

He sniffed and the corners of his mouth perked ever so slightly as he nodded. "Yes."

"Remember how you feel now. When you're feeling lost and alone, all you really need is a shoulder to cry on. Remember that, okay?"

Wiping his eyes, he attempted to pull himself together. "I'll try."

"You'd better." She tugged again at the tight bodice of the heavy dress. "I've got to get this corset off before it squeezes the life out of me." She giggled. "I guess it's a little too late for that, right? I'll see you later, sweetie."

He was about to reply when the plane touched down with a thud. An announcement came over the intercom. “Welcome to Las Vegas, and we apologize again for the disruption of our in-flight video system today.”

Chapter Twenty-Two

There are few destinations in the world where the vibe of the incoming flights is so different than the feeling on departures. Every plane that touches down in Las Vegas is filled with winners. The reality is in the long run, the house always wins. For every winner there are at least three losers, but they keep coming.

****

Jason and Anthony stood in the aisle of the stuffed plane between excited would-be gamblers as they all waited for the forward door to open. Now on the ground they were free to check their texts and emails. Jason nudged Anthony as he scrolled through the messages on his phone. "Guess who is waiting for me at the Bellagio?" Julie promised that Nikki would join them in Vegas and the text confirming her arrival put him in a good mood.

"You're a dog, you know. She's your first squeaky toy since…" Anthony cut his sentence short.

Jason gave him a playful elbow as the line moved toward the jetway. "It's okay, man. You can mention her name. I still think about Julie all the time, but it's all good now." He exaggerated, at least about the part of everything being all good, but he wanted to downplay the emotional rollercoaster he had been riding. "In some weird way it's as if she's looking down from heaven and watching over me."

They finally exited the plane and continued through the crowded concourse. "I'm glad to hear that." Anthony cast a concerned glance. "I've been worried about you, you know?"

Putting a hand on Anthony's shoulder, Jason responded sincerely. "I was just thinking how you are one of the few stable things in my life right now. I'm lucky to have such a good friend. I don't know what I would do without you."

Anthony now elbowed Jason, causing him to remove his hand. "Speaking of lucky, what's going on with you and Nikki? Anything more than bouncing back into the dating world?"

Pulling his carry-on bag past pretzel shops and flashing signs for the latest Cirque du Soleil show, Jason smiled. "So far, it's all been fun and games, if you know what I mean. I don't think either of us are looking for anything more right now, and that's fine with me because she's teaching me games I've never played before."

"You really are a dog."

"Dog? No, not me. I'm just another guy landing in Vegas hoping to get lucky."

Chapter Twenty-Three

In photography, perspective can make the Eiffel Tower appear to fit between one's finger and thumb. Just as easily, you can make a grain of sand seem as large as a planet. It's all about point of view, what your mind's eye thinks it sees.

****

Jason showered and changed into a black suit paired with a royal purple shirt. He hummed as the elevator took him down to the main level in the middle of a mash-up between authentic Italy and fantasy efficiency. Everything was geared toward maximizing gaming profits, so getting to the main restaurant required he go through the casino. As he strolled, more than a few thoughts about possible scenarios for the evening played out in his mind. The bling-bling-bling of slot machines provided a pure Las Vegas soundtrack to his imaginings as he covered the distance. Images of Nikki's long legs and perky breasts danced through his brain as he walked with an expectant bounce in his step.

The maître d' showed him to a table with an amazing view of the resort's famous fountains. The choreographed water show was reaching its climax, and he was so distracted he almost didn't recognize his date already sitting at the table. She was wearing a sleeveless floral patterned summer dress that seemed to come alive against an orange setting sun. She was beautiful, so how had he missed her? Then it registered. "You look fantastic. I love your hair."

Her voice shook in response to his compliment as her hand seemed to reflexively touch her brunette-colored locks. "Thanks. I felt I needed to do something different."

He took his seat across the table as the dazzling aquatic show completed its finale. His bouncy mood plummeted as reddened eyes stared at him. He realized that she had been crying. "What's wrong?"

The brash woman he knew was tonight apologetic. "You're early. I didn't want you to see me like this. I hoped I would have myself together before you arrived." She glanced away for a moment, then back. "I should go to my room."

"No." He reached for her hand. "You don't have to be alone." The touch of her warm skin spread from her hand through his entire body. Now his heart was pumping that warmth through every capillary and artery of his being. *When you're feeling lost and alone, all you really need is a shoulder to cry on.* Those were Julie's words that he interpreted to be applied to him. They echoed in his mind as he realized they were intended for Nikki. He looked deep into her emerald eyes. "Sometimes we all need a shoulder to cry on."

The words were simple and sincere and their impact was immediate. A torrent was released as if an emotional dam had been breached. She began sobbing and Jason stood from the table, still holding her hand. He wanted to shield her from the nosy eyes of other diners. "Hey, let's get out of here."

She let out a tear-muffled laugh, then muttered. "Yeah. These people only paid for one water show tonight."

He escorted her to the nearest exit and they soon found themselves by one of the many outdoor swimming pools. By this time, the sultry mid-October sun dipped below the horizon, but the stifling heat remained. He slid off his jacket and silently held her as she sobbed, soaking his shirt with salty tears. In time, her sobs softened, and then eventually stopped…for a few minutes, then the cycle repeated. She held onto him, and he held onto her as if each a life preserver for the other. Time passed silently as the blackness of night magnified the city's neon radiance, casting them in other-worldly shades of reds, blues and yellows.

His heart ached for her. "Do you want to talk? I'm a good listener."

She kept her head down, avoiding eye contact. “Not yet. If it’s okay with you, I just need someone to lean on.”

Now tears welled in his eyes. “I know how that feels. Let’s just stay here tonight and lean on each other.”

As the night air cooled, he put his jacket over her. Together, they cuddled on one of the chaise lounges that circled the pool, silently resting in each other’s arms. The time between rounds of crying increased, and after each one she snuggled closer, feeling like a perfect fit in his arms. While he wanted to understand the source of her pain and soothe it, in this moment it wasn’t important. All that mattered was being here for her when she needed him.

Chapter Twenty-Four

On planet Earth, all people are connected. The phenomena of six degrees of separation was first introduced in 1929, with the idea that a message could travel from any one person to any other in five conversations or less. If the assumption that six degrees has remained the average, then how does one think about total strangers connected by a single link? Coincidence?

****

Morning hues of blue and orange streaked the sky as the cuddled couple awoke to a bright desert dawn. Jason broke the overnight silence. "I don't know about you, but I'm starving." A tangerine sun powered its way through a thin layer of clouds and the morning temperature quickly surged past eighty degrees, on the way toward the century mark again. They sat up stiffly and surveyed their surroundings.

Stretching, Nikki responded playfully. "Me too. Somehow I missed dinner." Her laugh returned. "Guess that means I'm buying…again."

The pool attendant walked past with a net on the end of a pole as Jason gathered his jacket and Nikki reached for shoes that she slipped off in the wee hours of the night. They headed for the door, and after exposure to the morning heat, the air-conditioning inside the resort felt as if they had stepped into a giant walk-in freezer. She snuggled under his arm as they went in search of breakfast.

Soon, they were seated in a café just off the main gaming floor where they consumed buttermilk pancakes stacked high like poker chips. The twenty-topping-bar, which included his favorite of strawberries in thick sauce, completed their hotcake jackpot.

With their appetites for food and coffee sated, she broached the issue of her breakdown. “Sorry you had to witness that sloppy collapse last night. I’m not usually like that, you know.”

“You don’t have to explain anything to me. I’ve got some demons of my own.”

She raised her hand to her hair. “Like my new color? Well, it’s not exactly new. It’s the one I was born with.”

He took a studied look and compared it to what he had seen before. After all, this was the third variation since they met a few weeks ago. Gone was the jarring autumn explosion of reds and yellows that had replaced the garish deep pink she wore when they first met. They all made an impression, but the warm chestnut of today seemed perfect. “I love the look, but you are beautiful, regardless of the style or color.”

She responded to the compliment by moving her fingers from her hair to the puffiness under her eyes. “Thank you, but I’m sure I look a mess…It’s been a rough few days for me.” Her eyes seemed to question, perhaps deciding how much to open up to a man she really barely knew. After a long pause, she continued. “You see, five days ago I became an orphan, again, for real.”

Jason reached for her hand and held it lightly. He was unsure what she meant, but figured she would tell him if she wanted. What he knew for sure was that she was distressed, and he wanted to comfort her. “It hurts really bad when we lose people close to us.”

She sniffed and used her napkin to dab at the moisture gathering in the corners of her eyes, seemingly determined not to cry again. “That’s just it. I wasn’t close to any of them like I should have been, and now it’s too late. They’re all gone.”

They’re gone…unless they refuse to leave, like someone I know. He tried to shake off his own problems dealing with death, and be in the moment for her. “I’m so sorry for your loss. Sometimes it helps to talk about them, about the people we’ve lost. It’s another way to celebrate their life…and I'm a good listener." He felt like a hypocrite because this was the same advice he never followed.

Her bottom lip stiffened. "Have you ever felt there was a secret world out there? A secret world where decisions are made…decisions that affect our lives and we don't even have a clue it exists, much less who might be making them?"

An image of Julie in her blood-soaked white blouse briefly flashed in his mind. He squeezed her hand with sincerity. "More than you will ever know."

"I've always felt that way, too, but got my first real-world brush with it last year when my parents were killed. The visit from the Massachusetts State Police telling me of their murder brought me to my knees. I've been a rebel as long as I can remember, and we weren't particularly close anymore, but they always stuck with me through all my highs and lows."

He smiled in sympathy. "Sounds like they were good people."

"They were, and after they died, I felt pretty down, but not as low as I would go, not by a long shot. The next week at the reading of the will I got a surprise that changed everything. In addition to leaving me their entire estate, they left a message. In a recorded video they explained that while they always loved me with all their heart, I was not their biological child. I had been adopted days after my birth. They kept the truth hidden all those years."

"Wow. That must have been a shock."

She toyed with her napkin. "Yeah. It made my head spin, and it raised about a thousand questions I knew would never be answered." She took a deep breath and sniffed, seeming to try and draw strength from thin air. Her voice softened. "That's when this stretch of heavy drinking started."

Jason sat quietly with his head bowed, thinking about his own alcohol consumption during the past year, and Julie's lecture about what it was doing to his health. After a moment, his weary eyes met hers. "We've both been on a few benders lately."

She looked at him in a way that said she understood, like few others in the world could. “I took some of the small fortune they left me and hired a private detective to locate my birth mother. It took a while, but he found her. Any guesses where?”

He ran through their limited conversations and could only come up with one mention of a place other than The Blind Bat bar, or Heaven dance club. “Ireland?”

“Yep. Not only did I find out everything I thought I knew about myself was a lie, but I also learned I wasn’t even born an American. My entire life was built on lies.” Taking a sip of coffee, she continued. “I had lived feeling like I was the misunderstood daughter of a bedrock Boston family, but that wasn’t who I was at all. The investigator informed me that I’m the daughter of an unwed woman that has been institutionalized for most of her adult life. Schizophrenia compounded by early onset Alzheimer’s.”

“That must have really been tough news to hear.”

A glassy look came over her eyes. “It was, but somehow it didn’t surprise me, almost seeming to make perfect sense. Kind of an explanation of my own instability…and it only got more bizarre after that.”

Jason was almost afraid to ask. “There’s more?”

Nikki sat still, as if even she couldn’t believe the words she was about to speak. “I went to visit her, to meet the woman who gave me away when I was only three days old. She was mad as a hatter alright, couldn’t remember her own birthday, but she vividly remembered mine.”

She stopped and stared into the cavernous casino and Jason dared not say a word. She would continue when she was ready.

With her mouth closed, she pulled in another deep breath, and when she spoke the overwhelming lack of meaning that permeates every gaming floor seemed to infuse her voice. “She said she remembered it because it was the day she joined the order.”

His eyebrows rose. "The order?"

"Yes. See, my birth mother dumped me to become a Redemptoristine sister. They call them the Red Nuns." Head shaking, she continued, speaking with a flatness in her voice he had never heard. "My birth caused my mother, one Fiona O'Connell, to swear off ever having sex again. She chose a life of service to God over the awfulness of keeping a child like me."

Nikki yanked her hand away, and Jason immediately reached for it again as the image of her large Jesus tattoo flashed in his mind. *Now it makes sense…in a weird Nikki way.* "That's not true. You're a beautiful woman, inside and out. Sounds to me like she did you a favor."

Her face hardened into a mask. "Maybe. But I know when I have a child, I'll never cast her away like that. I would do whatever it took to keep her."

"I'm sure you'll make a great mother someday."

Now looking to be in firm control of her emotions, Nikki continued. "You want to know what else she told me? When I asked about my father, she told me he was the pope. Can you believe that?"

It was comical, but the woman's delusion was also deeply troubling. He found himself moved by her sad story and held her hand tightly. "I'm so, so sorry. Sounds like a disturbing reunion."

"Yeah, that's an understatement. Given her bed-ridden condition when I last saw her, it didn't come as much of a shock when I got the call the other morning that she was on her death bed. I arrived in time to hold her hand as she passed."

The telling of her story seemed like an emotional release, and feeling returned to her voice. "Now I understand why I always felt I didn't have anything in common with my folks. They weren't perfect, but they sure didn't deserve the never-ending hell I put them through."

Jason's next question was entirely off the cuff, a throw-away line really. "What happened to them, your folks? How did they die?"

"It was random and senseless, kind of like what happened to your wife. They were killed at a rest area on I-95. A couple from Maine found them murdered in the parking lot. The police said it was probably a mugging gone wrong."

Hearing the police speculate on what might have happened was something he knew well. "Did they catch who did it?"

"No. They didn't find much evidence at the crime scene. There was a lot of blood from their stab wounds and a vague description of two men that an over-the-road trucker had seen hanging around earlier in the day. All he really remembered was that one of them had a bandage on his face, or something."

Jason's stomach knotted. *No, there couldn't be a connection, could there?* His voice cracked. "Did you say stab wounds?"

"Yes, they were stabbed repeatedly and left to die beside their car, right there in the middle of the parking lot."

"Why didn't you bring this up earlier?" He was insistent as his emotions rose. "You knew that's how my wife died."

The snort surprised him. "We were flirting…and getting to know each other…intimately. Bringing up the deceased wife isn't usually a subject that fits that set of circumstances."

A shy smile eased onto his face, thinking of the intensity of their courtship. "You make a valid point." Still, his mind raced. *Two guys? Knives? It must be a coincidence, right?* Now he felt queasy. "This can't be…" Jason's words trailed off as he reached for his wallet, hoping he had saved Agent O'Reilly's card.

Chapter Twenty-Five

'About all you can do in life is be who you are.' This quote from Rita Mae Brown speaks to being content in one's own skin. And generally speaking, most of us also want others to like our authentic personalities. That's the majority of us, anyway. However, there is a minority who do their best to hide their real selves. For any number of reasons some people always hide behind a façade. But try as they might to conceal it, their true nature is just under the surface, occasionally peeking through and allowing others to catch a glimpse.

****

Jason's suspicion of a possible link between Julie's murder, Prescott Carver's assassination and Nikki's parents' death was not shared by Agent O'Reilly. His exact words were 'It's a long shot.' He did promise to look into it stating, 'You never know.' Nonetheless, Jason saved the agent's number in his phone in case something else came to mind. After breakfast, both Jason and Nikki went to their own rooms for some rest ahead of a busy night.

It was now evening, and nearly time for the first debate between William Brandt and Seymour Wellington. Brandt sent word asking both Jason and Nikki to join him backstage, a few minutes before the event. He had promised Nikki special access as part of the bargain to convince Jason to join the campaign, and now he was living up to his end of the deal.

Jason arrived first and waited for her, noting how his charcoal suit blended in with the sea of other guys dressed similarly. Nikki, on the other hand, stood out as singularly stunning and beautiful. Wearing a tailored white pant suit with cropped jacket and matching camisole, she looked fabulous. Her vibrant flamingo-pink shoes with four-inch heels matched her projected attitude. Jason's eyes widened upon seeing her. "You look amazing."

Before either could say anything else, Brandt approached in high spirits. "It's my pleasure to meet you, Ms. Broussard. I really loved your article speculating on my cabinet selections. I had a great laugh while reading it. It was totally wrong, of course, but it did make you the first to predict my entry into the race."

"Thank you, Mr. Brandt. You're an easy subject to write about, and to look at as well." She seemed back on her game.

Brandt chuckled and glanced at Jason. "You're a lucky man." He turned his attention back to Nikki. "I've only got a couple of minutes before I have to get back in the make-up chair for a last-minute touch up. I need to look my best for my fans, so go ahead, Ms. Broussard, ask me anything."

She appeared to radiate confidence, but Jason could tell she was nervous from the way her hands fidgeted. Her first couple of words betrayed her with a slight quiver. "Thank you, Mr. Brandt. My question is about what you will do after you are elected. The government has hidden proof of alien contact going back at least as far as Roswell. Would you go on the record as being in favor of declassifying those documents?" Moving her phone toward the candidate, she tapped the screen to record his reply.

He smiled broadly and answered her question seriously. "The readers of the *National Conversation* should know I am a champion of transparency. Too many secrets have been kept from our citizens. You have my commitment that, if elected, I will release more of those documents than all previous presidents combined. That includes both Roswell *and* Area Fifty-One."

As soon as he finished answering, he extended his hand. "I think you should be able to get a headline or two out of that, Ms. Broussard. Now, please excuse me. I've got a debate to win."

With Brandt's departure, Nikki and Jason stood alone amid a sea of technicians, advisors and security personnel. She sounded giddy. "That was pretty awesome. I usually have to make up headlines like that!"

Jason was glad to see her in such a terrific mood after the emotional crash he witnessed the night before. "Do you want to watch the debate, or do you need to start writing your story to meet a deadline?"

Her eyes lit. "If you don't mind watching alone, I can get this knocked out in a couple of hours." She batted her eyes. "Would you like to come by my room and proofread the piece before I hit submit? Maybe massage it a bit, perhaps help me work out a few kinks?"

Now it was his turn to brighten. "Yes, I could absolutely do that. I could give it a once over. Maybe suggest a few creative tweaks?"

She discreetly handed him a spare key card. "I'm in the Tower Suite."

Slipping the card in his pocket, he watched her walk away, then turned to find a good backstage vantage point where he could catch the debate. As he did, he bumped into Mesa Merino, the head of Brandt's Secret Service detail. "Sorry about that, I didn't see you standing there."

Merino had a touch of gray in his crisply trimmed sideburns, which stood out against his dark skin. A muscular build hinted at a lifetime commitment to the weight room. He spoke as he watched Nikki walk away. "I can see how you might be distracted."

Jason felt both proud and embarrassed by the comment, so he repeated Brandt's line from moments before. "Yeah. I'm a lucky guy." Seeing her exit, he turned his full attention to Merino. "It's nice to formally introduce myself. We crossed paths in New Orleans, but we were both kind of busy."

Before answering, the Secret Service agent scanned the backstage area again, as if his head pivoted on an automatic setting, like a programmed yard sprinkler. "That was Mr. Brandt's first event outside of New York and all of us in the detail were more than a bit on edge. To tell you the truth, I'm even more amped tonight, even though we have more agents on the ground. Having both candidates in the same location always makes me nervous."

An unfamiliar man approached before Jason could respond.

"No place I'd rather be. How about you, Merino?"

Agent Merino introduced the tall, willow-framed man with dull blond hair, styled straight back and held in place by too much gel. "Jason, this is Artimus Fraser. He's the agent in charge of Mr. Wellington's detail. My counterpart so to speak."

Jason noted his angular features as Fraser extended his hand. His nose was thin and pointed, and his cheekbones high and pronounced, giving him a bird-like appearance.

"I've heard about the Brandt campaign's new media approach. It's a pleasure to meet the architect of the latest losing strategy." The tone in his voice suggested haughtiness more than normal political competitiveness.

Jason's hand was already in his grip by the time he processed the insult. He was stunned at the rudeness and mumbled a weak reply. "Uh, the race isn't over yet."

What appeared to be a condescending smile graced Fraser's face as he nodded, then moved on like a shark swimming at its natural depth.

Jason looked at Merino. "Is he always such a prick?"

Merino cocked his head slightly and sighed. "Word around the water cooler is that he and Wellington are made for each other. Birds of a feather." Turning, he made another scan. "Looks like they're about to start the debate, so I need to get to my post." He pointed. "Stand over by that column and you'll be able to see everything."

"Thanks for the tip."

"Don't mention it. I'm sure we'll be seeing a lot more of each other in the next few weeks." With that, Agent Merino turned and walked away, scanning the backstage area with each step.

Jason went to the spot Agent Merino suggested and surveyed the scene. As promised, he had an all-encompassing view, including all the layers of security in the building. *I don't get Merino's nervousness. This must be the safest place in the world.*

Chapter Twenty-Six

Every election is framed by the issues of the day. In this century, some of the leading subjects have been war, the economy and a changing social landscape. Actually, that could be the same list of topics for almost every presidential election, beginning with George Washington's. While the candidate's stance on these issues is important, likability is usually just as significant. Nothing showcases both like a good debate.

****

The first face-to-face meeting between William Brandt and Seymour Wellington kicked off with a video tribute to Prescott Carver. It was the right thing to do, and Jason thought it made for awfully good theater as well. Regardless of his politics, Carver entered a private pantheon of political figures that began with Abraham Lincoln and currently ends with Bobby Kennedy. They are in the exclusive club of those slain while in, or seeking the office of the president. By the time the clip ended there were few dry eyes in the audience.

Following the homage, each candidate was given three minutes to make an opening statement, and William Brandt used his time to sing the praises of the late Prescott Carver. Seymour Wellington followed suit and commended his former foe. It's poor form to speak badly of the dead, even if he had called him a 'flip-flopping, two-faced carpetbagger' twenty days earlier. After his eulogy, he reverted to form against his new foe. Less than five minutes into the televised spectacle, he called Brandt a 'political debutante' and a 'Hollywood huckster.'

The man seems to know only one way to campaign. He could see Brandt's strategy immediately as well: focus on connecting with younger voters. Fans, in his vocabulary.

Brandt was coming off as far more relaxed in front of the camera compared to the stilted Wellington, and delivered perfectly intoned lines with grace and humor. "In this day and age, America deserves someone in the White House who actually believes in the science of climate change." And, "I don't need a consulting firm to tell me what young adults think. I actually work and socialize with them."

From his perfect viewpoint Jason could see nods from more than half of the attendees. *I give him credit, Brandt's really connecting.*

When the moderator steered the debate toward questions about the economy, the different strategic approaches were just as clear. Wellington focused on his experience in government by pointing out that Brandt himself was very wealthy. "Our party passed last year's tax reform bill saving American families billions of dollars." He then pointed to Brandt. "You should thank us, too. I bet it saved someone as rich as you a bundle."

"Touché." Jason whispered to himself as the barbs flew. "This isn't Wellington's first rodeo."

Brandt countered. "The companies I started have created tens of thousands of jobs for real people in fields as diverse as technology, manufacturing and banking. I guess those of us who can, do, and those that can't, legislate." After delivering the jab, Brandt looked directly into the camera and winked. "And some of us can do both. Did you see me in *Diary of a Congressman*?" The audience laughed, and polling would later show that those watching at home liked it too.

Parry and thrust. Brandt's looking sharp, and doing better than I thought he would.

There were more questions on subjects like interest rates and legalizing recreational marijuana before the debate ended, but the tone for the remainder of the campaign seemed set. Brandt was the hipper, media-savvy outsider, and Wellington was the walking embodiment of establishment politics. Both men seemed pleased by their performances as they shook hands to end the first of their two head-to-head encounters.

Jason milled about on the debate stage as advisors and well-wishers exchanged pleasantries. He felt energized by the magnitude and drama of the event as he greeted Brandt. His newsman blood was surging. "I thought you did great. I can't wait to talk about it tomorrow during our interview in Los Angeles."

Brandt smiled broadly, seeming aware that cameras might still be trained on him, but the determined look in his eyes signaled that he had already shifted from tonight's accomplishments to tomorrow's requirements. He shook Jason's hand and spoke with an edge in his voice. "Tomorrow, you get exactly one question about this debate. The rest of the time we'll spend talking to ABC's latest Bachelor. Remember, I'm in this to win votes, not a policy pissing contest. Keep your eyes on the prize."

Jason stammered. "But…but this is news."

The response was immediate. "And every word I spoke tonight will be sliced, diced and dissected by the network talking heads. A new cycle starts tomorrow, and my fans will be ready to be entertained again. So, that's what I'm going to deliver. Talking about tax policy for single men rolls eyeballs, while chatting with a single hunk-of-a-guy known as the Bachelor attracts them like magnets."

Brandt put his hand on Jason's shoulder. "We're doing this together, and we're going to win. It's our destiny." He then turned to Juanita Hernandez, the junior senator from Texas rumored to be on the shortlist of vice-presidential candidates. Her selection would bring even more interest and polled very well with the key demographics Brandt was targeting.

Standing alone on the crowded platform, Jason slumped, feeling deflated. He asked himself an existential question. *What the hell am I doing here?* Then he remembered his invitation to join Nikki in her suite and his outlook on the evening turned on a dime. He asked himself the same question, this time with very practical implications. *What the hell am I doing…here?*

Chapter Twenty-Seven

Mind and body, each with their own domain. One is deemed evolved and rational, the other primal and instinctual. Both are absolutely essential in defining what it means to be human. In most circumstances, they work in concert, like two sides of a coin. In certain situations, however, one realm dominates the other.

****

Jason knocked on the Tower Suite door, then used the key card Nikki passed to him at the debate. When he opened the door all of his senses were engaged. The darkened room was lit only by flickers of light emanating from candles placed strategically throughout the space. The flame dancing atop each warmed aromatic wax, and the sweet scent of vanilla engulfed him. Enchanting jazz music played in the background, filling the space with a palpably sensual vibe.

The frustration he felt minutes before dissipated rapidly, like a teaspoon of red food-coloring diffusing in an Olympic sized swimming pool. The tension was being replaced by different and even stronger emotions. She walked toward him as his eyes adjusted to the dim lighting. When they touched, he wrapped his arms around her bustier-clad body. "I guess you finished your piece?"

She looked up at him with a naughty grin, placing her index finger lightly on his lips. "Shhh."

He leaned down and gently kissed her luscious lips. Subtle hints of chocolate and mint registered on his tongue. Primal synapses fired in his brain, and any remaining conscious thoughts of Brandt or the debate were drowned by a surging flood of endorphins now coursing through his veins. The soaring sound of a soulful saxophone solo played on the speakers, amplifying the effect as she led him further into the room, stopping at the foot of the bed.

They shared another long, sumptuous kiss before they separated enough for him to once again behold her breathtaking beauty. The white satin bustier was knitted together with a pretty pink ribbon, taunt at the top, barely containing her ample breasts. A bow topped the ribbon like a special gift, waiting to be opened on Christmas morning.

He tugged firmly at the ends of the silky tie unwrapping this extraordinary present. One eyelet at a time he unthreaded the glossy strand, stopping after each rung to plant a small kiss on newly exposed skin. Slowly, methodically and expectantly he worked down her body, until the last filament holding the garment together slipped free of its mooring. The lacy teddy completed its mission of arousal and fell away. He ended his descent on his knees, repeatedly kissing the softest part of her feminine body, his tongue searching.

Her fingers ran through his loose locks and her soft moans added to the jazz composition echoing in his brain. When a new up-tempo track began, she fell backwards onto the bed, seeming ready for their next duet.

As he stood and unbuttoned his shirt his eyes beheld a beautiful woman surrounded by pillows situated around the bed, intended to be used in positions he had yet to imagine. By the time his pants hit the floor, his body throbbed and his mind ceased to register any thoughts other than anticipation of the pleasure of their union. He joined her on the king-sized bed and for the next hour they composed their own musical score.

Afterwards they ordered room service of oysters on the half shell. He enjoyed a couple shots of bourbon while she unexpectedly stayed with straight water. "I'm going for two days in a row."

That surprised him, but he was in such a perfect mood he simply accepted her decision. "Mixing things up is a good idea."

Giggling, she glanced at the bed. "I totally agree."

Red cheeks signaled his embarrassment, as their intense experience was not what he meant…although she was absolutely correct.

"Yeah." He grinned shyly. "But I was talking about life in general." He wasn't ready to say the 'L' word, but his feelings for her were deepening, so he ratcheted up his courage and tested the water. "I mean, life's short. Sometimes exploring a new path can lead to a better place." Now he waited, unsure how she might interpret his intentionally vague words.

She batted her eyes. "I know exactly what you mean." She moved closer. "It could be fun to discover new avenues with someone special." Closing her eyes, she kissed him deeply. Parting, she added to her previous comment. "And as long as the journey isn't rushed."

Jason could hear blood pounding in his ears. He tried not to stare too intently, but his emotions got the better of him. "I feel exactly the same way." He matched her movement toward him and they kissed again, then made their way back to the bed to make more music. By the time the clock struck midnight, both were contentedly asleep. One last thought filled his mind as he drifted off. *I haven't been this happy since*...He slipped closer to the abyss that separates wakefulness from sleep. With a satisfied exhale, he finished his final waking thought. ...*since before Julie passed away.*

Chapter Twenty-Eight

American lore holds that the feud between the Hatfield's and McCoy's started over the disputed ownership of a pig. Each act of revenge begat the next, until a dozen men died. Each clan wanted retribution for slights - real or perceived. Most of the time in the modern world, getting even is much less violent, but the emotions that drive the acts are the same.

****

Jason woke to light streaming into their suite and got up to draw the curtains. His casual glance out the window revealed something amiss. The fountains seemed frozen, with water hanging in the air, defying the laws of gravity. That's when it hit him - this wasn't a real window, but a prop on a sound stage. *Shit. Julie's back.* He turned around slowly to take in this dream's alternative reality. The Bellagio suite in which he had gone to sleep had been transformed into a movie set.

Julie was positioned off to the left in a tall director's chair wearing tight jeans and an even tighter Planet Hollywood tee-shirt. Another matching chair sat empty beside her. "Put your pants on, lover boy, and come join me. By the way, I like the jeans you gave me tonight, they fit like a second layer of skin."

By now he knew the uselessness of questioning her requests, so he angrily reached for his trousers. "Can't you give me a break…ever?"

"Oh, come on. Did I come see you while you and the princess slept by the pool last night? No, I did not." She seemed satisfied with her answer and stuck out her tongue. "So there."

He shook his head as he put one leg, then the other into his slacks before stepping out of the faux bedroom. Only two walls of the room stood on this transformed dream set, making it easier to film. The walk was short and he plopped into the empty director chair. Frustration dripped from his voice. “I give. What’s the deal this time?” His arm waved toward the two-sided bedroom. “What’s up with all this?”

“Duh…” She seemed genuinely excited. “We’re going to Hollywood in the morning.”

“Of course we are, it’s the next stop in the campaign. But you don’t have to go if you don’t want. Come to think of it, that’s a great idea. You can stay here and haunt tortured souls who have lost their life savings. There must be dozens in this very hotel.”

“As if. I go where you go. That’s the rules.” She chuckled. “Besides, you need me. Brandt put you in your place after the debate, and I can help you even the score.”

That got his attention. The burn from Brandt was still fresh. He watched Nikki breathe rhythmically as he considered Julie’s offer, then mumbled sullenly. “I’m listening.”

“Good, I knew you would see it my way.” She got out of her chair and motioned for him to follow. “Let’s get to work.”

Like a dutiful dog trailing his master, he tagged along behind. They walked ten yards from the imaginary Tower suite to another set that appeared, as if by magic. This one featured the Pacific Ocean as a backdrop. He recognized the location from his trip more than a year ago, when he pitched his idea for *Ghost Stories of the Stars*. That was the reason he was away from home the night Julie was killed. He couldn’t stop the thought that had burdened him with overwhelming guilt since her death. “I’m so sorry I wasn’t there.”

Before taking the next step, she responded to his grief. “We’re past that, remember? You’ve got to let it go. I have, and besides, we have more important things to discuss.”

His shoulders shuddered and he tried to clear his mind by focusing on what was in front of him. “Is this where we’re meeting Brandt tomorrow?”

"You're getting good at this, lover boy."

"Would you quit calling me that?" His hands gripped the armrest as her non-stop references to his relationship with Nikki were uncomfortable.

"Ease up, stud. I'm not concerned about her coming between us, we've got something eternal. Besides, I like the girl." A playful verbal jab followed. "And I noticed she abstained from partaking last night…unlike someone else I know."

"Get off my case." Jason paused. "I can handle my liquor."

Clearing her throat, she answered sarcastically. "Whatever you say. Anyway, I'm not here to bitch about your drinking, I'm here to talk about Brandt. Specifically, your interview with him tomorrow."

Jason's mood fouled further. "After watching the debate, I thought of at least a hundred follow-up questions. But he threw a bucket of cold water on that idea. This is a goddamn election and he's treating it like he's plugging a movie."

Putting her hands on her hips, Julie fired back. "To be fair, he did tell you he didn't want your interviews to be all about politics. He was up front about what he expected when you signed up. Besides, you'll see real movie hype in a couple of weeks when we get closer to the release of his vampire flick."

"I know." He felt the need to defend his surly disposition. "But he also agreed to my demand to have editorial control over these episodes." He paused, then calmed a bit. "It's just that tonight he came across as bossy and condescending. It rubbed me the wrong way, that's all."

The corners of her lips tipped up. "He's the one who wants to make these interviews entertainment." She giggled like someone about to pull a prank on a deserving foe. "Want to see what can happen when things get really personal with a president?" With that, she pulled a small tablet from a beach bag that just happened to be sitting beside the Pacific Ocean set. She hit play, and former President Bill Clinton appeared on the screen. The date of August 17, 1998 was superimposed on the bottom right corner as the playback began.

"This afternoon in this room, from this chair, I testified before the Office of Independent Counsel and the grand jury.

I answered questions truthfully, including questions about my private life, questions no American citizen would ever want to answer.

Still, I must take complete responsibility for all my actions, both public and private. And that is why I am speaking to you tonight.

As you know, in a deposition in January, I was asked questions about my relationship with Monica Lewinsky. While my answers were legally accurate, I did not volunteer information.

Indeed, I did have a relationship with Monica Lewinsky that was not appropriate."

Julie hit the pause button. "We can watch the rest, if you like, but I think you get the drift."

The beginnings of a smile touched Jason's lips. "It's not like I want to embarrass the guy, but…"

"Hey, he's the one who wants to talk to the Bachelor, so let him. And while he's at it, ask him about the first time he was in love. The first time he fell hard for a woman."

Jason glanced at her with suspicion. "Wouldn't that be more of a question for Nikki and the *National Conversation*? I mean, I still have *some* journalistic integrity."

She had a cat that ate the canary look as she answered. "Normally, I would agree with you. But last night I think he made it quite clear how he wants this Hollywood stop to go down. The man's telling you how to do your job, so give him what he thinks he wants."

He liked the logic. "So, just like that, ask him about his first love?" Julie reached for his hand. Her touch was always cold, but it still startled him.

"He'll probably give you some glossy answer about how many times his heart's been broken, that's when you press him a little and watch him squirm. Then, when you think the moment is right, ask him about the first woman that ever truly broke his heart."

"Shouldn't I know the answer to a question like that before I ask it?"

She chuckled. "Just ask him the question, let him answer, then you respond honestly. It will make great television, just like Bill Clinton's address to the American people. Don't you trust me?"

Without hesitation, he answered. "Of course I do."

Smiling, she touched his hand again. "*That's* what I've been waiting to hear."

Chapter Twenty-Nine

Emotions can be powerful, and force their expression, whether we want them to or not. And, as a species, humans almost always pick up on the nonverbal cues. One example is the facial expression of terror. With few exceptions, people around the world interpret bulging eyes as intense fear. But what if you don't wish to broadcast certain emotions to others, either physically or any other way? Scientists have devoted entire careers to the subject of masking true feelings.

****

The trip from Las Vegas to Los Angeles takes four hours by car, or just over an hour by plane. That's an hour if you don't have to arrive ninety minutes before your flight, stand in line for security checks, then wait another thirty minutes for your bags at your final destination. At a private airfield, Jason, Nikki and Anthony walked straight from a chauffeured limo onto William Brandt's campaign plane. The jet launched away from a blazing Nevada morning sun, then exactly sixty-three minutes later, touched down at an executive airport just outside of LA. The perks of wealth might grow old someday, but not yet for Jason and his travel mates.

They were in high spirits as they sauntered together, three across, through the small main building adjacent to the airfield. Jason and Nikki held hands as they strolled, with Nikki in cute pink shorts and matching halter top paired with sparkly sandals. The guys wore faded jeans, with Jason sporting a Foo Fighters concert tee and Anthony in his usual flannel shirt with sleeves rolled to his elbows. They were scheduled to shoot late in the afternoon to fit the candidate's schedule, and to capture a golden pacific sunset.

Turning a corner, Jason's stomach dropped, as if the airplane they just exited had hit an unexpected air pocket. He spotted a familiar face scanning the arriving passengers. *Agent Kevin O'Reilly. Damn it. What's he doing here?*

The agent had his badge out and held it for all to see as he motioned to their small group. "Mr. Simmons, remember me? Agent O'Reilly, from the FBI. We need to talk."

Nikki and Anthony looked first at the agent, and then at Jason, with wrinkled brows. Jason's good vibrations mood evaporated and his body stiffened. "You guys go to the hotel. I'll catch up in a few minutes. I'm sure this won't take too long."

O'Reilly interrupted. "Actually, I need to speak to you *and* Ms. Broussard. I have news."

Looking at Anthony as his stomach knotted tighter, Jason tried to act as nonchalant as possible with his friend. "Go ahead, buddy, take the limo. Nikki and I will get an Uber. We'll probably beat you there."

The agent addressed the odd man out. "I won't keep them too long."

Jason patted his friend's shoulder, and Anthony walked away slowly. He turned back with parting words. "Don't be late, we've got a Mexican appetizer on the menu this afternoon."

After Anthony was out of earshot the agent directed them toward a room with smooth concrete floors and high windows. It was cramped, secluded, and out of the flow of the small crowd of reporters and Brandt campaign staffers who had filled the plane. He pointed to two well-worn beige metal folding chairs, then waited for them to settle. "There have been developments in both of your cases."

Nikki went from what looked like nervous caution to excitement. "Jason was right. You've found my parent's killers, haven't you?"

"We haven't gotten all of the details from him yet, but yes. Powell Moberly has confessed to killing them."

The agent's words hung in the air as real as if they had taken on mass. Hearing Jason's hunch come true seemed to startle Nikki. "I thought Jason's theory was a stretch. I never dreamed…"

The agent glanced at Jason. “So did I.” Then he said it again, as if begrudgingly. “So did I. But when I questioned Moberly about their murders in Massachusetts, he knew things about the case that had never been released to the public. He seemed proud to take credit for being one of the two men who killed your parents.”

The well of tears that dried up two days before had evidently replenished, because with Agent O’Reilly’s pronouncement she wept again. This time the crying was softer, as if knowing who committed the deed was another step in her healing process. The streaming rivulets were washing over a deep wound that was finally beginning to scar, but was still very tender.

Jason held her as she gently shook, the only sound her muffled cries. After a few minutes, Jason looked toward O’Reilly. “You said you have news in both our cases.”

In his plain black suit and matching skinny tie, the agent seemed seven feet tall as he stood facing the sitting couple. “Yes, and I have a question for you as well. When we interrogated Moberly this time, he mentioned you, Mr. Simmons.”

Jason’s shoulders tensed. “What did that bastard say about me?”

The lawman’s hard steel-blue eyes narrowed. “We really leaned on him, trying to get him to give up his partner, but he wouldn’t do it, he stuck to his story. He said he never knew the other man’s name, or anything about him, and he even refused to give a physical description. He says they never met before killing your wife, or Ms. Broussard’s parents.”

O’Reilly took a step closer, now just a couple of feet in front of them. “Moberly claims they were both specifically chosen to commit these murders.”

“Chosen?” Jason hung open for a moment, then he repeated his question with more emphasis. “What do you mean, chosen?”

“He wouldn’t give that up either, said it’s the rules. Says he’s only told what he needs to know, when he needs to know it.”

Jason held Nikki close and kept his head down as her tears soaked his shirt. He stroked her short hair as his mind raced. *That's the same thing Julie says!* He didn't look up. "I'm afraid I don't understand."

"We're having a bit of difficulty as well, and hope you might be able to shed some light. Moberly claims all of his instructions came to him in his dreams, said his dead father told him what to do." O'Reilly paused for a moment then his tone seemed to turn accusatory. "He was pretty insistent you would know what he was talking about."

Jason could feel the agent's stare boring into the back of his skull, and he was about to freak out. That was *exactly* the same way Julie talked to him. Before he could come up with the right words to deny the accusation, Nikki came to his defense with a fierceness he had not yet seen.

"That son of a bitch is going to fry for what he's done, and now he's dragging a good man's name through the mud! I want to be there when they throw the switch. Hell, I want to be the one that lights him up!"

Jason nodded as he gathered his composure. "Let me get this right. This guy's claiming a dead man told him to kill my wife, then Nikki's parents? Then a year later kill a man who was campaigning to be the next president? On top of that he claims I'll understand what he's talking about?" Jason gave an exaggerated head shake. "The man's obviously insane."

The agent stared intently, as if looking for the slightest hint of…what? After a few long seconds, he broke the tension. "That's what we think as well. He's certifiable alright, but it's our duty to follow-up any lead we get because sometimes they pan out…like the crazy one you gave us."

Jason was shaken, but with the few extra seconds garnered by Nikki's outburst, he regained his control. "Anything else?"

The agent paused for an extra beat, which made Jason think he had more to cover, but O'Reilly ended the session. "Not today. But I'll check in every few days just in case, you know, you think of anything else."

Politely, Jason replied. "We're lucky to have men like you protecting our country."

O'Reilly gave him a sphinxlike look and an enigmatic response. "I'll be around."

Chapter Thirty

In a courtroom it's dangerous to ask a question to which you don't know the answer. Just look at what happened to the prosecutors in the O.J. Simpson trial. In what was called the 'Trial of the Century,' the prosecution asked him to try on a blood-soaked glove without knowing if the soaking changed the leather. His lead defense attorney uttered a line used over and over. "If it don't fit, you must acquit."

****

The secret service presence at the outdoor location for the Los Angeles William Brandt interview was almost as intense as it had been when both candidates were in the same location for the debate. Now in his blue blazer and a white shirt with subtle navy stripes, Jason paced with Nikki. As he walked, he silently rehearsed his prepared interview questions, trying to put the conversation with Agent Kevin O'Reilly out of his mind. She matched each step beside him in silence, her pink sleeveless dress flowing in the light ocean breeze. He guessed she was also mulling over what they had just learned.

Mesa Merino strode up to them with the confidence of an MMA fighter. He stood ramrod straight, wearing aviator glasses as he faced the Pacific. "The location is secure. You're clear to start the interview."

Jason mentally noted the difference in nervousness level between the debate last night and today. "Does an open space like this make your job easier?"

The muscular agent looked at Jason as the left corner of his mouth lifted. "I like these clear sightlines better than that zoo in Vegas. In that place a killer could have blended in with the crowd, biding his time, then put a bullet in either candidate from close range."

"He would have to get a gun past all the security checks, and that wouldn't be easy, would it?"

Merino glanced toward Brandt. "I guess we could ask the nut job who killed Carver."

"Oh…yeah." Jason blushed. "I see your point."

Merino's head pivoted, as if on some unseen timer, seeming to scour the surroundings for anything out of place. "That's why me and my team, as well as hundreds of other dedicated men and women are on the job. We have to keep Mr. Brandt and Mr. Wellington safe so that one of them can become the next president."

"You think Brandt's safe out here?"

"Each of us take a risk every time we get out of bed in the morning, but yeah, this place is about as protected as it gets."

"He's lucky to have a man like you on the job."

Mesa Merino answered simply. "I would protect William Brandt with the very last breath in my body."

Jason's mind split. On one hand he admired the dedication of the career agent. On the other, a divergent thought came to mind. *Where do they find these guys? Central casting?*

Merino cocked his head, seeming to listen to some sort of radio transmission, then extended his hand to Jason. "It's time. I hope you have a good interview." With that, he departed as Brandt and his entourage emerged from a billowy white tent that had been set up to serve as a temporary make-up room.

Jason greeted Brandt as he ambled onto their outdoor set wearing a stylish tan suit that surely cost more than most people make in a month. A hunky younger man with a chiseled chin stood just behind the candidate talking to a petite but well-endowed woman with a toothpaste commercial smile. The 'Bachelor,' in his dark gray athletically cut suit and matching tie, had been campaigning with Brandt in front of huge throngs all day, but Jason didn't immediately recognize the woman. He whispered to Brandt. "Who's the starlet?"

Brandt chuckled, as if everyone should recognize all the young faces that graced American television, even if they were of the 'Fifteen minutes of fame' variety. "That's Kyna Ulysses. She was the Bachelorette last season. I'd like her to join us on set, it will help balance the gender demographics."

What Jason said was, "Ah, I see…I'll give Anthony the update, and then we'll get right to the interview." What he was thinking was different. *Damn it. I'm having a hard enough time staying on task as is, especially with Julie in my head, so I would have appreciated a little advanced notice on the change.*

Unlike Jason, Anthony seemed to take the news in stride. "Cool." A lot of effort had gone into getting the camera angles perfect to capture the stunning seaside backdrop without having the lens' staring directly into the setting sun. He made a couple of quick adjustments, then spoke crisply into his mic. "Alright people, look sharp. We're making guacamole today."

Jason, sometimes kindly described as ruggedly handsome, gently herded the trio of truly beautiful people to the half-moon table. Anthony positioned it to include the breaking waves in the background, and Nikki took a seat near him to take notes on her tablet.

With everyone situated, Anthony spoke loud enough for all to hear. "Here we go. In three, two, one…" The cameras began rolling and the chef now spoke softly into his headset. "Our avocados are on the set."

On cue, everyone smiled and Jason kicked off the show by speaking excitedly to the audience that would be watching online in just a few hours. "Welcome to California. Today we again welcome our favorite presidential candidate, William Brandt. We're also thrilled to be joined by special guests Kyna Ulysses of the *Bachelorette*, and Cordell St. James from the *Bachelor*."

Kyna, in a tight red off-the-shoulder dress, spoke for both reality stars in a stereotypically high-pitched voice. Jason always referred to the sound as 'cheerleader voice.' "We're glad to be here in support of such a great man."

With no live audience, Jason decided to get his one political question in at the front of the interview. He would spend the rest of the time on celebrity chitchat. After all, he had his marching orders from both the candidate and his dead wife. "The pundits seemed surprised by your performance last night. What did you think of your first presidential debate?"

The polling data from all the networks showed Brandt had more than held his own. In fact, his overall approval rating had crept up a few percentage points. He was still lagging far behind in the polls, but the gap had closed. Brandt was obviously in a good mood. "Being onstage with cameras in your face, a live audience on hand and millions watching on television can cause a man to tense up. When my opponent has as many hours in front of cameras as me, maybe he'll loosen up a little."

He spoke the words with humor and ease. All on set, as well as those off screen chuckled at the quip. Jason still had an unsettled gut feeling about Brandt, but for the first time he could picture this man as president. *He could actually pull this off.*

The interview was off to a good start, so he decided to give the candidate what he wanted and get right to the celebrity portion of their chat. As much as he would have liked, nothing more would be said on the political front today. He looked squarely at Brandt as he delivered his first prepared Hollywood oriented line. "No other man alive has appeared on more magazine covers than you. You are a legend, one of a kind. This afternoon we have the pleasure of being joined by two of the next generation of fan favorites generating their own share of buzz. I know you three have had a fabulous day campaigning, so let's hear from them as we get started."

Anthony spoke into his headset. "Camera two, push in on the young gun, then pan to the eye candy beside him. We're adding the lime juice to our avocados."

On set, Jason became aware of how little his teeth showed when he smiled compared to Cordell St. James. He purposefully pulled his lips father apart as he asked the young star his first question. "It looked as if you found true love as your season came to an end. What's the latest on you and Natalie?"

Natalie Alfina had been the last woman standing in the final episode of the year, and Cordell expressed his unending love and devotion with a proposal of marriage. "It was such an emotional experience and I wouldn't trade it for anything, but the wedding plans are on hold at the moment. She's a special woman and we want to make the decision that's best for both of us."

Jason resisted his urge to speak them, but his thoughts were clear. *Dating sixteen women at the same time while being followed by a camera crew might not be the best way to find true love.* Instead, he went the safe route. "Relationships have their ups and downs. America is behind you every step of the way. Best of luck working things out."

His gaze turned next to Kyna. She was a petite pretty brunette with a bra size at least three times larger than normal for a woman of her height. He was guessing augmentation. Without any prep on this guest, Jason winged it. "Kyna, your romance was last season. How are things between you and your lucky guy?"

Her full lips pouted. "I'm afraid my story sounds a lot like Cordell's. Phillip and I actually set a wedding date, but things didn't work out."

With no better plan, he asked the obvious question. "Oh, what happened?"

She glanced at Cordell as if he were the only person in the world who could possibly understand. "We were great together on the show. Sure, we had cameras and crew around us, but were in a kind of protected bubble, our real-world problems kept away. When filming finished, our little slice of heaven disappeared almost overnight." Kyna's bottom lip quivered. "Phillip's old girlfriend came back into the picture." Her eyes shown as glassy as polished marbles.

Anthony whispered. "Push in on the Barbie doll, looks like we've added a little cayenne to the mixture."

Using the back of her hand, she wiped away the moisture on her cheek. "Sorry about that. It's just that love hurts. I'm okay now, and I'm a better woman because of the experience." Cordell reached for her hand, and they looked deeply into each other's eyes as if they were soulmates.

Jason would later learn that they met for the first time this morning. Watching and listening to these two Jason felt he and Anthony had truly gone to a new celebrity low, or high, depending on how one looked at it. He could sense a television special in the making with this pair as a new reality star couple. *Maybe that could be a side project for me and Anthony.*

Snapping out of his momentary lapse, Jason wrapped this part of the interview. "Thank you both for being so real and open with America." They nodded appreciatively as Cordell continued to hold Kyna's hand.

It was time to pivot to the candidate, time to ask William Brandt a few *personal* questions. "These two have given America a glimpse into their hearts. How about you? What's happening in your private life right now?"

Brandt answered these kinds of questions his entire professional life, so while a typical politician might be offended or find the question too intimate, Brandt appeared at ease. "Right now, I'm between relationships and that's probably for the best. It allows me to concentrate on the campaign. I can devote one-hundred percent of my efforts to working for America."

His smile seemed warmer and more genuine than Cordell's. Jason wasn't sure if that was because he was the real article, or because he was a far better actor. There was no distinction between the two choices for the camera, and maybe it didn't really matter.

Jason thought of Julie, and her advice. The time was right for the next question. "Fair enough. Then tell us about a time when you were in love. Tell America about the first real love in your life."

Anthony seemed to sense the moment. "Camera one, push in on Brandt. Here comes the cilantro."

Brandt's expression shifted, almost imperceptibly, but it was enough to signal this was not a question he expected. There was a long pause and the camera captured the Hollywood legend as his persona transformed from carefree to contemplative, featuring a distant stare. "I haven't thought about her in a long time."

Jason knew he had struck gold, and as an interviewer he sensed he needed to slow down. There would be a payoff as long as he didn't push too far, too fast. "Tell us how you met her."

Brandt listened to Jason's question, then turned in his seat to more squarely face the camera. Jason guessed he realized that if he was going to reveal intimate information, he might as well get maximum impact. His eyebrows lifted, and Jason interpreted that as Brandt changing from surprised, to now seeing this as an opportunistic moment.

"I met her on the set of my breakout film, *Iron Clover*. I was the nervous untested leading man on my first international location, and she was the pretty local woman hired as an extra for a few street scenes. We met the first day of shooting, and the chemistry was instant."

With no idea where this was going, for once Jason relaxed, determined to let it play out as Julie instructed. He nodded to the young reality stars still on set. "Mr. Brandt, why don't you remind some of our younger viewers, like these two, about that movie and how it impacted your career?"

"Sure. It was a romantic comedy about a young Irish steel mill worker who happened to look exactly like the spoiled son of an

American billionaire. Mistaken identity ensued in Dublin as I played both parts. The critics panned it, but it was a box office smash. The roles showcased my versatility and the movie became the springboard for my early career."

Jason prodded. "Tell us more about this mystery woman, this first true love of the man who may become president."

Brandt sat with an unfocused look, as if peering through time into his long-forgotten past. "I haven't thought about Fiona O'Connell in a long time."

Eyes widening, Jason stole a quick glance toward Nikki at the unexpected mention of the name of her birth mother. Nearly dropping her tablet, her jaw was slack.

Anthony was unaware why the name was important, but he seemed to pick up on Jason's change in vibes. His words were sharp and spoken quickly. "Camera one, tight on Jason. Camera two, push in even closer on Brandt. I think a clove of garlic just dropped into the bowl."

Leaning into the next question, Jason's relaxed demeanor from moments ago was replaced with an edge. "Your first love was named Fiona O'Connell, from Dublin?"

Seeming to sense Jason's alteration in tone, Brandt answered defensively. "Yes. It's a fairly common name."

This can't be a coincidence. Processing the bombshell, Jason reined in his emotions. "Of course it is. It's just that I've heard that name recently. It happens to be the same name of a friend of mine's relative. Small world, isn't it?" He steadied himself and asked another question to keep the interview going. After all, that's what Brandt wanted him to do. "What was Fiona like? How did she capture your heart?"

Brandt seemed to accept Jason's explanation and continued. "Fiona was beautiful, and sharp as a whip. She was also fiery and unpredictable, and that fueled my attraction. She wasn't like anyone I ever met…before or since."

The description reminded Jason a lot of Nikki, but he tried not to jump to any conclusions. Her surname was probably a coincidence in a nation overrun with O'Connell's and O'Connor's… and even O'Reilly's. And Fiona had to be one of the most common given names on the island. He glanced again at Nikki who was now on the edge of her seat, tablet on her lap. "Sounds like she was an exciting woman. What happened?"

Interlacing his fingers with the index ones extended, as if to emphasize a point, Brandt continued. "Fiery and unpredictable are great accelerants at the start of a relationship. Our passion burned bright from the day we met. I never experienced anything like the intensity of emotion we shared. But sometimes, when a fire roars too hot, it consumes everything around. That's especially true when both people involved were as young as we were."

With his breathing returning to near normal, Jason had his game face on again.

Anthony seemed to notice. "We've just added sea salt. Camera two, give me a quick shot of the reality airheads, then back to Mr. President."

Camera two captured a star-struck couple watching a master storyteller draw in a soon-to-be digital audience. The focus then went back to Brandt as Jason slowly herded him toward the conclusion of his saga of first love. "Why has this story never been told?"

Seeming back in his movie star comfort zone, he delivered a pure Hollywood answer. "I was a nobody. Who reports on a nobody?"

The reality stars laughed, as if knowing exactly what he was talking about. Three years ago, no one had heard of them, and today they were on a set with a presidential candidate.

Brandt proceeded in a more serious tone. "It was also the era before Twitter and TMZ, so a movie star could have a private side to their life."

Jason's gaze narrowed. "So, how did this torrid affair end?"

Opening his hands, Brandt shrugged. "We had a big fight and she threw a plate at me. Her temper exploded and she stormed out of the apartment. For the life of me, I can't even remember what we argued about that day. It was our first big blow-up, and I assumed she would cool down and come back the next morning. She didn't, nor the day after that. In fact, she never came back. We wrapped up shooting a couple of weeks later and I returned to the States with a hole in my heart."

Anthony rubbed his hands together. "It's time to mash these ingredients. Get the tortilla chips ready."

The interview continued as Jason probed. "Did you ever try to rekindle the fire?"

Brandt gave a sheepish half-smile in the moments before he answered. "When the movie hit the theaters, my career took off. I was in one project after another…and one public relationship followed the next. After one particularly bad ending to a romance I hired a private investigator to track her down. I wanted to see if she might be interested in seeing me again, especially now that I was a big star. He found her and reported back to me that she was involved with someone more important."

Jason sensed where this was going, but asked the question anyway so the actor could deliver his line. *If this is what Julie wants, this is what she's going to get.* "You were a major celebrity. Who was more important than you?"

He looked straight into the camera. "She became a nun. She chose a life of service dedicated to Jesus, over me."

"Ahhh." The couple responded at the same time.

Sneaking a peek at Nikki, Jason thought she looked like she had just seen a ghost.

Anthony let the cameras roll for a few seconds longer. "Cut. That's a wrap. Terrific episode everybody, and the margaritas are on me tonight."

Chapter Thirty-One

'Hell hath no fury like a woman scorned.' This quotation is often ascribed to William Shakespeare. Sounds right, doesn't it? Like so much in this world, it's almost right. The line as originally written goes like this. 'Heaven has no rage like love to hate turned, nor hell a fury like a woman scorned.' It was written by a William, William Congreve that is, a less famous English playwright. No matter, the line lives on because it speaks a certain truth about a woman's prerogative to go ballistic when appropriate.

****

The interview barely ended when Jason spied a determined Nikki heading straight toward Brandt. He stepped in front of her. "Whoa there. Slow down and take a minute to think about how you want to handle this before you say something you might regret."

She looked up at Jason, green eyes burning like sparklers on the Fourth of July, and pushed him sharply with a well-placed heel of her hand to his sternum. He took a forced step backwards. "Get the hell out of my way, if you know what's good for you."

He held up his hands and stepped aside as she resumed her bee-line to the candidate, who was now engaged in small talk with the two reality celebs. She reached the trio and interrupted their conversation the moment she arrived. "My mother? You had an affair with my mother?"

Jason followed in her wake and now observed Brandt's reaction. He could almost see the wheels turning in Brandt's brain, trying to make sense of Nikki's accusation.

Brandt responded tentatively. "You mean Fiona? Fiona O'Connell?"

Nikki answered loudly. “Yeah! She’s my…” She paused, seeming to search for the right words to describe her relationship to Fiona O’Connell, but her fury maintained its intensity. “She’s my birth mother!”

Cordell took a step back and searched for Kyna’s hand. They had both seen dramatic scenes like this on their shows and were trained in the appropriate protocol. “Hey, we’ll give you guys some space.”

Neither Brandt nor Nikki acknowledged them, so Jason addressed the couple. “You two did great in the interview.” They nodded, then walked away, hand in hand, seeming more interested in each other than anything else. Jason turned back to find Nikki continuing her interrogation.

Her words sounded sharp and barbed. “When were you and Fiona O’Connell together?”

Jason knew what she was really asking. ‘Are you my father?’

Brandt looked ashen and also seemed to understand the real question. “It’s been a long time. Give me a second to think.”

“Come on!” The veins in Nikki’s neck bulged. “Spit it out, and no fudging on the dates!”

“It was ‘85. I last saw your mother in 1985.” His brows raised and eyes widened. “When were you born?”

Nikki’s body shrank as her ancestral question was answered. “I was born in 1991.” Her fiery stare lost its spark. “For a moment there I thought…” She seemed unable to finish her thought.

Brandt reached out as if to comfort her, then spoke sympathetically. “Look, you probably have a lot of questions for me, and I have a few for you as well, but let’s save them for our flight to Cleveland tomorrow. I’ve got a black-tie dinner tonight with some party bigwigs, and I need to change into my tux. We’ll talk tomorrow. I promise.” He patted her shoulder, then walked away, leaving Nikki looking as if she had been knocked down by a big wave and was now trying to regain her footing.

Jason closed the gap between them and wrapped her in his arms. “That was a hell of an interview, wasn’t it?”

Her initial laugh turned into a soft sob. “I guess I won’t have to work too hard to come up with my next headline.”

He snorted involuntarily as he held her tight. “No, no you won’t. Truth really is stranger than fiction.”

Chapter Thirty-Two

People crave authenticity and purity. They want the real deal. That desire fuels causes as diverse as the organic food movement and extremist politics. Both have the same urge for truth, seeking assurances that what they see is what they get. Nothing but one-hundred-percent commitment to the ideal is permitted. The reality is the universe demands equilibrium between pure states and total disorder, and in the end the rules of physics always win.

****

Jason and Anthony kicked off the crew's afterparty with a margarita toast, then stepped away to work late into the night once again. In post-production they now referred to this as the Beach episode. Anthony tossed his drink in the trash while Jason switched to straight shots of tequila during the editing session. He reassured his friend with a wave of his hand. "I'll be fine."

By four in the morning, they were uploading their completed work from the hotel conference room they had used as a makeshift editing station. Anthony rubbed his eyes as he powered down his laptop. "Dude, we can still get in a couple hours of dreamtime before our wakeup call. Let's get out of here."

Jason gave Anthony a slap on the shoulder that was a bit too firm, in the way that guys do when they want to make a point without saying too much. He picked up the remaining half-full bottle of Jose Cuervo on the table and wobbled a bit, answering with a slight slur. "I'm going to sit on the beach with my friend. I don't feel much like dreaming tonight."

Anthony gave a heavy nod that seemed to scream pity. "That shit's going to kill you, you know. You can't live like that. Maybe you can get into an AA program when we get home. Like I've told you before, my dad couldn't put down the bottle either, and it eventually killed him." He paused, looking as if he wanted Jason to say something in response. When the time stretched to uncomfortable, Anthony finished his thought. "Look, I did ALANON when I was growing up, so I know those twelve steps have power. Please, Jason, think about getting some help. That's all I'm saying."

Jason shrugged and headed out the door into the nearly moonless night toward the rhythmical sound of the breaking waves. *The only thing I need tonight is a drink, not a lecture…from you or Julie. If I can't shut either of you up, maybe I can at least drown you out for a few hours.* He sat by the ocean with alternating thoughts of the two women in his life. Silently his mind replayed highlights of his years with Julie and of his short time with Nikki.

One particularly strong memory was the day he and Julie got caught in a surprise summer shower in Central Park. They ran to a nearby ice-cream shop and rode out the rain trying fifteen flavors between them.

He remembered her words. "This one is my favorite." Then, when she tasted the next scoop, she changed her mind. "No, this one is my favorite!" He could almost taste the salted caramel and blueberry flavors tonight. By the time all had been tested, she had declared ten of the fifteen varieties as the best.

The rain was steady that day and tapped the windows in a hypnotic pattern, inducing a warm feeling, like the incoming tide did now. Maybe it was all the senses involved that made that memory so strong.

The same could be said of his Vegas night with Nikki. He knew he would remember the hints of mint and chocolate in her kisses, and the vanilla scented candles from that night as long as he lived. Both memories made him smile and he wished he could live forever in either of those edited universes. He tipped the bottle after each new recollection and before long tears trickled down his cheeks.

He knew neither of those paths could be sustained. Julie had departed this world, never to return in physical form. She might visit him in his dreams until the day he died, but what they had when she was alive was gone. He knew that.

And then there was Nikki. White hot heat is a good way to start, but it can't remain at that pace, just as happened with Brandt and Fiona. In his heart, he knew that as well. But could there be a regular life with her, one that simmered instead of blazed? Was that what he wanted? As he pondered the question, he was honest with himself, realizing he barely knew her, and she, him. His mind formed a clear thought despite its drunken emotional state. *If she got to know me, the real me, could she love someone so screwed up?*

The waning crescent moon moved through the night sky as he continued thinking and drinking until morning. He stumbled onto the candidate's plane, ready to take off for the next stop, spent, both physically and emotionally. However, by the time the landing gear retracted into the belly of the aircraft, their newest campaign clip was already the top trending video on the internet.

As promised, Nikki was seated next to Brandt in the first-class section as the plane climbed to thirty-five thousand feet for the long flight to Cleveland. Jason and Anthony were further back, and when the bell chimed indicating they were free to move about the cabin, both men yawned. Jason selected classical music on his phone and slipped on headphones to help insure he would get at least a couple of hours of uninterrupted sleep on the way to Ohio.

Beethoven's Fifth Symphony faded and a familiar voice whispered in his ears in perfect stereo. "Jason, wake up. Guess who?"

He pried his eyes open and looked down at the screen. "There are rules about broadcasting on airplanes, you know."

She ignored him. "How do you like my look today?"

His bleary eyes focused on the details of today's outfit. "Hip hugger bell bottoms? Are those peace sign patches?"

"You outdid yourself this time. I love the crop-topped tie-dyed tee-shirt and my daisy chain headband. I look like a genuine hippy chick."

He was still grumpy about having his sleep interrupted, but he did havc to acknowledge she looked hot. "I like it, but why in the world would my imagination choose a Sixties theme?"

She put her hands on her exposed hips. "Duh, we're going to Cleveland…Rock and Roll Hall of Fame?"

"Ah, that's right. Brandt got permission to use the museum for our next episode. The reality stars from the beach are nothing compared to the real stars we'll sit down with tomorrow night."

Julie pointed a skinny finger at him. "The next time the celebrity part of this gig gets to you, just think about how excited you will be when you're on stage with those greats. You're going to sit down and talk with singers you admire and who have played every corner of the globe. Those two are the genuine articles."

He reclined the seat as far as it would go, which was about two inches. "Thanks for the reminder, but I'm really tired and could use some rest. Can we just get this over with?"

She brushed aside his gruffness and continued, chipper and upbeat. "Let's get a soundtrack going for our conversation. How about some classic rock?"

With her introduction, John Lennon's song, *Imagine*, started playing in his earphones. Jason closed his eyes and smiled. "I liked his solo stuff, but it's too bad Yoko Ono broke up The Beatles. Wonder what they would have created had they stayed together, you know, like the Rolling Stones?" Even though this music was from an earlier era than his youth, Jason always loved it.

Julie swayed to the beat. "He sang of a world where people shared their belongings, wiping out greed and hunger. What a place that would be."

Jason hummed along. "That's what a star sounds like. He had so much talent and vision."

"Yes, yes he did, and this very song got him killed."

“I almost forgot.” His head dropped. “He was assassinated too, right?”

“Of course, dear. Why else would I bring up John Lennon? His death ended all hope of there ever being a Beatles reunion, and it made Yoko a sympathetic figure to a lot of people. Not an easy task.”

“Here we go on the assassination thing again. Can’t you leave it alone for a while?”

“Your tutoring is almost over, just a few more lessons. I promise. Now, go ahead, ask me about the lyrics that got him killed.”

These kinds of questions still got under his skin, but his will to argue with her had been worn down like water smoothing stones in a stream over eons of time. “How did lyrics about imagining a better world get one of the greatest song writers and performers this world has ever known, killed?”

“Assassins often kill because they are true believers. They think killing their victims will advance their cause, or at the very least, make them famous. Mark David Chapman was a true believer who heard John Lennon sing about a world where possessions didn’t matter, then realized that the man who wrote and sung those words was one of the richest men in music. In his eyes, that made Lennon a hypocrite.”

Jason pondered her words. “That justified killing him?”

“Well, that and mental illness. He was a paranoid schizophrenic who was incensed that a man so rich could sing about a world where everyone shared their wealth, so he decided to do something about it. He was a deranged true believer, but a true believer nonetheless.”

“Are you going to try and convince me to believe in something so much that I will kill someone? Is that your plan? Is that what you’re trying to do?”

“Slow down. You misjudge me, because I’m not going to ask you to do anything. I’m just giving you an education. You, and only you, will decide what you will do when the time comes. I just want you to make an informed decision. That's part of the rules for this mission."

Sarcastically, Jason replied. "An education on assassination? Really?"

Julie held up two fingers. "Peace, man. Don't shoot the messenger."

A spontaneous laugh sprang forth. "Don't shoot the messenger? That's funny, considering our conversation. But, come on, Julie. This whole assassination thing is getting old. I've got my problems, but I'm not one of those nut jobs, those you call true believers. I won't plan and plot to kill someone. I'm just not that guy. I'm not."

"Good, then our lesson for today is over unless you would like to talk about something else…or someone else." From the screen, she motioned her flower ringed head toward the front of the plane. "Maybe you would like to know a little about what Brandt is telling Miss Suddenly Sober?"

He looked to the pair and could tell by the smiles and hand gestures that a friendly and animated conversation was underway. "I hope she can finally get some of the answers that she needs, but I don't think their discussion concerns me. It's none of my business. So, if you don't mind, I think I'll just go back to regular sleep."

"What if it does concern you? Would you at least like a heads up? I know you like her, and maybe you will be able to help her out as well."

Glancing toward the front again, his widened eyes betrayed him. "Well, you know, maybe if you have something to tell me that could help her…you know…maybe I might be interested."

"I thought you might want to talk a little more before going back to boring old regular dreams." She looked down her nose, chin lifted, as triumph curled on her lips. "Just a hunch."

"Come on, give it up." His frustration boiled. "What do you know?"

Dark, vacant eyes stared back. "Remember this when I visit you again. We have a relationship that you value."

"You've made your point. How can I help Nikki? Spill the beans."

"Right now, Brandt is regaling her with his stories of her mother's spirit and zest for life. He knew her before her mental illness came on strong, when her candle burned brightest. And he did love her."

A faint smile crept on Jason's face. "She needs to hear those kinds of stories. Until now, all she's known of her mother is the darkness of abandonment and insanity. But I fail to see how that involves me."

Adjusting her daisy headband, Julie continued. "With much of the mystery about her mother finally revealed, she's now going to obsess about finding her biological father, and she doesn't have any leads. She will fixate on that without making any progress and there is a good chance that she'll begin drinking again, heavily. Jason, you can point her in the right direction and save her from going to a very dark place."

"Why the sudden interest in Nikki's health? You've seemed amused by her, but I haven't sensed you have any particular interest in her overall wellbeing."

Swaying back and forth to the resumed sound track, she grinned. "Darling Jason, don't misunderstand my concern for her welfare. This is *all* about you. If she goes down the rabbit hole it's very likely she will take you with her, and that wouldn't be good for either of our futures."

He wasn't completely convinced. "I believe your main concern is that I'm able to do whatever it is that you want me to do when the time comes."

She winked. "I think of them as one and the same. If you start drinking any more than you do now, you'll go from a high functioning alcoholic to a falling down drunk. That won't help you or me, will it?"

Her bluntness hit him like a gust of wind on a sub-zero day. He was drinking more than ever in his life, and it wasn't hard to image her prophecy coming true. His answer was soft and honest. "I suppose you're on to something."

"Of course I am. Now, when she starts going on and on about her biological father just plant a thought. She'll take it from there."

He shrugged. "Sounds easy enough. What should I say?"

"When the time comes, just ask about the bishop. That's all you need to do."

Jason pondered her suggestion. "That seems a pretty odd thing to bring into a conversation. What if she questions me about it? Am I supposed to come out and say my dead wife gave me the idea?"

A giggle preceded her response. "You two have been close, but I'm not sure if you're ready for that level of intimacy. Trust me on this. The conversation will sound totally natural."

Looking at his bohemian-dressed wife on his phone screen, he sounded hopeful. "You'd better be right."

"Have I ever been wrong? And by the way, stay out of trouble." She held up her index and middle fingers. "It's time for me to go. Peace out."

He was about to ask her what she meant by that last part, about staying out of trouble, but her image and voice faded as the classic rock song, *Turn! Turn! Turn!* by the Byrd's, filled his headset. He mumbled as his weariness succumbed to sleep once again. "I guess I'll have to find out on my own."

Chapter Thirty-Three

Take the Long Way. These words are included in a classic Robert Frost poem, and in song titles from groups as diverse as Supertramp, Pearl Jam, and The Dixie Chicks. The appeal of the idea seems to be that by slowing down and going a different route, one might meet new people, explore interesting places, or simply enjoy the journey more. However, if speed is of the essence, the fastest way to get from point A to point B was figured out eons ago. It was Archimedes who first articulated that the shortest path between two points is a straight line.

****

The trio of Jason, Anthony and Nikki rolled out of the Cleveland airport in different states of mind. A tired Jason and Anthony were going directly to the Rock and Roll Hall of Fame to get started on the prep for their next episode. Meanwhile, Nikki seemed full of energy as she bounded to the next available taxi. Jason called out. "Let's get together for dinner tonight."

"Sounds good. Text me when you decide on a place. I'll be doing some more online research on my mother until then." They stepped into separate cars and their rides sped off in different directions.

A few hours later Jason arrived at a bar with a music theme, proudly wearing his newly purchased Hall of Fame tee-shirt. Surveying the joint, he saw furniture that was a little ragged around the edges, but his soft spot for the classic rock music playing in the background and vintage concert posters on the walls made up for the rough decor. Exhausted, he found a table, and by the time Nikki joined him he was on his second bourbon. Seeing her, his weariness eased a bit as he asked about her day. "How did your ancestry search go?"

Wearing a tight-fitting spaghetti strapped top and matching black denim jeans, she slid into the worn booth across from him. "My head is spinning. Thanks to Mr. Brandt, I know more about Fiona than I ever dreamed possible. Little things, like the fact that she loved to soften squares of chocolate over candles before eating them, and she enjoyed sipping champagne while soaking in the tub. I now think of her as a real person, not just some crazy old witch who gave me away."

"He's 'Mr. Brandt' to you now? Sounds like someone is star struck." Jason's dog-tired mental and physical state started their evening out on a sour note.

The snap back was immediate. "That's not fair! He did me a huge favor, and he's probably going to be our next president. Everybody better get used to calling him mister, even you."

Holding his tongue, he finished his second drink and signaled the waiter for another. "You want to compare their dirty martinis to the Blind Bat's, or are you still on the wagon?"

"I'm sticking to water for a while. I'm on a cleanse."

"A cleanse?" He could hardly believe his ears. "Who are you, and what have you done with the real Nikki Broussard?"

There was an air of mystery in her voice as her head cocked. "I pride myself on being unpredictable, apparently like my mother." She glanced toward the ceiling for a moment, then locked eyes with him. "I just hope I don't go off the deep end, like she did. You've only seen one side of me, and it might be my best, but I'm a complicated woman."

His eyes drew in her raw beauty, looking absolutely radiant in her form-fitting outfit. His mind wondered longingly as he answered. "Yes, you are. You're gorgeous, smart and fascinating. A one-of-a-kind original."

She blushed at the compliment as the waiter returned with his third drink, and they placed an order for a jalapeno-calamari appetizer. She then turned the conversation in a new direction. "Now that I know so much more about my birth mother, I'm channeling my energy toward finding my biological father. I don't have much to go on, and so far, all of my research has been a dead end."

Julie told me this would be the next obsession, and so it is. Play it cool. "What about a private detective again? It worked to find your mother."

"I called the guy I used last time, but he's on a high-profile divorce case stakeout. He can't start on it until next month, and I don't want to wait. I want answers now. The problem is that my only clue is from my crazed mother, who claimed the pope is my father."

Jason teased. "Hmm. As beautiful as you are, I sincerely doubt that Pope John Paul the Second was your father. I don't see any family resemblance at all. Go ahead, look it up."

She didn't catch that he was joking and pulled her phone from her pocket. A few taps on the screen soon produced the image of the man who was pope the year she was born. "You're right. I look nothing like him. The shape of his egg head…the eyes…nothing seems right. Besides, it says that he was in Ireland once, but it was in 1978. That's not the right timeline. I may never find out who my biological father is, but I'm fairly certain it wasn't the pope."

What the hell, this is as good of a time as any to try what Julie suggested. "I guess you're right." He paused and swallowed. "Maybe, in her confused state, Fiona just got the level of detail wrong. What if your father was another kind of holy man? Maybe like a priest, or even a bishop? It wouldn't be the first time a man of the cloth strayed from their vow of celibacy. Give that a whirl."

Once again, Nikki bowed her head to the god of the internet and tapped away. After a long couple of minutes, her eyes raised and an ashen face met his buzzed stare. Her words sounded ominous. "This can't be good."

Oh no, Julie. What the hell did Nikki stumble onto? And why do you keep doing this to me? "Surely it can't be that bad." He rocked his ice cubes against the side of the tumbler, chilling the bourbon further as he gathered his composure. “What did you find?”

Someone behind the bar chose this moment to turn up the volume of the music playing in the background. Bob Marley wailed his song, *I Shot the Sheriff*, as she fired him a wild look. “Remember Powell Moberly and his religious connection?”

“Something called…” Physically drained and half drunk, he struggled to remember the name of the fringe group. “What was it?” He closed his eyes and finally the right words found his tongue. “It was sort of like, The Friends of Fatima, right?”

She nodded.

“What do *they* have to do with your search for your father?” He had a sick feeling he wasn’t going to like the answer.

Placing her phone carefully on the table, she turned it around so he could see the screen. A photo captioned, ‘Cardinal Michael O’Cleary’ looked back at him with piercing green eyes, just like hers. “Not only do we have similar looks, but he’s a priest who became the Bishop of Dublin in 1985, and was there until 1992. The timeline fits since I was born in ninety-one.” Her eyes cut to him as her words trembled. “Want to know the spooky part? Guess what he’s been up to in Rome the past few decades?”

Incredulously, Jason stared hard. “Don’t tell me he’s involved with that organization. I thought they were a bunch of religious extremists, not part of the official Church hierarchy.”

Taking a deep breath, she continued. “He’s mainstream alright, as far as I can tell, but he’s the cardinal charged with safeguarding the original *Three Secrets of Fatima* documents in the Vatican archives. Sound like a coincidence to you?”

He felt his cheeks getting hot as he tried to connect the dots in his mind. “What? How can that be?”

“Jeez, you suck as an investigative journalist. This is real, and there is no way it’s a coincidence. That dude is probably linked to the murder of your wife, my adoptive parents, and Prescott Carver." She paused, then lowered her voice. "It also seems likely he's my biological father."

Jason tried to see the hidden patterns like Nikki, but the cogs in his head were slowed by exhaustion and eighty-proof liquid gunk. "What are you going to do? Walk right in to St. Peters and demand a meeting, the same way you did with me? I'd buy a ticket to see that."

"Thanks for the vote of confidence, Mr. Optimistic. While that approach works more often than you would ever imagine, I've found the bigger the organization and the higher the target, the more layers of protection are built into the system. Just walking through the front door like I did at your office won't work here. I'll need to take a different approach."

He took another sip, then spoke words he immediately regretted. "I was an easy mark, wasn't I? Even when I knew you were coming, you just blew right into my world."

She seemed ready to explain her plan, but his comment stopped her. "Hey! What do you mean you knew I was coming?"

Damn it! Me and my big mouth! He contained his panic, then deflected. "I'm joking. I mean, it had been a year since Julie…you know…and I knew I would meet someone new sooner or later. That's all." He leaned forward while rolling his hand, motioning for her to continue. "Now, what's your plan. How are you going to get to this cardinal?" Her eyes dropped back to the screen, giving him a moment to recompose. *That was close. I don't need to be explaining this whole, dead Julie in my dreams, thing tonight.*

Pecking away, she seemed to accept his explanation, then waved her phone in front of him. "Sometimes the direct approach is best. Just watch a pro at work." She tapped a few more times, then smiled broadly. "Got his email address from the Vatican directory. Let's begin."

She spoke as she typed. "Dear Cardinal O'Cleary. My name is Nicole Broussard and I am the daughter of Fiona O'Connell, of

Dublin Ireland. I think you knew her VERY well. I have an interest in the *Three Secrets of Fatima*, and I believe you are the man to answer ALL of my questions. I am traveling with the media group covering U.S. presidential candidate, William Brandt, but can alter my itinerary as necessary. I think we should arrange a meeting as soon as possible. Regards, Nicole Broussard." She flashed an impish grin as she hit, 'Send.' "That ought to rattle his Catholic cage. Any bets on how long it takes him to respond?"

Jason caught the waiter's attention and ordered yet another round by pointing to his nearly empty glass, then faced her with bloodshot eyes. He didn't intend it, but his voice carried an edge. "It's the middle of the night over there, so it will be quite a while. If he's got any smarts, he'll not respond…ever."

As soon as he finished his sentence, her phone dinged, indicating a new email. As she read, a wry smile crept onto her face. "Guess who's a night owl?" Pausing, her eyes scanned from side to side as she continued reading. The corners of her mouth twitched either nervously, or in intense concentration, he couldn't tell. "He says he's been expecting to hear from me for some time, and he would like me to come to Rome as soon as possible…like leave in the morning as soon as possible. How's that for moving the investigation along at warp speed?"

Blinking slowly, Jason shook his head. "What the hell? Just like that, he invites you to the Vatican…without any questions? Amazing."

She reread the email and her bottom lip trembled. This whole discussion about her father had started only a few minutes ago, and the exhilaration of chasing down a longshot lead seemed to be replaced by the realization that all her questions could really be answered in the next few days. "I guess I'm heading to Rome…maybe to meet my father…a man who could be involved in an international murder conspiracy."

The evening crowd began to fill the place and *Sweet Child of Mine*, the classic rock song from Guns and Roses, blasted from the speakers. Jason reached for her hand. "Let's get out of here and go someplace a little quieter."

She squeezed his and nodded.

Standing, he looked around the room for the waiter and accidentally bumped into a burly man wearing a black-leather patch-covered motorcycle vest. The beer in the man's mug splashed all over his ample belly.

"Hey, asshole. Watch where you're going."

Jason grabbed a napkin from the table and offered it to him. "Sorry. I didn't see you."

The biker dude responded unexpectedly. "I know you. You're the punk who made Krissy Antonio cry, aren't you?"

Appearing regularly on television has its perks as well as its problems. This was an example of a problem. Even with four drinks in his system, Jason recalled the incident immediately. "We made up. I promise." Krissy had been upset about a mean tweet from a friend when she arrived on set that night, and he pushed a little too aggressively in the interview. The combination proved too much as she broke down and cried on national TV, and he looked like a jerk. "Things just got a little out of hand for a few minutes, that's all."

The bulky man's full cheeks flushed as red as chili peppers. "I'll show you what it's like to pick on a defenseless woman." With that remark, he poured the remainder of his beer over Nikki's head.

A loud gasp escaped her lips as the cold liquid doused her. She grabbed the tumbler on the table that contained the dregs of Jason's drink and flung it toward the biker. Her aim was not completely true, and some of it landed on another customer with a graying ponytail and receding hairline.

The ponytail guy glared at her. "You bitch!"

Two hours later at the police station, none of the twenty people hauled in could say with absolute certainty who had thrown the first punch in the ensuing brawl.

Chapter Thirty-Four

Most people care what others think of them. With enough visible good deeds, one can build a virtuous reputation, but a single bad step can shatter a person's public image. A wise man once said, 'Character is like a tree and reputation is like a shadow. The shadow is what we think of it; the tree is the real thing.' Who said this? Abraham Lincoln, the first president of the United States to be assassinated.

****

Jason fell into bed at three-thirty in the morning. After seven hours in the Cleveland justice system, he now had a court date scheduled three months hence, and had been released on his own recognizance. When the night began, he hoped for another torrid experience with Nikki, but she was headed straight to the airport to catch her flight to Rome, with a stern warning from him to be careful meeting with O'Cleary. This was certainly not the kind of evening he expected, but having Julie appear in his dream wearing a judge's robe was no surprise at all. *Here we go…again.*

She swung her gavel three times. *Bam, bam, bam.* "Court is now in session. The Honorable Julie Simmons presiding. Will the defendant please rise?"

"Arghhh! Please stop this crap once and for all!" He was tired, pissed-off and sexually frustrated. The best he could hope for now was a few hours of much needed sleep before final preparation for perhaps the most interesting interview of his career. The last thing he wanted was a dream visit from her.

From her elevated judicial bench, she swung down hard again, creating a deafening boom. "Order in the court! I will have order in the court or you'll be sentenced to a lifetime of dreaming only of me."

His mood swings had become more frequent, and now he laughed uncontrollably, stopping only when she interrupted.

"I fail to see the humor in this situation."

Subduing his outburst, he replied. "It's kind of an empty threat if your presence in my dreams for eternity is what I already expect."

Winking, she shot back. "You've got a good point there, dear." Sounding more serious, she continued. "But we're coming closer to the day that will decide all of our futures, including whether I continue to visit your dreams in perpetuity."

Jason's head snapped. "How soon? This is my life and I have a right to know what's going to happen, and when."

"Slow down, slugger. We've got to settle this court case before we talk about the future. You stand accused of striking a man in defense of your girlfriend. How do you plead?" She leaned forward on the bench, and combined with her judge's robe, her dark eyes appeared blacker than usual.

Tonight, he was having a hard time taking her seriously, and he couldn't contain a snort. "Guilty. I plead guilty to defending the honor of one Nicole Broussard."

Winking again, she continued. "Good. I'm glad you admitted your role in this sordid affair. Now, let's talk about her part in this crime."

Jason shook his head in amusement. "I guess she's guilty of the same thing. She's a gamer alright, and she had my back."

Judge Julie nodded. "That should be a sign to you about this girl. She's more than just a good lay."

Cheeks flushing, he answered softly. "She's smart, funny, and I always feel better around her. Plus, she's tough as nails. I already know she's special."

The gavel banged again. "Case dismissed. The court will now hear the next charge against this defendant."

"Hey, what did I do now?"

"It's what you're not doing now that's going to get you in trouble. You've left Anthony high and dry to do the prep for tonight's interview with William Brandt and his two famous guests."

The realization hit Jason like one of those famous 'walls of sound' from a 1960's Phil Spector produced record. "Holy shit. I've always had a thing for classic rock, and I'll be interviewing two of my favorite recording artists in just a few hours. I'm sleeping, and I've got to wake up. Now!"

Laying her gavel down, she looked at him with relaxed, sympathetic eyes. "Interviewing singers is easier than interviewing movie stars. You'll be ready, don't worry. What you need to be prepared for is how to incorporate Brandt into the discussion. As excited as you are, this show is still all about him."

"Do I have to?" He frowned. "These guys are legends, and I'll never have another chance like this."

"You can do both, wait and see." Her words softened his discontent. "You've got to get their candidate endorsement first, then everything else will take care of itself."

While her instructions sometimes took him places he didn't plan to go, they had never been boring. He looked up at her, perched behind the dark-stained wooden bench, in submission. "Okay. What's the plan?"

"For starters, one little known fact is that William Brandt is the only major star to have had a song from each in one of his movie's soundtracks. He's a big fan of both, and now a personal friend. The interview will be really simple. Ask each of the artists about their latest project outside of music, then why they are supporting William Brandt for president. After they give their endorsement, turn to Brandt and ask him his favorite song from each of them. The interview will be to die for."

His head bobbed like a toy dog riding in the back window of a car. “Why do you always mention death, like just now? You said, ‘To die for,’ when you could have said the same basic thing ten other ways and not conjure that image.”

Demurring, her voice almost purred. “Quit being so sensitive. It’s just a figure of speech. We’ll be talking about death for real soon enough, and we won’t be using metaphors.” She waved her hand. “But we’ll have that conversation another time, when we find out what you’re really made of. Right now, you need to get your ass out of bed before your partner blows a gasket.”

Raising her gavel, she swung it again and again without stopping. *Bam, bam, bam, bam, bam, bam.*

Covering his ears, he yelled. “Stop making all that noise.”

Anthony shouted from the other side of the hotel room door on which he was pounding. “Get up, dude. You’re late…again.”

Chapter Thirty-Five

In astronomy, stars can be judged by their luminosity, how bright they appear from earth. Entertainment stars can be gauged similarly. The most basic measurement is box office gross, or record sales. Of course, there are other standards for the greatest of greats, such as being known worldwide by a single name, like Elvis.

****

Jason didn't come of age in the classic rock era, but he always loved the music. It was the link between the early sounds of artists like Chuck Berry, and the alternative bands of the nineties, like Nirvana. His credit card was still warm from all of his purchases from the gift shop, and now he paced backstage in the Foster Theater before the interview in his new Rock and Roll Hall of Fame leather jacket, too excited to sit. *This is going to be a terrific night.* He heard Anthony call for everyone to take their places, so he headed to center stage in front of an expectant audience.

Due to Jason's tardiness, Anthony didn't seem to be in the mood to shoot tonight, and Jason understood, but his partner was a professional. So, like any good producer, or chef for that matter, he knew the audience would always get his very best. Anthony's attitude about Jason, however, did not seem nearly as friendly, as he refused to speak to his partner most of the day. "Alright people, we're making pierogi in three, two, one..."

Despite getting the cold shoulder from Anthony, Jason was pumped and he spoke as brightly as anytime on this tour. "Good evening, everyone. Tonight is one of the most special nights of my life, and I hope it will be for you as well. We have the honor and privilege of coming to you from the Rock and Roll Hall of Fame, and that's a big deal for a music fan like me."

Anthony directed the crew. "Let's get the basics covered. Camera two, get me a close-up of the cardboard cutouts of our two Hall of Fame inductees. They're the basic dough we're building from tonight."

On set, the introductions continued in the intimate semi-circle theater style setting of just over one-hundred and sixty of the candidate's most influential supporters. "This evening Mr. Brandt will be joined by a couple of good friends who happen to be members of this very exclusive club. They have fans of all ages and from every corner of the globe. So, without any further delay, let's bring them on stage."

He took a deep breath and began the intro for one of rock and roll's greatest recording stars. "Our first guest really needs no introduction, but we'll do it anyway. He's one of my favorite artists and his induction into the Hall of Fame proves he's one of yours as well. Please give a big welcome to the one, the only…the Duce…Duce Ripley!"

Duce walked out, waving to the crowd in jeans and denim shirt, perfectly on brand for the Americana rock sound he honed in his music. The small crowd went bonkers, making more noise than seemed possible for a group of this size. Jason smiled broadly, knowing this had the makings of one of the biggest nights in political history.

As the applause finally subsided, it was time to call out the next star. Jason could barely contain his nerves. Up until this point on the campaign trail, he had been interviewing stars that were not necessarily his favorites. This show featured some of his idols, and the butterflies in his stomach confirmed it.

Now he really wished he had prepared better, but this was not the time for reflection, it was time for him to do his job and fire up the crowd again. "All the way from Glasgow Scotland, please give a warm welcome to the front man for a band that has sold over one-hundred-million albums. He needs only a one-name introduction. Give it up for Timooooo!"

Extending the last letter of the singer's name had the intended effect. As Timo walked out in black jeans and collared shirt, the energy of the crowd soared to new heights, like at a championship sporting event. The normally cool political elite in attendance were cheering like they were in the Roman Colosseum awaiting a spectacle.

After greeting both stars with his most sincere handshake, Jason stood smiling like a four-year-old on Christmas morning. The moment was truly big, and he didn't have to exaggerate his emotions. He remembered Julie's words about who needed to remain the biggest star of the show, so he continued his introductions. "Let's get to the reason we're gathered here tonight. As people, we all desire to be part of something bigger than ourselves. We share the wish to be part of history. In fact, we all want to *make* history, and with your help and support, that's what we can do."

He paused for dramatic effect as he sensed the crowd's pent-up energy, ready to light up the place. In his best ringside announcer imitation, he pushed forward. "Please put your hands together for the next president of the United States, William Brandt!"

In the enclosed space, the partisan crowd's roar was deafening. History *was* being made, and they all knew they were witnesses. Jason and Anthony caught each other's eye, and smiled. They were back in sync, and while Jason had never publicly introduced Brandt as the next president before, he couldn't help getting swept up in the excitement.

Anthony spoke into the headset and Jason nodded, hearing the conversation in his earpiece. "Time to cut the dough into little circles. Maybe Jason can fling this dish together after all."

All four men took a seat on stools onstage, and for the first time since this whole circus began, Jason felt small among these entertainment giants. Between the two musicians they had sold over three-hundred-million albums. As for Brandt, Jason knew his audience appeal well by now. He drew on the energy of the crowd and a new vitality coursed through his veins.

Julie's advice calmed his nerves as he tried playing it cool, calling Mr. Ripley by his stage name, like they had been friends for years. "Duce, it's great to see you tonight. Why don't you tell us a little about your latest work outside the studio, and why you're here?"

Anthony seemed revved as well. "Camera two, push in on Duce. Looks like Jason's going straight for the cheese and sauerkraut stuffing. Is that water boiling?"

He asked about the water as seriously as if they were in a real kitchen and Eddie, on camera two, replied matter-of-factly. "Almost."

Duce answered in his gravelly voice with a grin and a wisecrack. "I'm from New Jersey, in case you didn't know."

The audience chuckled. Thanks to many of his hit songs mentioning the Garden State, they were forever linked. "The virus really hit us hard and a lot of people, regular people who have supported me for years, suffered devastating loss. I've made it my mission to help them financially and emotionally to rebuild their lives. We've made progress, and the cause has been supported by people like William Brandt, who has generously given both time and money."

Jason looked at the candidate while the singer addressed the crowd. This sounded remarkably like the testimonials in New Orleans. *Maybe my gut is wrong. Perhaps the man's the real deal and could be a president for the ages.* The audience applauded politely and Brandt blushed and waved in acknowledgment of the recognition.

Duce smiled as he addressed the crowd. "I've never forgotten where I came from, or who my fans are. I believe that William Brandt is cut from the same cloth. He was born to a working-class single mother and has donated more of his wealth and personal attention than any celebrity I know. As an American, a voter, and also as a fan of his work, I'm supporting this man and believe he will not only be the next president, but I think he will be the next *great* president of the United States." This brought the party faithful to their feet in a loud and sustained ovation for both Duce and the candidate.

Anthony seized the moment. "Camera one, tighter on Brandt. Camera two, pan the audience. We've added the browned ground beef to our cheese and kraut. Only a couple more steps to go. We're rockin' tonight, baby." The audience continued their applause until both Brandt and Duce stood.

The energy buzzed in the room, and like a good host, Jason kept the action moving. He turned to the second musician. "So, Timo, we appreciate you being here as well. Tell us a little about what you've been up to outside the studio, and why a Scot like yourself has an interest in American politics?"

The front man for the band 2much did what came naturally and played to the audience. "What a great crowd we've got here tonight. A great crowd for a great man."

The audience cheered again as the electric vibe in the room went to a new level. Brandt waved once more, but this time there was no blushing, as if he understood there was no need for modesty with these people in this room tonight. He was surrounded by fans, and the stars were literally lining up behind him. He appeared to bathe in the adoration.

Jason finally saw Brandt as the man who could, and would wear the mantle of responsibility as leader of the free world. *Maybe I'm seeing what everyone else seems to already know.*

With the crowd settled, Timo made his case. "I've been active in political causes for freedom around the world. I've championed democracy in places like South Africa, and lately in Darfur. Those struggles are important, but they're contained by lines on a map. The fact of the matter is that without a healthy planet for all of us, those other efforts won't matter. We need men and women like William Brandt, who are doing real work to help us reach a sustainable future. We need them, and we need them in places of power. Even though I'm not a citizen of this country and can't vote for him, I am a citizen of the world, so I feel it's my duty to support his candidacy in any way I can."

Timo glanced at Brandt, then back to the audience. "So, Cleveland, do you feel the same way?" The response was a frenzy that took almost two full minutes to subside.

Anthony whispered excitedly to Eddie. "The water is boiling; I can feel it. Pinch the edges of the dough together and drop those pierogis into the pot. Put the skillet on the burner and melt the butter. We're almost ready for the final step."

Jason let the cheering last as long as it could sustain itself. *This is what it feels like to make history...and it feels pretty damn good.* After a couple of final whoops from the crowd, he followed Julie's advice. "Mr. Brandt, tell us a little about your connection with these two musicians."

Scooting to the edge of his stool, Brandt glanced at each quickly before turning to the audience. "I've known these guys for a really long time, and we've worked on a lot of projects together over the years. While we may not always agree on every issue, we're in sync on the big ideas. Things like the dignity of the working man and woman, and hope for our common future. I guess my favorite all-time memories for both were when they introduced each other into this exclusive Hall of Fame. I was truly honored that each of them invited me to attend as their special guests. They're terrific musicians, wonderful people, and will forever be my friends."

The audience applauded the sincerity of Brandt's comments before Jason clarified. "Duce, you introduced Timo? And Timo, you introduced Duce when you each were inducted here?"

They nodded and Brandt spoke for the three of them. "Those were magical nights, just like tonight. I guess you could say that destiny brought us all back here together on this stage."

There was another mention of destiny, and even Jason considered the idea. *Is this all pre-ordained to happen?* Now was not the time to ponder that question as the audience waited for Jason to move to the next segment of the event. Julie's advice ran in his head like a beacon guiding him, and he looked toward Brandt. "Between them they've had dozens of hits and you probably have a lot you really like. Of all their songs, which has been your most favorite from each?"

The candidate glanced up for a moment, seeming to study the question. "That's a tough one, like asking an uncle to choose a favorite niece. But if I have to choose then I'm going with, *From the USA*, for Duce and, *Name That Love*, from 2much and Timo."

There were polite applause and nods with Brandt's selections and Jason knew a set up when he saw one. *I guess I walked right into that one, Julie Simmons. A patriotic tribute that could be used as a campaign theme song, and a song with lyrics referencing Robert Kennedy's assassination. This is almost too rich.*

Duce now took over the interview. "How about we play a few tunes for our candidate?" The audience again went over the top as a stagehand brought guitars to the musicians.

Anthony knew what time it was as well. "Toss those little boiled crescents of goodness into that hot melted butter for a final sear. It's time to eat."

Duce kicked off the first song, "One, two, three, four." With that lead in, he began belting his hit, *From the USA*.

For the next two hours the two musicians traded leads, covered each other's songs, did duets and in general put on a hell of a show. Julie was right again. It was an interview to die for.

Chapter Thirty-Six

There's a love song from the sixties that includes the idea that you can't be anywhere you aren't fated to be. It's speaking to the belief that life isn't random, but plays out exactly as it is preordained, that destiny rules all. The song? *All You Need is Love*, co-written by John Lennon, who was assassinated on December 8, 1980.

****

Two weeks had flown by at an unrelenting pace, and tonight Jason and Anthony landed in Houston. They dragged themselves from the airport to the downtown Marriott in time for a late dinner. Jason made an offer to his friend. "You want to grab a bite before turning in?"

"Nah, dude, I'm bushed. I think I'll order room service and call it a night. We've got a big day tomorrow."

Nodding, Jason answered. "Sounds like what I should do as well."

Anthony gave him a hard stare. "Should do…or will do?"

"Look, I haven't been sleeping well lately." Jason missed Nikki, who was still in Rome, and spoke with an edge. "I won't do anything stupid, it's just that I'm not ready to call it a night. Tell you what, I won't even go out. I'll stay here at the hotel bar."

Glancing at the key card holder indicating his room number, Anthony growled. "Just be ready in the morning. We've got to get to the mystery location, set up, then be ready to shoot by three."

Depositing his bag just inside his room, Jason immediately turned and headed toward the main floor bar. Rhythmic world music played softly, setting a calm mood in the darkened, mostly empty space, making the one person eating at the mahogany bar stand out. "Can I buy my favorite secret service agent a drink?"

Mesa Merino looked up from his salmon salad and pointed to his glass. “Straight club soda tonight, but you’re welcome to join me.”

Jason slid onto a barstool and the cute bartender took his order for a Maker’s on the rocks. He turned his attention to the agent for some company. “What’s it like guarding the man who might become the next president of the United States?”

The automatic half-laugh sounded as if he had thought about the question a lot. “You ever feel like you were destined to do something, that you’ve had a purpose in life even before you knew what it was?”

The prompt barkeep brought his drink just as Merino finished speaking. That gave Jason a moment to mask his tension, as yet another person brought up fate and destiny in casual conversation. He recovered, responding neutrally but honestly. “I’ve thought about it, once or twice.”

“If you went back in time and told my second-grade teacher this is where I would land, she wouldn’t be surprised. I mean, I was the youngest student ever allowed to join the flag raising squad, and I kept my spot all the way through high school. I’m still proud of that.”

Savoring his first sip, Jason pondered the agent’s words. “So, you’ve always been a patriot?”

The veteran agent raised his napkin and wiped his mouth. “That’s the way my life has played out. I went to college and majored in criminal justice, then right after I graduated, 9/11 happened.”

“Let me guess, you were at the recruiting station the next morning.” Jason had heard similar stories from many of the soldiers he profiled during his time in both Afghanistan and Iraq.

Merino nodded as he smiled. “Two tours. I thought about going career military until I met Meredith. She changed everything.”

Jason signaled the woman behind the bar for another round as he thought about Julie. His voice was quieter as he spoke from the heart. "The right woman can have that effect."

Now it was Merino's turn to speak softly. "She was a good woman and I miss her something fierce. This job, this calling, it's the only thing I have left to get up for in the mornings."

That familiar sinking feeling in the pit of Jason's stomach returned in full force as he processed Merino's words. The agent's wife was dead. *Please tell me she wasn't murdered and this is all connected.* Respectfully, he asked the question. "I'm sorry for your loss. What happened?"

"Breast cancer. It runs in her family. She fought like a warrior, but in the end, it won. That was four months ago and her passing hit me hard. Don't get me wrong, I've seen people die. On the battlefield one guy even caught a bullet while standing right beside me…but this was different. I felt my life lost its meaning, its purpose, and I wasn't sure what would come next. You ever feel like that?"

The memories of the doom and emptiness that swallowed him in the days and weeks following Julie's death returned. In the months after her murder, all of his senses were dulled and he felt as if everyone else moved through life free as a bird, while he labored like a man slogging through waist deep water. He took another sip. "My wife passed just over a year ago."

Merino nodded. "Then you know what I'm talking about. Even the job that I loved seemed pointless, until I got the call that Brandt was entering the race and I'm assigned to his detail. Nothing has been the same since. Every day is a whirlwind, and I have a sense of peace when I close my eyes at night, like I've been training for this my entire life. It's as if this is exactly where I'm supposed to be. I believe this is the reason for my existence, that I was put on earth to protect William Brandt. I've never been surer of anything in my life."

Jason thought there were some faults in his reasoning, but who was he to question someone else's state of mind. "He's lucky to have you covering his back. There's a world full of crazy out there."

Folding his napkin and dropping it on his plate, Merino agreed. "You got that right. Now, if you'll excuse me, I'm going to head to my room and get some shut eye. We've got another packed schedule tomorrow."

"Yeah, packed schedule. I'll see you in the morning." Jason stayed bolted to his barstool as Merino departed.

The cute bartender reappeared. "Interested in seeing the menu, sweetie?"

He didn't even consider that option. "Nah, just bring me a double."

Chapter Thirty-Seven

'What would you do?' It's a simple question that asks you to place yourself in someone else's shoes. A network took the concept and made a show of the same name. Christians took the phrase and changed it to, 'What would Jesus do?' That made WWJD bracelets a fad for a time. The question implies weighing the pros and cons. But what about those split-second choices, when introspection gets bowled over by the moment? That's more about reflex than decision.

****

Jason stumbled from the elevator into the hallway, and then to the door of his room shortly after midnight. After fumbling with the keycard, he entered and flipped on the television. He could hear the advertisements for pay-per-view movies playing as he stood urinating in the partially lit bathroom. His aim was aided by the glow of a nightlight designed to help disoriented travelers, though not necessarily while they were drunk like him, find their way to the toilet in an unfamiliar location. After emptying his bladder, he grabbed a short, sanitized glass from the countertop and filled it from the tap. Past experience told him that he would wake at some point with a parched tongue, and that he should be prepared. He only spilled a little as he made his way back to the bed, carefully placing the water on the chunky nightstand. "I've got to set my alarm. Anthony will kill me if I'm late in the morning."

He double checked his phone, making sure he chose AM instead of PM, then laid down on the bed watching the hypnotically recurring loop of movie previews. Fully clothed, he fell asleep atop the soft white duvet by the second cycle. He awoke to the sound of a familiar voice calling from the flatscreen. "Wake up! You're going to be late!"

Bolting upright with arms flailing, he knocked the glass of water off the table, soaking a plate-sized area of the tan, short-napped carpet. "Shit. Look what you made me do."

"Look what I made you do? Who's the dumbass that put a glass of water so close to the edge of the nightstand? Don't go blaming me for your carelessness."

Her logic made him madder and in his intoxicated, sleep deprived state, he snapped at her. "Why don't you just get the hell out of my life!"

Onscreen, she placed a hand to her ear and he realized she was dressed just like the on-duty version of Mesa Merino. Her black eyes were covered with reflective Aviator sunglasses and she wore a standard government issued black suit, with an earpiece in her left ear.

Her head tilted as she appeared to listen intently. "What's that? His mission here is almost complete? Yes, I'll tell him."

His rage faded. "Did I just hear you say this…this…mission is almost over?"

Imitating Merino, she continued. "As God is my witness, we are about to complete this mission. It's the fulfillment of my destiny." Then she giggled. "You've got to admit, that was pretty good."

Joining her in a laugh, his mood mellowed. "That was pitch perfect."

Taking a bow, she acknowledged the compliment. "Thank you, he's an easy mark. The thing that makes it so fun is that everyone sees it but him. You should hear Meredith's impression."

The mention of Merino's dead wife vaporized his good mood like the first drop from a summer shower hitting a sizzling hot Texas sidewalk. "Why did you have to go and do that?"

She scoffed. "I'm a dead woman. Who do you think I talk to at night while you're out drinking?"

He sighed heavily. "Just tell me why the hell you're here tonight, and if you're serious about all this dream crap almost being finished."

"Jason, just chill out. You've got to find a new hobby or something. You're wound way too tight."

"Get to the point. I've got an important day about to start."

Julie's attention turned to a point offscreen and she again appeared to be listening intently to her earpiece. "Roger that, I'll tell him." Her smile broadened as she faced him again. "Good news. This will be quick, less than five seconds of live action. Let's watch."

Before he could say anything, her image disappeared from the television, replaced by a film clip labeled, March 30, 1981. Without any setup, the action began. President Ronald Reagan strode confidently past a small crowd, headed for an open limousine door. A shot rang out and chaos engulfed the scene. In less than five seconds, four more shots were fired and Reagan had been shoved into a waiting car that sped away.

The scene faded to black, and after a second or two of silence, Julie reappeared on the TV. "Did you see how close Hinkley got to Reagan? It's lucky for America he was such a piss-poor shot. He hit everything but the president."

In disgust, Jason picked up the spilled glass and walked toward the sink. He answered while refilling it. "I thought he did hit Reagan."

She waited for him to come back into the room. "That crazy son of a bitch hit the President's Press Secretary in the head, causing partial paralysis and permanent brain damage. He also hit a DC Police Officer, and a secret service agent, but the bullet that hit Reagan was a ricochet. It was a glancing shot off the armored side of the car. Let's watch it again."

Before he could protest, the short clip ran again, this time in slow motion, with her commentary. "He looked just like a president, didn't he?"

Jason noticed Reagan's demeanor. He always looked like the American idea of the leader of our nation. The way he walked projected an air of confidence, with his broad shoulders pulled back, and his facial expressions hinting at optimism and humor. Most voters saw these traits in the one-time actor and elected him to two terms. Jason couldn't help but see the resemblances to William Brandt as the few seconds of footage rolled. "He's remembered more for the way he changed America's self-image as for any of his actual policies or legislative achievement."

The tape continued as Julie narrated. "As Reagan walks by Hinkley, you can see him raise his pistol. See it, there on the bottom right side of the frame?"

Jason nodded, as her commentary continued.

"Let's pay special attention to the secret service agents as they go automatically into action protecting the leader of the free world. As soon as the first shot is fired, Jerry Parr starts shoving the president into the open door of the waiting car, while Timothy McCarthy spreads himself as wide as possible, acting as a human shield. He caught a bullet to the chest with that move, and he's lucky he survived. They screwed up by letting a killer get so close, but at crunch time, they redeemed themselves."

The clip didn't take long to run even at the reduced speed. Jason glanced at the clock on the nightstand. "Interesting stuff, but I've got to get ready for our shoot today. I can't be late again. Like I said before, get to the point. Why are you showing this to me?"

Once more, she listened intently to her earpiece as she appeared to stare into the distance. "Roger that. I'll tell him." Her gaze focused back to him. "The point? Isn't it obvious?" She shook her head with a look of frustration. "It's really simple, Jason. Know that every secret service agent alive will take a bullet for the president, and second, if *you* have to take a shot, take it and don't miss, like that screw-up, Hinkley."

Now it was he who shook his head in frustration. "Haven't we covered this all before? You're a freaking lunatic if you think I'm going to take a shot at anyone, much less someone running for president."

Lowering her reflective sunglasses, she peered at him with her black eyes. "You, of all people, should know the futility of guessing what anyone will do in the future. Just be ready when the time comes. Got it?"

He was about to speak when he heard an annoying, repetitive beeping. *Damn it...that's my alarm.* He flicked on the light and saw the empty waterglass, and just as in his dream, there was a soggy area of carpet spread-out in a teardrop shape. *At least some of it was real.*

The television had remained on the recurring loop of movie previews all night, and with a couple more clicks, he turned on a morning news show broadcasting live from Houston. An excited reporter prattled on with breaking news. "While extremely late in the process due to the assassination of Prescott Carver, multiple sources say William Brandt will name Juanita Hernandez as his running mate at a rally this afternoon. Hernandez will be the first Hispanic Vice-Presidential Candidate, and the third woman nominated by a major party ticket."

He spoke aloud to the TV. "I guess I know who we'll be interviewing this afternoon. The only question is where?"

Chapter Thirty-Eight

'It's just like riding a bike.' Most of us have heard the phrase and know the feeling of doing something learned a long time ago, but not practiced since. It's the kind of muscle memory that reminds us that the mind and body are entwined like the strands of a thick rope. What's learned and experienced is sometimes forgotten, but never really gone.

****

Even with a sophisticated ventilation system, traces of gunpowder, cleaning solvents and lubricating oil permeated the showroom of the Lone Star Firing Range. It was as if a battlefield scented candle had been burning since the day the place opened. To some, the smell was the embodiment of power, excitement and control, but for Jason the odor triggered memories he tried to suppress. His skin crawled as he thought about the roadside explosion that rocked the lives of himself and his partner that fateful day, and his recurring visions now. *Julie's not real, I've just got a rattled noggin.* Shaking his head, he tried to clear his hungover brain. *No time to think about those things, we've got a deadline to meet.*

The location had been kept secret, and now Jason knew why. The place would be swarming with protesters if the site had been revealed. That would definitely not be the kind of unscripted coverage Brandt would want. But, if they could pull off the interview and get out quickly, then the buzz of choosing this location, with his spin of course, would dominate the next news cycle. And as they say in show business, 'all publicity is good publicity.'

Regardless of the campaign momentum this might generate, Jason found focusing difficult. He and Anthony took a tour through the facility trying to find an ideal backdrop. Every turn they took put

Jason just a little more on edge, like on patrol in Iraq. "I don't like this."

"This place gives me the willies." Anthony's shoulders rolled forward, making him look smaller. "Why do you think Brandt wants to do this episode at a business with over a thousand handguns?" He pointed to a wall display ten feet high and thirty feet long. "Especially after what happened at that shopping center last month."

They opened the door to the shooting range situated behind the showroom and goose bumps ran down Jason's arms as the rat-a-tat-tat of an AK-47 emanated from one of the partitioned lanes. He answered sarcastically. "The election is getting close and I guess he's trying to shore up his conservative street cred. Nothing says 'Real American' like firing off a few hundred rounds in Texas."

Shrugging, Anthony replied. "I guess, but whatever his reasons, we've got to be ready in a few hours. The lighting is definitely better in the showroom, but the vibe is so much more intense back here. Let's set up in front of the lane partitions." He pointed. "Over there in that open space. Maybe position some human silhouette targets as a backdrop. As much as I don't like this place, it will be visually stunning…I can't wait to shoot it."

A wry smile crept across Jason's face. "This represents a pretty good analogy for every election, but especially this one. Because of what happened to Prescott Carver, Brandt will catch a ton of crap from the gun control crowd for this stunt, but do you think they'll vote for Mr. War, also known as Seymour Wellington? I don't think so. The NRA is backing Wellington, but after this they can't exactly slam Brandt, claiming he would take Americans' guns away, can they?"

Rubbing the back of his neck everything fell into place for Jason. "He's done the election math and knows this will be a net vote gainer. He's aiming at the sweet spot in the middle of America's political war. From the beginning he's said he's in this to win, so let's do our part. You do your magic with the set, and I'll do final interview prep for him and his new Veep."

Four hours later the place crawled with secret service agents, and Jason felt a little naked as one of the few people on the premises not packing a weapon.

The ever-present Mesa Merino led Brandt and the newly selected VP candidate, Juanita Hernandez, into the shooting range. The agent took a long look around and nodded to Jason. “It’s great to be an American, isn’t it?”

Jason cocked his head. “No other country like it. How have things gone with the newcomer today?”

Taking a quick glance over his shoulder at Hernandez in the make-up chair, Merino answered. “I didn’t think Mr. Brandt’s crowds could get any bigger, or have more energy, but I was wrong. It’s been completely bananas out there today.”

That report matched what Jason had been reading about the rising political star. She was a firecracker. He teased Merino. “You ready to spend the next few years standing guard outside the Oval Office?”

Anthony took control of the set before Merino could answer. “Alright, everyone. Kids are starving in Ethiopia and we’ve had ribs smoking all day.”

The make-up artist was just finishing with Mrs. Hernandez, who now glanced toward Brandt in the next chair. “What the hell?”

Laughing as the final brush strokes were applied to his face, Brandt replied. “Half the time I’m not sure what he’s talking about, but he captures a moment like no other. The maestro is ready for us.”

The crew scuttled about getting microphones adjusted as Jason sat down wearing a black blazer with an open-collared white shirt. He was situated at one point of the stark white triangle table that Anthony had assembled earlier. As last-minute lighting adjustments were made, Jason could see the set was a study in contrast and shadows.

Human silhouette targets were staggered at varying distances behind the table and lit with different effects, framing what the cameras would see. Everything was black, white or residing in some shade of gray between the extremes. The vibe was crisp, clean and slightly haunting, like a dystopian set from a sci-fi movie.

Jason was positioned at one end and Brandt, in a black suit, at the other. With Hernandez at the middle point of the triangle-shaped table, this made her the literal as well as figurative focus for the cameras tonight. She dressed in a tailored black and white blocked business dress that complemented the wardrobe of Jason and Brandt.

Her brown skin stood out amid the black and white color scheme, contrasting as if a different lens filter had been applied to her alone. Her bright red lipstick popped like a 3-D effect had been added, and the total imagery was as if she were transported in from a different world. She was different, in fact, and if the rest of the world didn't already know it, they would after this interview. Visually, the set was breathtaking. Anthony had outdone himself.

From his director's chair, the chef counted down. "In three, two, one…"

The light on camera one glowed red and Jason smiled confidently. For the first time in a while, he felt comfortable as he kicked off the show. "Welcome everyone, to the Lone Star Firing Range just outside Houston Texas, home city of Senator Juanita Hernandez. This morning she joined William Brandt as his vice-presidential running mate in what has been the most unusual race in our nation's history. Welcome to the campaign, Mrs. Hernandez."

"Thank you, Jason. I'm proud to join one of my heroes on the ticket, and I'm honored by the opportunity to serve my country this way."

As Hernandez rattled on about her excitement on joining the race, her red lips caught Jason's eye. It wasn't that they were red, it was that they were a certain shade. Signal Red, to be exact. It was the same that Julie always wore. He chilled, even under the hot lights. *What are the odds?* His thoughts tumbled down from his mind's stable plateau like a boulder bounding toward a valley floor.

She finished speaking, and Jason realized he hadn't heard a word she said. An uncomfortable silence reigned as he gathered his thoughts.

Whispers from Anthony went out to the crew. "Camera one, push in on Jason, he's going off recipe for our Texas slaw. Damn it, Jason. I tried to keep it simple tonight."

After what seemed like an eternity, but in reality, was only three seconds, Jason attempted to reengage. "America is lucky to have leaders like you that step up when destiny calls."

He paused again. *What the hell am I saying? Focus Jason! Destiny? Really? When all else fails, let Brandt do the talking.* He looked at Brandt with wide eyes, hoping he understood his plea for a bailout. "Mr. Brandt. What did you see in Senator Hernandez that made you confident she was the right choice to be vice president?"

The unflappable Brandt came through. He glanced at Hernandez, then straight into camera two. His smile exuded stability and confidence as he spoke glowingly of his running mate. "I'm going to lead America with a team that looks and thinks like the people of this great nation. I value diversity in age, race and sex. I especially value a diversity of ideas, and Juanita Hernandez brings all those things to my team. While we don't agree on every issue, I respect her opinion and willingness to fight for her beliefs. We will have the kind of open and honest dialogue that Americans want and deserve from their leaders."

Those few seconds allowed Jason to regain his composure. He took a deep breath and nodded a silent 'thank you' to Brandt. As he resumed, Jason turned his focus back to the new VP candidate. "Senator Hernandez, tell us a little about your family. Maybe something that might surprise people outside of your home state?"

Her smile dazzled in both size and brilliance. The Signal Red lipstick magnified the whiteness of her ample mouthful of large teeth. "Well, I shot my first wild boar on my daddy's ranch when I was five years old. He was so proud he had the head stuffed and mounted. In fact, it still hangs on the wall of their den."

Anthony whispered into his headset. "I'm glad we already had the cabbage chopped, because she just added the vinegar. Stay on your toes because we're having a Texas-sized barbeque tonight."

A slow grin formed on Brandt's face as Jason asked Hernandez a follow-up question. "Do you still hunt on your family's ranch?" Brandt's smile broadened, seeming to like where the interview was heading.

Widening eyes reflected the light from the senator's dark pupils that twinkled like twin stars. "I bagged another feral pig last week." She twisted, pointing to one of the silhouettes hanging behind her. "Would you like to see me fill one of those targets with holes? I'm a pretty good shot."

This wasn't in the plan, and Jason glanced first at Anthony, then Brandt. She was offering to blow Anthony's carefully crafted backdrop to smithereens, and an assassination had brought the candidate into the race. A suggestion to fire live rounds on set had been made and Jason wasn't going to make that call. "Mr. Brandt, in light of all that's happened in this race, what do you think?"

There was no hesitation. "This campaign has been different from the beginning. I say, why change that now? Let's show the nation a different side of our future vice president."

Anthony must have agreed as he hopped up from his director's chair. "Cut. Alright people, we're adding some jalapenos to our slaw. Let's set up on lane five because Annie Oakley is going to put on a show and make us all famous. Stay close, because we'll be ready to shoot in a few minutes."

The crew immediately began repositioning cameras and adjusting lighting as Jason approached the newly minted VP candidate. "Sounds like you had an exciting childhood."

One of the crew presented a selection of handguns on a red-velvet covered board for her consideration. "I wouldn't trade those days for any amount of money. I'm the luckiest woman in the world." She paused, holding one of the guns and looking pleased by the weight and balance. "What do you think of the Glock 19 Gen 5, Mr. Simmons? It's the weapon of choice for secret service agents."

Shrugging, he answered. "Fine, I guess. I'm not really into guns." He glanced at the buzz of activity and realized this might be the only private moment he would have with the woman whose schedule was about to get very busy. He had to know. "I noticed your lipstick. Signal Red, right?"

Juanita tilted her head for a moment. "I'm not sure what it's called, but thanks for noticing. One of the make-up assistants suggested it today."

"One of the assistants?"

She stroked the gun. "Yeah…I think her name was Julie…maybe?"

He tensed, stunned by her reply, then Anthony called from his new position. "I need everyone in their places. We're adding mayonnaise to hold this show together."

"What the hell is that guy talking about?" Hernandez looked at Jason with a scrunched face. "Is this a picnic or a set location?"

His composure partially regained, he answered. "With Anthony there's no distinction. I've learned to trust him and everything always turns out better than I imagine, and I often get a great meal."

The chef called again. "Come on people. We haven't got all night."

With everything ready, Juanita headed to her spot. Jason walked behind with one thought repeating over and over in his brain. *No, it can't be. Julie's not real, she's only in my head.*

The call to begin came from Anthony. "We go to Jason in three, two, one…"

There was no time to think of Julie now, he needed to give Brandt what he wanted. Jason went on autopilot and hoped his preparation and Anthony's direction would keep the interview headed in the right way. "Mr. Brandt, it looks like you've added firepower to the ticket, both literally and figuratively."

Tonight's episode was not so much about him as his new running mate. He did, however, seem to want to show America his decision-making approach, and hammered that point home again. "My administration will include strong men and women. The choice of Senator Hernandez is an example of the broad spectrum of experience and backgrounds that I will seek to include in my cabinet."

It was clear to Jason that Brandt was shifting his narrative as the election neared. He had solidified his image as beloved actor, industrialist and environmentalist who had risen above his humble beginnings, and was now focusing the attention of America on what a Brandt run White House would look like. With the choice of a gun toting Texas woman, he was signaling that it would be different than any other, but still mainstream, not like those wild four years earlier in the nation's recent history.

Jason turned to the star of the evening. "Senator, for those of us who haven't spent much time at a firing range, what should we expect to see?"

"Please, Jason. Just call me Juanita." She continued to handle the pistol confidently as she sighted one of the targets and pretended to pull the trigger, before lowering the gun. "I've always liked to be in control, and if you're five-foot-five and one-hundred and twenty pounds soaking wet, being handy with a firearm levels the field with any man in the world. The old saying goes, 'God made man, but Sam Colt made them equal.'"

Admiring her spunk, Jason threw in his own quote. "I see. I thought the old saying was, 'education is the great equalizer of men'…and women, so to speak."

The huge smile returned to her face. "America won't have to choose between the two with me. I've got a PhD from Harvard in Public Policy, and I can hit a tin can at fifty paces. If they let me carry a gun on the campaign trail, I can be both the VP candidate, and an extra member of Mr. Brandt's protection detail."

That comment gave rise to chill bumps, and while not his intended next question, she had opened the door to the sensitive subject. "Are you implying you could help prevent another assassination, like we saw with Prescott Carver?" Out of the corner of his eye, Jason saw Brandt nodding as if he were expecting, even hoping this question would be asked.

Raising the gun, Juanita Hernandez pointed it downrange and fired ten of the magazine's fifteen rounds in rapid succession. She then pushed a button, retrieving the target via a pulley system. "God ultimately decides our fate, but if I'm ever in a situation to be the instrument of his will, I won't miss."

Anthony directed. "Camera two, push in on the target. This is the money shot."

"Six to the chest, and four to the head." Jason's eyebrows lifted. "You don't mess around, do you?"

"Stir everything and top with paprika." Anthony spoke excitedly. "Anything after this is garnish."

Juanita laughed. "I mess around all the time. How about you? Do you ever mess around? Why don't you step up here and pop off a few rounds?"

Whispering, Anthony changed courses. "Hold the paprika. She just added onions to our recipe. Camera one, push in on Jason."

Jason felt the blood drain from his face. "I haven't held a gun since I got back from Iraq."

The effervescent force of Juanita Hernandez didn't bend. "Step up and face your fears. Let's see what you've got."

Camera two pushed in tight on the handgun as Juanita inserted a fully loaded magazine, while camera one focused on Jason's vacant stare. In a flash, scenes from his time as a war correspondent played in his mind, only to be quickly pushed aside by a more recent event. His repeated dream of Julie's murder rushed back in full 3-D effect. He mumbled. "Uh…I don't think this is such a good idea."

She wouldn't take no for an answer. "Take control, Jason. Own your destiny."

Destiny...Destiny? Here we go again.

Anthony licked his lips, as if trying to produce moisture in a suddenly dry mouth. "Camera one, stay on Jason. He's either going to add some brown sugar, or drop the bowl. Either way, we're going to capture the moment."

Juanita clipped a new target in place and sent it downrange. "Just stand beside me and do what comes natural. I find shooting therapeutic, helps me clear my mind."

Walking like a zombie, Jason stood beside her. He could feel her buzzing energy as she placed the gun in his hand. He had been trained in handgun safety as part of his network preparation to go to a war zone, and he acquitted himself well. Unexpectedly, the gun felt natural, like he held it only yesterday.

She talked soothingly. "In this moment, look at the target and forget everything else. See only what's in front of you, as if it's the only thing that exists."

Feeling like someone else were controlling his body, Jason raised his arm steadily and deliberately. Suddenly, he was on the street where Julie was murdered, and instead of watching helplessly, as he had so many times in his dream, he had a Glock 19 in his hand. The taller of the two assailants raised the deadly blade and prepared to plunge it into Julie's chest. Now, the aggressor's hooded shape came into soft focus on the target, and instead of watching a repeat of her murder, he squeezed the trigger again, and again. He pulled until the magazine was empty.

The senator was hooting as the pulley system zipped the target back to them. "You've been sandbagging me! Look at this grouping!"

Anthony gulped. "Camera two, be ready for a shot of the target."

Juanita held it up for the world to see. "Fifteen straight to the head. I want you on my side if we ever play paintball."

Standing, Anthony waved his arms like a matador inviting a bull. "Cut! The ribs are smoked and the slaw is perfect. The feast is ready."

Chapter Thirty-Nine

Predicting the future is tricky business, but that doesn't stop us from trying. As far back as 634 BCE, people have gone on record predicting the end of the world, and so far, have always been wrong. Pope Sylvester II predicted the end would occur on January 1, 1000, but he was wrong, as was Pope Innocent III in 1284. Even the Mayan calendar missed in 2012. But some things are easier to predict, you just know them in your gut.

****

The editing was completed in Houston, and as expected, the online video proved to be the most controversial yet…and the most viewed. The posted comments ran the gamut from, 'Utterly tasteless,' to 'Love a hot babe with a gun.' Like it or hate it, people watched, and as Jason had come to accept, this was the basic strategy in William Brandt's campaign.

Jason and Anthony landed at La Guardia, dog tired from living on the campaign trail. Outside the terminal, Jason breathed in the scent of automobile exhaust mixed with hints of fried food. "I'm glad to be back in the city. It's good to be home."

As Anthony prepared to enter the first cab in the queue, he gave Jason some advice. "I'm going to crash for sixteen straight hours. You should do the same, bro."

Catching the not-so-subtle jab, Jason replied. "Yeah, I hear you. I'll see you at Brandt's office tomorrow night for our last interview. Let's set up around nine."

Anthony's yellow taxi pulled away and Jason slid into the next one in line. He gave his address, then leaned back resting his eyes, until he heard the driver speak. "I know where we're going. I know where we live."

Blinking hard, he looked in the rectangular rearview mirror, catching Julie's face as the car sped away into the stream of vehicles. "Am I asleep already?"

"Of course. I think you just set a new personal record for fastest drift-off. Don't worry though, you're entering the final stages of your mission, then you'll have plenty of time to catch up on your Z's."

Checking the mirror again, he saw the cabbie ID card dangling on a lanyard. It confirmed he was riding in the taxi of one Samuel Adebayo, but his eyes saw Julie Simmons looking back at him. "Now I know I'm insane."

She whipped the car in and out of traffic at high speed, even compared to the normal hustling drivers. "Sit back and relax, enjoy the ride because you're going to need to conserve your energy. Your little chick-a-dee is back from Rome and she's hot to see you."

"Damn it, Julie. Give it a rest."

Glancing at him, she snickered. "Don't you have a dirty mind this afternoon? I meant that she has news for you from her investigation. You'll be one step closer to understanding how all the pieces will fit together in these final days."

Jason sulked in the backseat, tired of talking about destiny and missions. His head whipped back and forth as Samuel, or Julie, or whoever was driving, rapidly switched lanes. After enduring a couple of more violent jerks on the wheel he spoke softly. "I'll be glad to see her again."

Julie resumed her commentary. "You should know this is a double date. Agent O'Reilly will also be joining."

"Great. That should really help set the mood." He caught a glimpse of the meter that ticked upward in this expensive market.

She braked hard for a light, then hit the gas again when it turned green. After another sharp turn, the cab neared his building. "You'll take care of resetting the mood all on your own, but the agent will have news…and a warning, so pay attention."

He opened his mouth to speak as she hit the brakes in front of his building, waking him. He saw Nikki sitting on the stoop, just as Julie had promised, then looked in the mirror. A dark-skinned man with an accent spoke. "That will be thirty-seven dollars, please."

Jason tapped a credit card and added a tip, rounding up to an even forty. "I guess I dozed off back here." A smile and silence reflected back in the mirror as Jason prepared to get out. He mumbled. "My wife could learn a thing or two from you."

As he stepped onto the sidewalk, Jason faced Nikki like a puppy that had been lost for a week- excited but bedraggled. He was still wearing the same clothes from the Juanita Hernandez interview the night before, and his beard was in the no-man's land between clean shaven and cool stubble. The dark circles under his eyes were a seldom seen shade of river-bottom brown.

He looked a mess, but she looked radiant in a pink halter dress with lime-green straps. They made her eyes appear even more dazzling. Jason was so glad to see her he dropped his bag and sprinted up the stairs, grabbing her in a blind embrace. Even in his rush of emotions, he sensed her hesitancy. "What's wrong?"

Nikki's head tilted toward the door of his building where a silhouette of a man was visible through the glass. "We're not alone."

Hanging his head, Jason sighed. "O'Reilly?"

"He's been waiting to talk to both of us…together."

"Jeez." His shoulders sagged. Since Powell Moberly started talking, he felt the agent was more interested in tying him to the killing of presidential candidate Carver, than in finding Julie's other killer. "That man. What the hell can he want now?"

They entered the building and the agent greeted them in the lobby. "Mind if we do this in your apartment, Mr. Simmons, or would you prefer to go downtown?"

Glancing at the ceiling, Jason knew that really wasn't a choice. He shot an exhausted glare at the agent. "Let's just get this over with."

The elevator deposited them on the tenth floor and Jason invited them into his apartment. "Sorry about the mess." His stare hardened. "Someone tossed the place and the enchanted housecleaning fairy is running late."

Nikki sat beside Jason on the sofa, while the agent stood in front of them and got right to the point. "Powell Moberly has been talking again. Talking about you two."

Jason gripped the back of his neck in frustration. "I thought we agreed he was a stark raving lunatic. Something change?"

The G-man rubbed his hands together slowly, as if deciding how to proceed. "We've been working under that assumption, but every time we're about to stop listening to his rants, he says something that can't be ignored. Something unexplainable."

Now Nikki joined in a weak voice. "And this concerns us, how?"

"Well, for instance, he's been talking about you." He paused as he pointed toward Nikki. "He seems to be aware of things about you someone held in solitary confinement shouldn't know."

Shifting closer to the edge of the sofa, Nikki answered with a tremble in her voice. "Like…what?"

O'Reilly paced slowly in front of the pair. "Like your travel itinerary." He shot a spiked glare at her. "He told us you were in Rome, and when we did a passport check, guess what we found? That's right, you've been there for the past several days. Coincidence?"

Jason interrupted. "This is insane."

O'Reilly pivoted and faced the disheveled television host and answered with a sneer. "Oh, he knows all about you. He has you nailed."

"I don't like your tone." Jason paused and took a deep breath, recalling Julie's advice to pay attention to the agent. "What did he say…what did he say about me?"

"He told us you would be getting loaded. Naturally, we assumed that to mean you would be drinking again and let the comment pass, no clairvoyance needed there." A wry smile indicated he enjoyed the poke at Jason. Then he swung back to cop mode and the condescending look disappeared, replaced by a more menacing one. "This morning we see your video from the firing range and watch you destroy that target. I decided to have another chat with Mr. Moberly about our interpretation of his comments."

"Oh, and what did the remarkable Mr. Moberly have to say?"

Eyes darting between them, he continued. "He was all grins and giggles today. By the way, he's taken to calling you two the Crown Prince and Princess of the Next Millennium, whatever that means. But he did have some predictions."

Nikki stood. "I know my rights, so either tell us why we're here, or leave. This interrogation is over."

Agent O'Reilly laughed. "This isn't an interrogation, Ms. Broussard, this is a courtesy call. A warning, so to speak."

Jason stood as well. "Warning? Look, we're the victims here, remember? My wife and Nikki's parents were killed by that psycho. We're just trying to get on with our lives as best we can. Powell Moberly just keeps making that harder."

Pausing, Jason felt he had appropriately described the killer as the monster he was, but Julie's direction nagged at him. Rather than end the discussion with the agent, Jason asked another question. "What kind of gibberish is he spouting that would bring you here to warn us?"

Seconds ticked by as a palpable tension raced between the three of them as O'Reilly now seemed less sure of what he should say. "He's talking about some kind of final mission that's soon to be completed.

Says that God has ordained that you two will be at the center of all that happens next."

Nikki breathed a sigh of relief. "Is that all? I've interviewed dozens of crazies that said they knew the future, and they always give vague predictions like that. Did he give you anything more than general babble or are you just amped up on his gobbledygook? I never trust people who say they can predict the future unless they give me something specific to verify. You shouldn't either." She stared at the agent with fierce green eyes.

Jason shot her a furtive glance, remembering their conversation on the balcony of Heaven, when she professed her faith in the psychic informer with precise insights. He turned toward the man. "He told you something, didn't he? He told you something, and now you're here on a fishing trip."

It was O'Reilly's turn to appear defensive. "As a matter of fact, he has been very specific, and after what he said…" His voice trailed off, as if deciding whether he should tell them of the prisoner's predictions. He gave a soft head shake, then continued. "He said that…he said that you, Mr. Simmons, you would cast the only vote that mattered in the upcoming presidential election, deciding by yourself who would hold the office."

O'Reilly took a beat, as if for dramatic effect before glaring at Nikki. "And you, Ms. Broussard, here's what he said about you. He says you will tell the world why Mr. Simmons made the right choice."

Jason hung his head, and as he did, he caught the slimmest glimpse of Nikki. Her eyes were full and she was ringing her hands. It looked as if she were barely holding it together. In the short time he had known Nicole Broussard he had seen her face express a range of emotions. He had seen ecstasy and agony and a whole lot in between, but there was one emotion he had never seen from the adventurous reporter. Fear.

That startled him, but right now he had an FBI agent to deal with, who hadn't noticed his glance toward Nikki. Jason decided the best course of action was to let this standoff play out, and keep the agent's attention on him, not Nikki. He would find out what was going on with her after this was over.

Laughing softly, he addressed O'Reilly. "Let me see if I've got all of this straight. First, an insane inmate locked in solitary confinement, who I must add has killed four people, including a presidential candidate, claims to have mysterious powers. As proof, he tells you about our travel itineraries. What's your theory on that? Does he really have supernatural abilities, like he's a real psychic? Or maybe he's the world's luckiest guesser? Or maybe, better yet, someone is feeding him information? Wouldn't that be the best theory, Agent O'Reilly?"

A forceful reply returned. "*Something* is going on, and we're working all the angles."

Jason continued with an extra dose of sarcasm in his voice. "Hmm. Secondly, what the hell do you think it means when he says that I will decide who will be president? I'm a TV host for God's sake! That's all! How could I possibly decide who will be the next leader of the free world?"

The agent fired back. "Obviously, we don't have those answers, or this would be a different kind of conversation. What we do think, is that something's going on, something we're not seeing. And every time we have a new tidbit of a lead, it involves you two. We don't think that's a coincidence."

There it is. This is what they believe, and O'Reilly said it aloud. The FBI considers us suspects is some kind of conspiracy, but don't have evidence to prove anything. Lowering his voice, Jason attempted to diffuse the tension that was building in the room and continue to keep the agent focused on him, instead of the crumbling Nikki. "Look, I get it. You're running out of leads in the Carver assassination. It's a high-profile case and the heat is coming from above. You need to come up with a break…so you're grasping for something…anything to advance the case. But giving credence to a madman who claims to know the future…really?"

O'Reilly grabbed his belt, and with a tug on each side, reasserted his point. "Just know we're watching you two…for anything." He gave a hard glare to each of them. "Now, if you'll excuse me, I have work to do."

Jason escorted him to the door. As soon as it closed behind the agent, Jason turned to Nikki. "Did that really just happen, or was it a dream?"

Nikki sat on the couch, buried her face in her hands and wept softly. "Why does everything have to be so damned weird? Why?"

Her reaction shocked him and he rushed to her side. "Shh. Don't let him bother you. He's just desperate and swinging in the dark, trying to make contact with something…anything."

She inhaled and her body straightened, then she wiped tears from her cheeks. "It's not just him, it's everything. Your wife, my parents, Brandt…O'Cleary." Her words trailed away.

Jason's mind snapped back to Nikki's travels. "Your trip. You just got back. What happened in Rome?"

"Oh, nothing much. Just that I found out I'm going to be an orphan again."

Pulling her close to offer support, Jason was confused. "What do you mean?"

Patting his chest gently, she let his messy shirt absorb some of her tears. "The good news is that I did find my biological father and got to spend some time with him, but the bad news is that he's dying. He's on his deathbed at this very moment, and insisted I return to the States. Says it would be impossible to explain my presence at his funeral without the truth of our relationship coming out." A tearful laugh confirmed her agreement with that statement. "I'm glad I met him before he died, he filled in a lot of blanks about my mother and my birth. But he's right, there is no need to put myself in that kind of spotlight, and ruin his reputation after his death."

Jason groaned in sympathy. "So, it's true. The cardinal really is your father?"

She remained pressed against his chest and he could feel her nod. "Why is this happening to me again? Why does the universe hate me?"

Holding her tight, the next words flowed spontaneously. "No, no, no. This is just a rough patch. You're too beautiful, on the inside and out, for the universe to hold a grudge forever. Just hang in there. Everything will be okay. Your best days…our best days are ahead of us."

Inhaling loudly, she sat up straight, as if to gain control of her emotions. "Funny you say that. That's almost exactly the same thing he told me. After literally swearing on a stack of Bibles in his Vatican office that he has no links to Moberly or those conspiracy people, he said great things are right around the corner."

Jason fidgeted with his index finger on the bottom of his lip, deciding how to ask his next question. "Do you think he said that in the 'I know the future' kind of way, like Moberly is doing, or was he just trying to be nice?" Her silence spoke volumes and he dared not say anything else until she answered.

"He said a lot of nice things…things like how he and Fiona agreed to keep their affair secret and find the best possible home for me they could. And they did…and I appreciate that now more than ever. He told me how he kept up with me through my parents as I grew up, and how he prayed for me when I…when things went bad." Nikki's words choked, as if recalling one of the darkest moments among the many in her past. Her shoulders sagged lower. "Like my second OD."

She sniffed, then continued, sounding as empty and hollow as a fallen tree in a desolate forest. "And he also told me how proud he was of my writing career. He had clippings or printouts of everything I've ever had published."

"He's right." Jason tried to be supportive. "I've read your work, and you do have a way with the written word. I'm sure there's a novel in there somewhere."

Her laugh was light and airy, as if channeled from a dream in another dimension. "Just like every other writer I know, I think I'm the one to produce the next great American novel, but that's not what he was talking about." Like the flip of a switch, her voice turned serious. "He was very, very specific."

Jason watched her transformation, unsure of what would come next.

Taking a deep breath, Nikki continued slowly, as if hand selecting each word like picking the perfect tomato at a produce stand. "He told me I was going to win the Pulitzer Prize for Investigative Journalism. Let that sink in after what we just heard from O'Reilly."

Silence engulfed the couple as Jason processed what Nikki said. She leaned into him again, and he wished their thoughts could merge, that they might decipher everything together without speaking a word. The physical world intruded into his silent meditation as his stomach growled loudly. "Hey, how about we go down to the Blind Bat and grab a bite?"

Nikki's spine stiffened, and she pulled away. "I've been thinking, Jason, about a lot of things over the past couple of days." Her next words sounded ominous. "We need to talk."

Jason's stomach really knotted now, as if suddenly punched. He responded hesitantly, guessing where the conversation was heading, but hoping he was wrong. "Oh?"

Looking up at him, her eyes stared with a weariness etched in dilated red capillaries surrounding emerald green pupils. "These last few weeks…these last few weeks have changed my life…literally changed my life. I feel like I'm being swallowed up in some vast uncharted ocean, unseen currents pull me one way, then another. Right now, I need some firm ground under my feet. I hope you understand."

Tears welled up in his eyes. "I do understand. It's just that I've been holding onto you as my rock in the same dark sea. You're the only one who understands me. Please don't leave me…please don't leave me…" His heart ached as one more word escaped his lips. "Alone."

With eyes averted, Nikki slowly stood as she continued to lightly hold his hand. "It's not forever, I promise. I just need some time to take care of myself, take care of things." She squeezed his hand. "And I hope you'll do the same."

His breaking heart hardened. "What's that supposed to mean, Nikki? You're the one who barged into my life with tales of Brandt's occult leanings and a thirst for perfect martinis. You're the one who pushed our life into an alternate universe."

Looking down toward him, she released his hand and her gaze went to the ceiling. "Touché. I deserved that." Nikki took a step back, wiping her cheek with her hand as her eyes now met his. "You're right. You are absolutely right, and that's my point. I poured gasoline on a fire. What we've had these past few weeks was like a flare burning brightly…on both ends. We made white-hot heat, and blazing light, but if I don't take a step back, I'm going to be consumed in the flames."

He sat somberly as her words of truth penetrated to his core. *How can I argue with her when she's right?*

She turned back toward him when she reached the door. "Will you call me, sometime?"

The verbal gut punch made it hard to breath and left him barely able to speak. He replied weakly. "Yes, I'll call. I promise."

Chapter Forty

Each bottle of Marker's Mark Bourbon has the cap, and a portion of the neck, hand dipped in bright red wax. This serves three distinct purposes. The first is as a seal, guaranteeing the product is pure and has not been tampered with. The second is to signify this is a premium product, with each bottle inspected by hand. The third is perhaps the most important. The red wax is a branding signature, visually screaming for attention on crowded shelves. Whether in lipstick or bourbon, red always makes an impression.

****

Jason fixated on the one-point-seven-five-liter bottle nestled between two competing brands. *You've been a part of some of the happiest occasions in my life, like my last anniversary with Julie. And you've been part of some of the saddest as well.* He blinked a few times, not wanting to call up tears. The crushing depression in the days after Julie's death seemed to be lurking, ready to take over his life again with the slightest misstep. *I couldn't survive that again.* He did a little math in his head and calculated he had purchased over a thousand bottles of his favorite brand, yet, he couldn't recall being entranced, like he was tonight.

The bright red wax wasn't exactly the same as the Signal Red lipstick worn by Julie, but it was close enough, and when he squinted, he could almost see her reflection in the exposed glass on the neck of the bottle. He remembered the living, vibrant version of his wife and smiled. As he continued gazing at the bottle, he considered the wax itself. When this bottle was dipped, the wax was hot, bubbling and vibrant, like Julie had been. Now, the wax was hard and cold, an echo of what it once was, just like the Julie that haunted his dreams. He snatched the bottle from the shelf, paid the clerk, then watched her slide the bottle into a brown paper bag. Jason walked home silently, gripping it tightly around the long neck, perhaps squeezing a little more firmly than necessary.

Almost as soon as the door closed behind him, Jason pulled the tab that broke the wax seal around the cap. He poured a double shot and kicked it back, trading a savoring of the complex set of tastes for a quicker jolt to his system. Only then did he sit down in his overstuffed leather chair, with exactly two cubes of ice in his favorite tumbler and a triple shot. The bottle, ready to refill the glass as needed, was placed within arm's reach on the side table. He sipped the dark golden Kentucky spirit in the way it should be enjoyed as he flipped on the TV. Two football teams with lackluster records, and neither representing a rooting interest, was the perfect choice to get him to his destination faster. The non-stop chatter of the announcers helped even more, and soon he dropped off to sleep, just like he knew he would.

When he opened his eyes, it took a moment to focus. An unfamiliar picture hung on the off-white wall beside him as he came to understand he was lying on his back on some sort of daybed. A soft light diffused through the sheer curtains in front of tall windows in a room he didn't recognize. It was difficult to clearly see the details of the figure seated in the chair beside his prone body. He kept his gaze fixed, and slowly the visage of a female figure dressed in a men's gray three-piece wool suit emerged from the shadows. As his eyes further adjusted, he could see the distinctive shade of her lipstick, then noticed she was holding a cigar.

"Good evening, Julie, I've been expecting you."

She picked up the notepad that rested on her lap and spoke with a Viennese accent. "The patient reports vivid dreams of undetermined cause. The likely sources of these night-terrors include post-traumatic stress disorder, brain injury associated with prior concussions, and of course, alcohol abuse. Recommendations for treatment include psychotherapy, an advanced MRI of previous injuries, and cessation of the consumption of liquor."

He folded his hands over his stomach and stared at the ceiling. "Sigmund Freud. How fitting."

She looked down on him from her seated position with an impassive expression that seemed to barely mask a giggle. "The founding father of psychoanalysis did say, 'The interpretation of dreams is the royal road to a knowledge of the unconscious activities of the mind.' I can't think of a more fitting way to talk about what comes next."

Laughing aloud, Jason's voice sounded as if a dash of crazy had been mixed with a pinch of amusement. "Did I get it right with the suit? I think it does something for you."

Julie answered in her phony accent. "Yes. It's great. I'm buttoned up, in control and interpret people's dreams for a living. What's not to like?"

Shaking his head, he continued to play along. "So, Dr. Julie. I've been having these dreams, interesting dreams, dreams that always feature my deceased wife. What could those possibly mean?"

"Hmm." She continued in her Freudian role play. "Tell me more about these visions that feature what I can only assume is an extraordinarily beautiful woman."

The game was on again. "Well, there's been a lot of talk about assassinations, I mean a whole lot. We've talked about John Kennedy and John Lennon and many, many more. It's been graphic at times too, if you know what I mean. I've become an expert on the subject, especially on the ways these killings have changed the course of history. But truthfully, it's more than I ever wanted to know."

Scribbling in her notepad, she questioned. "I see. Have there been any other subjects in these dreams? I mean anything other than assassinations?"

Smiling, he thought back on his first evening with Nikki. "There has been one subject that I've particularly enjoyed." Then his mind fast forwarded to earlier in the day when she walked out. "But I don't want to talk about her right now."

More notes were written. "I see, then we'll move on. Tell me, have these dreams helped you in other ways, say professionally?"

"That's easy. My wife, my dead wife that is, has given me specific interview questions to ask that have been spot on. There have been times when an interview was headed for the crapper, and a bit of advice from one of those dreams saved the day. So, yes, these dreams have had a positive impact on my career."

After placing the cap on her pen, Julie set it and the notepad on a side table with delicate spindly legs. Her accent remained as she summarized. "It sounds to me, Mr. Simmons, that all in all, this has been a positive experience. Would you agree?"

There was a long pause as Jason carefully considered his answer. The soft sunlight streaming in and the barely-tinted walls lent the room a gauzy feel, which calmed him. "At times I have been scared, angry, grateful and frustrated. I've felt my life was spiraling out of control, and sometimes I have even been embarrassed. But, when I think back over it all, I mean when I consider everything that's happened in the past few weeks, this has been one of the most productive and exciting times of my life." Taking a deep breath, he continued. "I guess I have you to thank for a big part of it."

She dropped the accent. "Awe, Jason. That's so sweet. I'm glad you feel that way. That's going to make the end of this mission sad for me as well."

Now Jason sat up and looked her squarely in the eye. This discussion was the reason he was so anxious to see her tonight. "That seems to be the consensus. I hear Powell Moberly is predicting the same thing."

Even in this moment of connection, her cool touch startled him as she reached for his hand. "Yes. We both see the end coming, but from different perspectives. Just so you know, if things go the way he predicts, you'll die."

Reflexively, he pushed her hand away, arms flailing. "Whoa now! That's the first I'm hearing about this! What do you mean, if things go his way I die?"

Julie smiled reassuringly as her black eyes stared unblinkingly into his. "I've always told you that you don't have to do anything you don't want to do, right? That means the future is not set. You'll have free choice in this matter."

"Then I'm choosing the way where I make it out alive."

Now it was her turn to reply immediately. "Good. That leads us to our next subject, your last interview with one William Brandt, the man who might be the next president."

"Let's not go changing the subject. I need to know how I stay alive. Let's stay on topic here."

Leaning in closer, she touched his shoulder. "Baby, you should know by now that all of this is connected. This last interview with him tomorrow night is for all the marbles. It will be your final chance to ask him questions that will determine who lives, and who dies. You will have the opportunity to ask him anything you want to help you decide if he should be president."

Jason felt his heart should be racing based on the seriousness of the discussion, but instead, the beat was steady, like a metronome pacing a musician. "I think I know the answer, but I'll ask anyway. Someone's going to die, maybe even me, but whatever happens, I'll have a hand in deciding who will be the next president. That's what's going to happen, isn't it?"

She smiled her biggest smile yet. "You finally understand! You've come to accept your role in history. You won't just have a hand in the matter, you've been chosen to cast the only vote that counts."

Hearing her words echo her killer's, his heart now pounded and he had a hard time catching his breath. "It's just as Moberly said!" His emotions roiled. "This can't be happening! This can't be real!"

With her hand still on his shoulder, she squeezed. "This is your dream, so that's for you to decide. Just be ready for Brandt, the world will remember what you say and do."

A long silence stretched as he calmed and considered everything, until finally asking the big question. "If all of this is true, tell me, if you know…why me? Why is this decision being forced on me, of all people? I mean, look at my life! It's a mess! Why would God, or Satan, or the universe or whoever want *me* to make this decision?"

Standing, she walked toward the door, then stopped, turning to face him. "Darling, as the great Sigmund himself once said, 'Sometimes a cigar is just a cigar.'"

Her delivery of the supposed quote seemed off, and her reply was not really an answer to his query. He readied to question her further when he became aware of another voice in the room, the voice of William Brandt. This startled him, and he awoke, finding himself seated in front of his television.

The trailer for *Dracula- A Time to Reap*, played with a narrator overdub. "Playing now in a theater near you."

This was the opening weekend and the movie would be the topic of his interview tomorrow night, his last interview in the series. He knew exactly what he needed to do. As soon as the clip concluded, he pulled out his phone and purchased a ticket for the next showing.

Chapter Forty-One

A night devoted to celebrating departed souls and dressing like ghouls sounds like the antithesis of modern America. Yet, Halloween is by some accounts the second most popular holiday in the country. It was appropriated from pagans in the same way Christians latched onto winter solstice celebrations as the date they chose to honor the birth of Christ. Whatever the origins, modern Americans revel in the theater of the night.

****

Jason arrived early and mumbled to himself as he waited for Anthony. "This is too important for me to screw it up."

When Anthony pulled in with a van full of equipment, he seemed surprised. "You're on time."

Picking up the heaviest cable bundle, Jason hoisted it on his shoulder. "Yeah. On time and ready to work." He reached down and grabbed a lighting case with his free hand. "Thanks again for carrying more than your fair share these past few weeks. You're the best friend a guy could have."

Anthony didn't smile. "Hmph."

They worked quickly, and mostly silently, knowing each other's preferences from their years of filming together. By the time Brandt arrived for make-up they were doing final checks on the lights and sound with the crew in place. Even with the stress Jason had put on their friendship lately, they still made a good team, and at the stroke of midnight they were ready to begin the interview.

Tonight's set was simple, but fitting for an interview with the star of a vampire movie. The boardroom of Brandtco Enterprises featured floor to ceiling windows overlooking Manhattan, and this evening an icy-blue full moon hung over the city. Jason and Anthony had arranged the seating and lights to place the glowing sphere just over the star's shoulder. Jason and Brandt would face each other seated in the same oxblood red club chairs as in their first interview. As Jason sat in his black suit and Halloween themed, purple and orange diagonal striped tie, it felt to him as if their story had come full circle.

Anthony called out the countdown in the darkened room. "In three, two, one…" With the cameras rolling, he whispered his first direction. "Camera one, push in slowly on Brandt, he's the yeast in our dough tonight. The show rises or falls based on him."

Looking into camera one, Jason introduced his guest for the last time. "Mr. Brandt, it's my pleasure to welcome you to this, our final meeting before the election. This interview, and your debate tomorrow night are all that remain of your campaign, a campaign for the ages. On top of that, you have a new movie that's just been released, so we have a lot to talk about. Are you ready to get started?"

On cue, the always stage aware actor connected with camera two. "I've been looking forward to talking with you all day."

Jason began with a softball question in what he hoped would be the best interview of his life. "Reports are that your latest film, *Dracula – A Time to Reap*, did very well on opening night. In fact, they say it might be the biggest opening weekend for a movie ever. How does that make you feel?" Jason noted that Brandt was wearing the same black suit and narrow red tie he had worn in the movie. *Always on brand.*

Brandt smiled his perfect smile, the one that put him on more covers than any other person in history. "Jason, I feel fortunate. I have the best fans in the world, and they came out in force. I can't thank them enough." He paused for a moment and then stated the obvious. "And it also helps it's a horror movie opening on Halloween weekend."

Nodding, Jason added another reason for the success. "That, and the fact that you've been in the public eye every day for the past few weeks."

A tip of the head acknowledged the comment. "It's certainly been an interesting few weeks, hasn't it? Three months ago, you would have had to be a psychic to have predicted I would be sitting here with you tonight discussing my new movie, as well as my hopes of becoming the next president of the United States. It's been an amazing turn of events."

Anthony spoke to the crew. "There's the yeast, right off the bat. Brandt's wasting no time getting this dough rising. We might be making the best pizza pie in the city tonight."

A queasy feeling hit Jason's stomach as he processed Brandt's words, and black thoughts raced through his mind. *Come on, man. Did you have to go straight to weird right from the beginning, or are you just messing with me? Because yes, I did predict you would run for president, and so did Nikki's psychic friend.*

Instead of asking those questions, he held it together and asked another easy one, trying to keep the interview on track. After all, he did have a job to do, and a decision to make. "For those who haven't seen the movie yet, tell them about the character you play."

Brandt leaned back and rested his elbows comfortably on the arms of the chair with his hands clasped in his lap. "To tell you the truth, the role of Dracula was one of the most interesting of my career. The script was quirky, yet inspiring, and the character's range of emotion was extreme. It stretched from passionate lover to cold blooded killer, and almost everything in between. Each scene required a unique and nuanced approach. It took the sum of my experience to bring this character to life in an interesting way, and not just a rendering of a caricature." He paused. "In some ways, I've been preparing for this role my entire life."

Jason felt the apparent sincerity, whether it was real or not, and asked a follow-up question. "Without spoiling it for those who haven't seen the movie, how did you feel playing the prince of the undead?"

Without missing a beat, the actor replied. "It was a blast. One minute I'm on the precipice of ruling the underworld with controlled aggression on full display, then the next I'm desperately sprinting through a forest trying to outrun the first rays of dawn. It was a rush."

Anthony leaned forward and spoke quietly. "Alright, Jason. Add a compliment with some salt and oil and knead this baby."

Jason heard his partner and was on the same wavelength. "Well, the critics love it. A reviewer for the *Times* claims you have, and I'll quote here, 'Transcended the genre.' That's pretty high praise, especially for a horror flick."

The actor blushed ever so lightly. "I appreciate the kind words, but that's not my motivation for acting, nor was it my motivation for launching Brandtco Enterprises. It certainly isn't the reason I'm running for president. I simply always strive to do my best and make a difference, regardless of what the critics might say."

With that response, Brandt deftly accepted the praise, and at the same time, deflected it by claiming a higher calling. Jason made a mental note that Brandt's time on the campaign trail had only made him better at striking that delicate public balance of basking in adulation while appearing not to need it. He also took notice this was his second mention of his run for the top office and judged it a hint that it would be okay to talk a little more about his campaign. Especially since the election was only days away.

Here we go. "Your fans are coming out in droves to support you in the movie's opening weekend. Do you think they will come out and support you Tuesday, on Election Day?"

Anthony called out direction. "Camera two, push in on the prince of the undead. Camera one, pull out a bit on Jason. He's spun the dough in the air and now we'll see if he catches it, or if it hits the floor."

Brandt sat a bit straighter, then leaned toward Jason. It was the same as when he first agreed to take the gig, here in these same offices. Just like then, Jason could sense the pull of the man's presence as much as register the movement with his eyes. When Brandt spoke, Jason felt like they were the only two people in the world.

"Would it be okay with you if we had a conversation, a conversation where you ask me the most important questions a voter might have? Ask me the questions you want answered to help you decide if you want me to be *your* president."

Barely containing himself, Anthony gave excited commands. "Camera one, push in on Jason, now! We're getting extra toppings tonight. The dough is on the pizza stone, and the brick oven is almost hot. Go for the sauce, Jason, go for the sauce!"

Jason tried to swallow, but his mouth was suddenly dry. This was exactly the decision Julie told him about, and Brandt was serving up the opportunity on a silver platter. Finally, enough saliva was produced, and he was able to respond in measured tones. "I've been waiting to have this conversation. Shall we begin?" The candidate relaxed outwardly, but Jason had the feeling he was in the room with a dangerous animal hidden behind a flimsy curtain.

"I've been waiting as well. You can ask me anything."

Caution ruled Jason's emotions, at least for now. "Alright then, let's get the basics out of the way. Are you qualified to be the leader of the free world?"

Shifting, as if to get comfortable, Brandt smiled again. "You're right. This is the easiest part, at least on the surface. The constitution spells out two requirements for the job - be a natural born citizen and at least thirty-five years old. So, strictly speaking, I'm qualified. But that wasn't really your question, was it?"

Jason remained cool and in control. "You're a political newcomer who has never been elected to any public office, not even a local schoolboard. Now you expect America to believe you're qualified for the top job in the land?"

Opening his hands, Brandt accepted Jason's direct challenge to his credentials. "In our great country's history, we've had lawyers, soldiers, businessmen and even another actor rise to become president. Many, like me, never held elected office before either, so I won't be breaking new ground on the first Tuesday in November. But I sense your question runs deeper. You want to know if I've got the abilities and toughness to lead our nation, in good times and bad. Is that right?"

With an unyielding stare, Jason nodded. "Do you?"

The trained actor looked directly into camera two. "No man can honestly look you in the eye and say they know they can handle every possible emergency or crisis perfectly. We're all human, and I'm sure whatever decisions I make as president will be second guessed by some, no matter how favorable history may later judge."

Now he turned his gaze to Jason. "What I think you really want to know is, 'Who is this guy and does he really have the right stuff?' I can assure you that I get the people of this country. I've been poor and forced to worry about an uncertain future. I've worked hard and started a business, and over the course of years I've hired many thousands of fine people and provided good benefits with excellent wages. But even that's not the full answer."

He turned to face camera two again, looking straight into the living rooms of America. "What's most important is that I get what this generation does now affects every generation that will follow. That's why I gave away that carbon trapping technology. This race is bigger than either candidate, and the world needs a president with that perspective. This is who I am, and these are my experiences."

The answer seemed to silence even the hum of equipment in the room, until Anthony whispered. "Camera two, the moon is rising above our candidate's shoulder. Pull out to keep that big pepperoni in frame, and while we're at it, add some to our pie."

Jason audibly exhaled. "That was some speech, and if I were your typical political reporter, I would want to talk more policy. But, as you and I have discussed, I bring a unique set of experiences myself to this interview. Let's go unconventional, into uncharted waters. Would that be alright with you?"

The biggest smile of the night met Jason's stare. "I would like nothing better, and I'm sure my fans will agree."

A half-crazed grin formed on Jason's face. "Let's talk about the real unknowns then, the unknowable. For example, do you believe in spirits and the afterworld?"

Anthony almost came out of his director's chair. "Did he just throw sardines on our perfectly good pizza?"

"That's more like it." The candidate beamed. "Any politician can talk about safe stuff like deficits and terrorism, but my fans want to know where I stand on these kinds of issues as well, so let's talk about them. Polling suggests that more than ninety percent of Americans believe in God, or a universal spirit, and you can count me in that number. The same poll suggests that just over half of us believe in the probability of extra-terrestrial life as well. So, yes, I do agree with most Americans that there are things out there that are real, even if we can't see them."

His answer indicated to Jason that Brandt had practiced his response to questions like these, and he had turned a potentially negative issue into a political plus by siding with the majority of voter's beliefs. Not for the first time, a thought came to mind. *Damn, he's good.*

Jason decided to take another shot. "I understand your general thoughts on the matter, but let's get specific. During our first conversation before the campaign began, you mentioned your dreams of your mother, dreams where she told you things. Dreams where she even gave you specific advice. Do you remember us talking about that?"

Brandt looked more comfortable than any candidate should when answering questions like these. "Of course, like it was yesterday. What would you like to know?"

Anthony leaned back with a look of resignation. "Camera one, push in on Jason. Thank God those were pineapples instead of sardines a moment ago, but Jason's going to shove this pizza in the oven, whether the toppings or temperature are ready or not."

Jason paused as the camera zoomed in. "You've said that you have those dreams, and that over time, you've come to believe her visits are just projections of your unconscious mind. You said that it's just how your brain works to help you process information. But what if she exists as some kind of spirit, like ninety percent of Americans believe?"

William Brandt didn't hesitate. "Jason, have you ever had a dream that was so intense, and seemed so real, you would swear it really happened? Has anything like that ever happened to *you*?"

While William Brandt didn't hesitate, Jason did. *He knows. He knows about Julie. The son-of-a-bitch knows.* Silence built tension, and Jason knew he had to say something. "Uh, yeah. I suppose I've had that kind of dream. I suppose everyone has."

Brandt nodded like he was in the catbird seat. "Well Jason. That's what those dreams are like. Then I wake up and know that no matter how intense the vision, or how real it seems at the time, this is the world of the living. Only the living make decisions here."

Anthony sniffed loudly, then spoke to the team. "Camera two, pull out and get them both in frame. Smells like the crust is perfect and sounds like the pepperoni is sizzling. Let's hope Jason doesn't burn us all down."

Jason realized he had been played into checkmate. Brandt framed the issue as even if he were to believe his mother was a spirit, only us on this side of the veil actually make decisions for the living. All that was left to do was gracefully end the interview. "We're down to the final days of the campaign and I want to thank you for inviting me and this crew along for the ride. This has been an experience I'll never forget. I hope these conversations have helped America get to know you better as the nation prepares to vote on Tuesday. I would also like to add my congratulations to you on the opening of your latest movie. I personally think it's your best work to date. Do you have any last words for your fans tonight?"

The candidate squared to the lens as the Hunter's Moon perched over his shoulder. "Jason, we set out to do something different. These interviews weren't supposed to be the same old, same old where everything is scripted and canned and the candidate talks from their bulleted points. I think we succeeded. There has never been another campaign like ours, and America owes you and this crew a debt of gratitude."

He paused, and his smile nudged up in the slightest way. "In closing, I would like to ask that my fans and supporters look at me for who I am, and what I stand for. If you would like to see someone real like me get elected, then please go to the polls on Tuesday."

Anthony stood with a smile on his face. "That's a wrap, everyone. The pie is perfect and there are plenty of slices to go around."

Chapter Forty-Two

Humans have the ability to see things from different points of view. The phrase, 'Walk a mile in someone else's shoes,' is an example of trying to look at a situating from another vantage point. Our founding fathers took this concept further, putting a 'third eye,' on the one-dollar bill. They were implying that God sees all. Nothing is hidden.

****

Jason stood cradling a tumbler of bourbon, looking out the living room window of his apartment. His eyes were locked on his typical New York City view of the building next door as it was slowly illuminated by the rising Sunday morning sun. That was what his eyes saw, but his mind overrode the visual input, drifting from one stored memory to the next. Hazy vignettes of hanging out with Julie on lazy weekend afternoons blended seamlessly into vivid flashbacks of waking with the vivacious Nikki at the Ritz. Clips from his bizarre dreams joined his cycling memory loop, as did snippets from his interview series with Brandt. When the tumbler emptied, he refilled it and everything played again as the building next door was bathed in ever brighter sunlight.

He started drinking as soon as he returned home, after finishing the editing with Anthony of the Halloween interview and uploading it to the internet. He hadn't even bothered with changing out of his suit, simply taking off his jacket and loosening the purple and orange tie. On his third refill he sensed a presence standing beside him, and he knew who it was. "Hello, Julie. I've been expecting you."

She answered serenely in her basic little black dress. "I know." She smiled at their reflection in the glass. "And look at you. You've leveled up to be able to see me while you're awake."

Her words didn't ruffle him at all as he rocked the ice cubes against the side of the tumbler. "I suppose I've been working pretty hard to reach this state." Together they stood silently, watching the last shadows of the prior night disappear. He finally spoke again. "Tonight's the night, isn't it?"

"Yes." The response was spoken softly, but direct.

Taking a long sip, he savored the distinctive caramel and vanilla notes. "Any last lessons from history? Maybe a reenactment of John Wilkes Booth killing Abraham Lincoln?"

She touched his arm as if to reassure him. "Only one more lesson to go, but first, tell me what you've learned from our time together."

The next sip was longer than most, and his mind rewound to the first lesson Julie had taught on the subject of assassinations. "Ari Salzman taught me that sometimes you have a chance to kill a monster before the beast begins devouring thousands, or perhaps even millions of souls. It's a hard choice that must be made, that is if you are truly dealing with a monster." He stood quietly in thought. "Is William Brandt a monster?"

"The rules are clear in this matter. That is for you to decide." Julie redirected the conversation. "What else have you gleaned?"

The sun continued its daily mission of blanching the bricks of the adjacent building, turning their dew dampened hue to a paler, baked version of themselves. "Jerome Jordan taught me that simply changing jobs can change history. Lee Harvey Oswald gets into the Texas Book Depository because Jerome's not there, and a year later America gets a Civil Rights Bill passed. Maybe I shouldn't even go to the debate tonight?"

She purred. "That decision is entirely yours, dear. But there's no need to decide right now, it doesn't start for hours."

A few minutes of silence passed before Jason spoke again. "I'm still deciding what lessons I learned from the Prescott Carver assassination. All I know for sure is that it seems to be the fulcrum for everything. Your murder, Nikki's folks, Brandt entering the race. They're all tied to that event. That can't be a coincidence, can it?"

A head tilt preceded her answer. "The full investigative powers of the FBI haven't figured it out either, so don't beat yourself up, just focus on what you do know." Her dark eyes met his in the glass again. "Of what else are you certain?"

Jason answered more quickly this time. "I know that Leni Riefenstahl had choices. We…I mean I, asked Brandt different questions than the mainstream media. All in all, I'm proud of what me and Anthony put out there. Only history will tell if we got it right."

"I'm proud of you, too." She rubbed his arm. "What you did will be remembered forever."

That response made him swallow hard. "And what exactly does that mean? Will I be remembered like Leni? As a tool of evil?"

"That's above my pay grade. I just know your work will be remembered. Now, come on. Tell me, what else do you recall?"

He sighed as he replayed the highlights from the past few weeks in his mind. "I know the fact that William Brandt had an affair with Nikki's birth mother is the biggest coincidence ever, or…or…or William Brandt is involved in something much bigger, something I haven't figured out yet."

She stared at the window, just like her husband. "What else you got?"

His left hand joined his right in holding the tumbler. He strummed his fingers on the cool, sweaty glass. "I know that true believers and the mentally ill are often the perpetrators of these kinds of public killings." He stopped talking and looked at his reflection more closely, especially the dark circles under his eyes. "Am I mentally ill?" He smiled at himself. "On second thought, don't answer that."

She punched the side of his arm as she teased back. “Don’t talk like that. I’m the most real thing in your life right now. Keep going, tell me all you’ve learned. Everything.”

Closing his eyes, he replayed the past few weeks. “Let’s see, what came after John Lennon? Hmm. That’s right, Ronald Reagan. I learned that Hinkley was a terrible shot, and that a secret service agent will gladly trade his life for that of the president’s. That about sum it up?”

She leaned against his shoulder and spoke jokingly. “You’ve learned so much more than that, haven’t you? Like how much you love hanging around reality stars from dating shows.”

Lowering his head, he chuckled. “Kyna and Cordell. How could I forget them? Am I supposed to learn something from them, or are you just busting on me?”

The giggle told him all he needed to know.

Turning to face her, he took another drink. “So, task master, am I ready? Is your work complete? Am I ready to meet my destiny?” He felt her lean in close and put her arm around his waist, and it comforted him.

“Almost, darling, almost. Before you go to the debate there are a couple of facts I’m allowed to tell you…now.”

His left arm wrapped around her, matching her embrace and he could feel her coolness even through his long-sleeve shirt. Today, it didn’t faze him. In fact, it felt reassuring and natural. “Somehow I knew this was coming.”

She glanced up for a moment, and her red lips smiled. “Now you’re ready to hear it all, I know it. You’ll have every bit of information you need to make your choice. You ready?”

His pulse remained steady. “It’s time.”

She looked back at their reflection in the window and their eyes locked. “If elected, Seymour Wellington would live up to his nickname of ‘Mr. War.’ He would go down as the second president to launch a nuclear attack. Unlike in Harry Truman's day, we're no longer the only world power to have those kinds of weapons. It would be bad."

Jason didn't blink, but he did swallow. "And Brandt, what kind of president would he be?"

Julie squeezed his waist ever so gently. "If elected, the world would see relatively peaceful days. There will even be progress in Mid-East peace. Prosperity and a reduction in greenhouse gasses would happen, just like he said."

Time seemed to stand still as he considered her prophecies. "Sounds like a no brainer, so I know there's a catch." His voice lowered, sounding gravelly. "Why must there always be a catch?"

She leaned her head against him, still in his embrace. "That's just life, Jason. That's just life."

Once again, he thought it funny that a dead woman was explaining the nature of life, and he laughed softly. "I guess you have a perspective on things I can't match. Go ahead and tell me, what's the hidden thing that turns everything upside down?"

Cold hands clinched a little tighter. "Now, don't be mad when I tell you this. My instructions were clear you could only be told after you completed all your courses. Promise me you won't be mad."

Jason sighed. "I've waited long enough, just tell me."

"Alright. Now remember, you promised. Okay, here goes. Remember your promise."

He raised his voice in frustration. "Just tell me already."

Her words were brief and to the point. "William Brandt is directly responsible for my death. It wasn't his idea, and he didn't want it to happen, but he didn't stop it when he could have."

The contents of Jason's stomach surged upward and it was all he could do to keep from puking. He yelled. "Did you say what I think you said? William Brandt? He's responsible? I sat beside him on set after set…he looked me right in the eye…and he…he knew? I was certain something about him was off!"

She nodded. "They do say he's the greatest actor of his generation."

Jason's cheeks burned and anger quickly became his primary emotion. "That bastard…that bastard will pay!"

Julie pursed her lips. "There's more, if you think you can handle it."

For a moment he thought his knees might buckle, but her embrace kept him upright. His vision blurred. "More? There's more?"

"Yeah. You sure you don't want to sit for a minute?"

Rage ran through his veins and Jason answered through gritted teeth. "I can handle it, just tell me the truth. Tell me everything."

"You know I would have told you sooner if I could, it's just the rules made me wait."

"Whatever, just tell me everything! Now!"

She steadied her enraged, wobbly husband. "Brandt signed off on the killings, but Moberly and his partner actually did the deeds. Guess who swung the knife that ended my life?"

Beads of perspiration now ran down Jason's face. "Quit beating around the bush! Just tell me. I have the right to know!"

Speaking softly in the face of his outburst, she filled in the final piece of her murder mystery. "I've told you before that your instincts are quite good. You thought he was bad news the first time you met him. Secret Service Agent Artimus Fraser isn't just a jerk, he's a killer. My killer."

Jason's head swam, filled with images of Seymour Wellington's lead security agent. "I'm going to gut that son-of-a-bitch!" His rage bloomed in full technicolor as he broke free of Julie's embrace. In a profanity laced rant, his foot caught the edge of the Persian rug, sending him and his drink in a freefall. The tumbler crashed into shards of crystal glass on the floor, as his head hit the coffee table simultaneously, bringing stillness to the room.

Chapter Forty-Three

Each person on the planet makes tens of thousands of decisions every day, and they mainly fall into three categories. The vast majority will have a barely perceptible impact on an individual's life trajectory. Choosing between red wine vinaigrette or ranch dressing at lunch rarely changes a person's future.

The second category is when one of those routine decisions has unexpected major consequences. You decide to try a different coffee shop, and the cute barista smiles, then chats with you. It leads to marriage a year later. How could you have seen that coming?

The third class of decisions is the one most people think of as 'decisions.' We all know this type. Should I go to the state university, or go deeply in debt to attend an Ivy League institution? Do I take the job that moves me across the country? These are the big decisions, and we know that whatever path we take, our lives will never be the same.

****

After clearing the security line at the journalist's entrance near the back of Radio City Music Hall, Jason's mood was immediately lifted. Nikki Broussard stood before him glowing. He took in a deep breath and approached her. "Hey, I wasn't sure you would be here tonight. You look great."

Standing statuesquely, she wore a creamy coffee-colored wool suit with matching cape. When she smiled, a dimple formed in her right cheek. "How are you doing, Jason? Better, I hope."

He lied. "Yeah, I'm feeling good." He was excited to see her and he spoke without thinking. "Now that the campaign is over, I can finally catch up on my sleep. Perhaps we can get together sometime, maybe have dinner or something?" He immediately regretted his words. *Too fast...* Her eyes seemed to size him up, and he knew that even after a shower and shave, he still looked like crap.

"Yeah…sometime. Listen, I need to find my seat. Mr. Brandt has invited me to watch the debate from his guest box. Says he wants his favorite reporter to have one of the best seats in the house."

His cheeks reddened. "Of course, go find your seat. It was good seeing you again, and I mean it, you really do look great."

She walked away and his shoulders slumped in his slightly rumpled black suit. He felt alone in a sea of backstage activity. Because of the assassination of Prescott Carver and the late entry of William Brant as his replacement, this final debate had been pushed back as far as possible, just like his selection of Senator Juanita Hernandez as his running mate. Jason stood as still as a totem pole as what he learned from Julie left him unsure of his next step.

A familiar voice boomed from behind. "Mr. Simmons, there you are."

He turned slowly and tried to mask his growing internal turmoil with a smile. "Agent Merino. Looks like we made it to the end. Are you ready for some fireworks tonight?"

Merino smiled broadly. "I know agents aren't supposed to talk politics, but I really hope Mr. Brandt does well this evening. From what I've heard, he's still down in the polls." His gaze lifted. "Would you like a word with him? He's over there, in make-up."

A wry grin crept across Jason's face. "I'd love a word with the man."

The candidate caught a glimpse of Jason as he stood beside Agent Merino in faded light, just beyond the high-wattage lights ringing the large mirror on the opposite wall. "My good luck charm is finally here. Come closer, Jason. I'm stuck in this chair until Linda gets done. She's an artist with a powder-puff."

The young woman, with a lime green ponytail sprouting from a bleach blond mop of hair, looked up from her work and winked into the mirror at both Jason and Brandt. "I'll bet you say that to all the girls."

He smiled his million-dollar smile as he spoke to her by way of the mirror. "Only to the most talented, my dear, only to the best." She blushed and went back to her work with what looked to be even more concentration.

Brandt turned his head ever so slightly to address Jason. "We're almost to the finish line and I couldn't have done it without you. Our unconventional campaign has allowed us to almost pull even, and that wouldn't have been possible without you and Anthony." His eyes darted. "Speaking of the chef, where is he? I thought you two were joined at the hip."

Play it cool, don't make a scene...yet. He rubbed his forehead, trying to assuage his throbbing head. The gesture also occupied one of his hands to keep him from reaching out to strangle the man responsible for his wife's murder. "He's on vacation. Stowe Mountain, I believe. He was ready for a break."

The head bob from Brandt was barely perceptible. "Good for him, he deserves it. But you, you are here. Why didn't you join him? Your work is done, isn't it?"

The hair on the back of Jason's neck bristled and he could feel his face reddening. His head lowered, and he continued to rub the spot that pounded hardest until he was sure of how he wanted to answer. "I felt I needed to be here, after all, how many times will I have the chance to see history made?"

Linda added finishing touches and removed the protective smock, wishing the actor good luck. "Break a leg!"

Those two exchanged a few words, then Brandt turned and extended his hand toward Jason, who didn't respond. "Something the matter?"

Jason glanced around at the swarm of secret service agents milling about the backstage area. He leaned close to Brandt and whispered. "I know. I know *everything*."

Brandt stiffened a bit then grinned curiously. "Oh, do you now?" The grin lingered, then his face changed as if hearing a director countdown to begin filming. "I'm glad someone does, because I don't know what you're talking about. I'm just a guy trying to do what's right for his country. Thanks again for all that you did to get me this far. Now, if you'll excuse me, I have a debate to win."

With those parting words, Brandt walked away, leaving Jason standing beside the chatty Agent Merino. "The debate will be starting in just a few minutes and it's going to be a war, an all-out war. Wellington will be gunning for Mr. Brandt, and he'll be firing right back. When the smoke clears only one of them will be standing, and it will be clear to America who should be president."

Jason felt unsteady. *War...gunning...firing back...when the smoke clears.* The words repeated and swirled as he tried to gain his balance. *Why! Why does everyone have to talk like that?* Jason realized he was about to pass out, like the day Agent O'Reilly came to his office.

Merino must have noticed the signs. "You okay? You look a little green."

Nodding, Jason recalled the doctor's admonitions from his hospital visit a few weeks earlier. "Yeah, I think I'm alright. Just a little dehydrated from all the travel."

The agent had a look of concern, or pity, Jason couldn't tell which. "I think you'll be comfortable over here, Mr. Simmons. You'll be out of the hubbub, but you'll still be able to see everything. I've scouted the building and I personally think it's the best seat in the house." Merino made sure Jason was seated, then excused himself and was back in seconds with a glass of cool water.

Jason kept his feelings in check, but responded sincerely. "Thanks man. I haven't been feeling myself lately."

Merino listened, while at the same time keeping his eyes on his assigned candidate. "I know what you mean. This venue has my senses on high alert, like when I was in Afghanistan. You know what that's like, you were there. This place has too many people, too many doors, too many places to hide. I'll be glad when the night is over. You never know who might have planted a bomb or something."

Jason shivered once. *Damn it, Merino! Bombs? After what happened to me over there, that's the last image I want in my head.* Taking a few deep breaths, he regained his composure. Drinking some water had a positive effect and he was better able to take stock of his vantage point. Curtains, and the scaffolding supporting the lighting kept him hidden from the audience, though he could see them. He spotted Nikki in the second level balcony box, just off stage right, and she looked amazing as she mingled with media tycoons and other invited Brandt pals.

Turning, he could also see the beehive of activity behind the stage. Secret service agents guarding both candidates had taken posts at strategic locations, as crew members made final adjustments to light and sound. He was also hidden from most of them as well. Most importantly, he had an unobstructed view of the debate stage.

His stomach knotted as a voice came from behind. "Is this where the losers hang out?" Secret Service Agent Artimus Fraser strode up as if he were the landlord. "After tonight, you can both go back to your little worlds."

Jason's thought was to charge the man, but for some reason his legs wouldn't respond.

Merino stepped into the breach. "So says the man who has seen a twenty-point lead dwindle to less than five. This debate will settle things once and for all. By the way, my guy is as loose as I've ever seen. How's yours?"

Fraser's sneer didn't come on all at once, instead it appeared in slow-motion, as if he had spent years of practice in front of a mirror, perfecting the look. "Don't worry about Wellington, he's ready." He stepped back. "I'll see you also-rans later. I've got work to do."

After he walked away, Jason shared his true feelings. “That man’s pure evil.”

Sighing, Merino shook his head. “I don’t know if I would go that far, but I’ve never understood people like that. I meant what I said. Mr. Brandt does seem to have an energy surrounding him today, even more than usual. I think he’s going to crush Wellington.” After a half-beat, Merino changed the subject. “Will you be alright here, Mr. Simmons? Like Fraser, I need to get back to work.”

Jason was more than happy to wave him off. “I’ll be fine. You’ve wasted too much time on me already. Go take care of whatever it is you need to do.” Now he could sit by himself in his hidden nest, alone with his thoughts amid the growing crowd. His mind whirled with visions of personal revenge. *Fraser is easy. Live by the blade, die by the blade. Exactly thirteen thrusts, one for each that he put into Julie, and I have to put my weight into them, too. An eye for an eye, as they say.*

From his vantage point he could see the comings and goings of technicians, journalists and well-wishers as the pace of events quickened leading up to the announcements instructing everyone to take their seats or go to their assigned locations. *Brandt’s not as simple. A knife would do, but that seems too... seems too kind. He could have stopped Julie’s murder and he didn’t. Just killing him won’t be enough, he has to suffer. He has to hurt for a long time, then beg for mercy, but none will be given.*

The stage lighting changed, signaling the networks had gone to their last commercials before the event began. Jason now saw mushroom clouds in his mind. *But, if Brandt is dead, then what? Would Wellington really push the button...send the missiles? Start a nuclear war?*

The moderator kicked off the evening and Jason strained to hear the words. They were muffled, like an invisible woolen wall were between him and the stage. *Please, no! Please don’t let this happen to me now!*

The dream started like it always did. Julie stood up from the table at Luigi's preparing to leave…

Chapter Forty-Four

Dreams have always fascinated humans. In the earliest recorded writings of our species there are mentions of dreams and their interpretations. In many cultures, dreams are not episodic events, but other realms of existence. Depending on the peoples, that realm can be inhabited by dead relatives, strange animals or even gods.

****

Jason's dream universe was inhabited by a single entity, and now he felt her cool presence beside him. "Why did I have to watch that dream again? Why did I have to see all that blood, your blood, one more time?"

Julie again wore the same black leggings and white blouse she was wearing the night she was murdered. Tonight, she looked paler than usual, making her lipstick seem all the brighter. She also seemed subdued instead of her bossy, bouncy dead self. "It's important to remember how we got here."

The debate raged on in the haze of the other realm, and occasionally Jason could hear the roar of the audience in support of one candidate or the other. "It's all about tonight, isn't it? It's somehow up to me. Whatever decision I make settles everything, right?"

Julie touched his cheek with the tips of her fingers, then gently slid them down his neck until her hand rested on his shoulder. "Yes. That's why you're here, but it's also why everyone is here." She gripped gently. "It's why Brandt and Wellington are here. It's why Nikki is here, as well as Fraser and Merino. It's why everyone's here. They have all played their parts bringing us to this point. All is as it should be tonight."

Jason heard a loud outburst from the audience and turned his gaze. "Sounds exciting out there."

She slowly joined his stare. “The audience is certainly getting a show. Both candidates brought their A-Game, it’s nip and tuck. Punch and counter-punch. It’s really quite a performance from both men, but don’t worry, you’ll *probably* have plenty of opportunities to see the replay.”

“You mean there’s still a chance I don’t make it out of here alive, right?” They sat in silence as he waited for whatever came next.

Finally, Julie pointed to an open case used to carry the biggest lights for the set. “There’s a hidden compartment under a false bottom. If you pull that black tab, you’ll find a surprise.”

He studied the case, and in the low light behind the stage it took a moment to pick out the tab from the matching black case lining. “There’s a gun in there, isn’t there?”

She moved her head up and down, confirming his guess. “It’s a Glock 19 Gen 5. I think you know how to handle one of those.”

Jason’s eyes bounced between the black case and his wife’s equally dark eyes. “Who put that there, and what are you asking me to do?”

Julie tilted her head as she stared back. “It doesn’t matter who put it there. You just need to know someone else did their job, and got the gun here. As for what to do with it, we’ve covered that subject at length.”

Another cheer went up from the audience, but Jason’s eyes remained locked on Julie’s. “Just to be clear, I’m supposed to kill either Brandt or Wellington?”

The hand that had been resting on his shoulder slipped off. “As I’ve said from the beginning, this is your choice. But tonight, you will decide each man’s fate, as well as the course of history.” Applause emanated from the auditorium. “It’s time to make a decision, Jason, the debate is almost over. It’s simple, really. Kill one, or the other…or neither.”

His primal desire was to pick up the pistol and gun down Brandt. "He could have prevented your death, and didn't. How can a man who murders be allowed to win?"

Vacant eyes locked with his. "It's your decision, Jason. You can't miss from this distance. One shot and my death will be vindicated."

Walking over to the case, Jason pulled the tab and picked up the gun. It felt cold, like Julie. He took aim at William Brandt and put his finger on the trigger. With a firm squeeze the deed would be done. His wife's murder would be avenged…and he would be killed or spend the rest of his life in prison…while the rest of the world experimented with tactical nuclear warfare.

His still hands began to quiver and he lowered the weapon. "As much as I want him dead, I can't do it. Can you forgive me?"

"I've accepted what happened to me, and hope you can as well." She pointed. "Would you like to kill Wellington? I've told you what he's going to do if elected."

Jason's shoulders shrugged. "I'm worse than Ari Salzman. I'm not even going to aim, because I know if I didn't have enough anger to kill Brandt, there's no way I can kill Wellington. I guess I'm banking on Brandt pulling out a come from behind win and save the world."

She stood in blood-soaked clothes and returned an enigmatic Mona Lisa smile. "Then would you kill Agent Fraser? He's the one who actually put the knife in me, and as I recall he seemed to enjoy it."

Jason's stomach roiled. "I'll deal with him later. I promise you that. He will pay."

Touching his shoulder, she added new information. "There is no later, only this moment. You are the person that decides, but you must know that other actors are taking their cues from your action or inaction. Your decisions have consequences."

"I don't understand. He's gotten away with it for a long time. What will a few more days matter?"

Her eyes widened. "If you wish to *personally* avenge my death, now is the time. Take your shot, or don't. It's your choice."

Swallowing hard, he raised the weapon again. In his mind he could see Fraser bringing the knife down into Julie's body over and over. Her blood spilling faster with each blow. He felt sweat beading on his forehead as his finger bent around the trigger. *One squeeze and it's done.* His heart raced. *I have to...* He stood with Fraser in the sight and considered the method and timing of his retaliation. "I'll get him, he'll get his due all right. But not now…later, when I can do it with a knife. He needs to experience his death exactly as you did. An eye for an eye."

The Mona Lisa smile returned. "You've been given the opportunity for revenge, and you passed. Your responsibility was to decide, and you have. Put the gun away and watch history unfold."

As instructed, he put the pistol back into its hidden compartment. As soon as he secured the lid, a movement behind the curtain caught his eye. Agent Fraser was breathing rapidly and his right hand was flexing.

Julie pointed. "Just watch. He's going to take matters into his own hands. In less than thirty seconds he's going to kill again."

"What?" Jason's head whipped toward Julie. "What did you say?"

As calmly as reading the directions of a recipe, she repeated herself. "I said, in less than thirty seconds he's going to kill again. He's going to kill William Brandt. You made your decision, and it's final. Now others are free to make theirs."

Looking back toward the agent, Jason saw a man who seemed more agitated with each passing second. "Is he that crazy?"

She nodded. "He's a true believer, and he also has dreams. Unless you stop him, he's going to do exactly as he's been told. Even though you've stashed the Glock, you still have agency over how this ends."

Jason stood frozen as Fraser discreetly pulled his pistol from its holster.

He grabbed Julie's shoulders and shook. "What do I do? What do you want me to do?"

The response was as firm as it was predictable. "You know the rules. This is your decision."

He wanted everything to slow down, give him time to think, but Fraser had his own timetable and the gun was now fully exposed. A sound came forth from Jason's mouth as if it had sprung to life of its own accord. His voice exploding in the loudest volume achieved in the entirety of his life. "Nooo!!!"

Fraser spat an angry two-syllables toward Jason. "Los-er!"

The few seconds of their interaction gave another man time to react. Agent Mesa Merino flung his body halfway across the stage. He was spread mid-air in front of William Brandt when Fraser pulled the trigger. The bullet exploded in Merino's chest and pandemonium engulfed Radio City Music Hall. Blood spatters covered the stage as some agents trained their weapons on Fraser in a hail of gunfire as others rushed both candidates to safety.

Chapter Forty-Five

Riddles and puzzles are as old as mankind. Our most ancient written texts include Samson's riddle in the Old Testament of the Bible, and the Greek riddle of the Sphinx. They can be sources of amusement, like working a crossword puzzle, or be entertaining as with a night playing charades with friends. The human mind naturally enjoys figuring things out.

****

Over the last forty-eight hours, Jason endured six multi-hour interrogations as the FBI tried to figure things out. He hadn't been charged with a crime, so he wasn't required to don prison garb, but he hadn't been allowed to go home either. The suit that was slightly rumpled upon his entry into the facility now looked as if a bum had slept in it for a week. Before his seventh grilling, he was allowed time alone in a holding cell. The bed was a concrete bunk covered by a wafer-thin mattress. Sleep came quickly.

Julie sat beside him in an orange jumpsuit, rubbing his hand. "How are you holding up?"

Joining her in sitting, he took a deep breath, then exhaled slowly. "I haven't had a drink in two days…it's been rough."

"I'm sorry, sweetie. I know it can't be easy."

"That's an understatement." He gave a head tilt, with a weak grin. "But I think the worst is behind me. The mother-of-all-hangover-headaches is better today, and my hands are barely shaking now." He held them out and the tremors were scarcely noticeable. "See?"

After he lowered them, she patted his left hand and voiced what sounded to be genuine relief. "That's all I ever wanted. To see you make it through this mission in one piece was my goal all along."

With assurances of his physical health, she changed subjects. "How are the interviews going?"

"Being questioned by the FBI is remarkably easy when you tell them the truth. I've told them everything I know, everything I'm sure I know anyway. I'm still not sure about this part." He shot her a wicked grin. "They had a doctor check me out, and he said hallucinations can be another symptom of alcohol withdrawal." He paused for a beat. "Are you even real?"

A giggle indicated her mood. "Believe whatever you need to believe." Her easy attitude turned serious on a dime. "What are they asking?"

"It's the same questions over and over, asked in slightly different ways. I know they're just doing their jobs, but there is nothing left to tell… Well, nothing I could tell them that could be corroborated."

Red lips widened into a knowing smile. "The truth will set you free, just like Martin Luther King said. So, exactly which truths have you told them?"

Jason massaged his temples as he summarized what he had repeated hundreds of times already. "Let's see. First of all, I've told them I've met the now deceased Agent Artimus Fraser exactly twice in my life, once at each debate. That I haven't had any other contact with him…ever. That's a biggie."

Julie squeezed his hand. "Yeah, that's huge. You need distance between you and the men who assassinated one presidential candidate and almost killed another."

Jason rubbed his stubbled chin. "They've questioned me about how I seemed to be the only one who saw Fraser draw his gun in a backstage full of law enforcement." He shrugged. "I tell them over and over again, I sat where Agent Merino told me, and I happened to have a good view."

"Good. It's easy to keep your story straight when you're being truthful." A grin eased on Julie's face. "Speaking of stories, I've heard that since this last assassination attempt, Powell Moberly is singing like a parakeet in an opera house. His description of Agent Fraser is dead on as the same man that helped him kill me and Nikki's parents. He knew some things, but he's been kept mostly in the dark about the big picture, you know, rules and all. Moberly and Fraser's names are now among the most famous of political assassins of all time."

Pondering the thought, Jason shook his head. "I guess it takes all kinds." He contemplated the idea for some time. "Speaking of those two, I've been turning something over and over in my head and I can't figure it out. Both the FBI and I want to know the same thing. Why did Moberly and Fraser kill you? It makes no sense."

The dull eyes seemed soulful. "You know the rules. I can only tell you what I'm allowed to tell you. How about we talk some more and I bet you figure most of it out on your own. What else have you told them?"

"Really? We're going to stick with this rules crap? The mission is over, for God's sake. You've said so yourself. Give me a break."

Silently, she kept rubbing the back of his hand. After a few minutes she continued. "These rules are in place for a reason. They've protected you so far, and because of them you're going to walk out of here a free man, with the rest of your life ahead of you." She persisted. "What else have you told them?"

This sigh was one of resignation, knowing she wouldn't stop until she got her way. "Fraser and Moberly also killed Nikki's folks, and obviously they know about my relationship with her. They've done everything short of water boarding me with questions about that seemingly random murder and how it can't be a coincidence that I'm connected to it as well. It's really easy to answer their questions, because again, I don't know anything."

She clasped his hand in encouragement. "You're doing great. Just hang in there and keep telling them the truth. What else are they asking?"

He thought for a moment. "Oh, yeah. They're really questioning me hard on that religious thing, that Friends of Fatima group. From what I've pieced together, both Fraser and Moberly must have been members of some super-secret society, a splinter group bent on keeping Brandt from becoming president. The way they're asking their questions, it sounds to me like it was one of those groups like QAnon, who takes a couple of facts, then spins them wildly, sucking in the gullible, or those seeking answers in a confusing world. Am I right?"

"Rules." She shrugged.

He was sick and tired of hearing that word, but let it slide. "Anyway, those have been really quick discussions because I know absolutely nothing about those nuts. They've asked me about a million questions, but generally they are related to those three things. My relationship to Fraser and Moberly, how does yours and Nikki's parents' murders fit in, and what do I know about that fringe group. That's what they want to know."

Lacing her pale slender fingers together, she beamed. "Terrific. You are safe and their investigation will end here. Fraser was shot and killed by another secret service agent, and Moberly will spend the rest of his life behind bars."

Hearing the word 'agent,' Jason's thoughts went to the other man who died that night. "It sucks that Fraser killed Merino, he was one of the good guys."

Julie's head tilted. "On the plus side, he's being revered as a national hero, and he's reunited with Meredith. There are worse fates." Her expression changed as she smiled. "And after the polls close tonight this will all be over for everyone."

Jason's interest was piqued. "I haven't exactly been able to keep up with the news in here. Is Brandt going to win?"

"He was just behind Wellington before the shooting, but by surviving an assassination attempt by the bodyguard of his rival, he's expected to get more than eighty percent of the vote. How do you feel about that?"

Sitting as still as a tombstone, he examined his feelings. "I hate the bastard for killing you…and yet."

She waited in silence as he collected his thoughts.

"I hate him, but hearing Wellington's not going to win and plunge the world into a nuclear nightmare…that seems right."

She leaned back against the wall. "Good, I'm glad you've got at least some level of peace about all this, and just so you know, Brandt's calling you his lucky charm. While you're getting grilled in here, he's portraying you as a national hero out there, almost on the same level as Agent Merino. It should really help your career." Her smile transformed from relief to mischief. "Would you like to know how this all fits together?"

Jason pounced on her words like a cheetah on a gazelle. "Of course I would, but what about your precious rules? I thought you couldn't tell me stuff like that."

"You're right. I can't *tell* you anything, but I can *ask* you questions. I'm willing to bet you know more than you think. You just need a little help connecting the dots. Shall we give it a go?"

Suspicious, he answered her question with a question. "Why are you doing this? Why are you helping me?"

"Jason, in everything we've been through, one thing has remained constant. I'm your wife, and I care about you, even if I am dead. Would you like a little closure or not? Personally, I think it would do you some good."

His misgivings were not completely allayed, but unanswered questions gnawed at him. "Go ahead, ask away."

Rubbing her hands together, she began. "Let's see, where do we start? I know, we'll do this chronologically. What's the earliest event you can connect to Brandt ending up in the White House?"

Closing his eyes, he thought. "I guess your murder. That's what started it all."

She shook her head in apparent frustration. "No, no. no. That's where we came into the story. My question to you is, what is the earliest event, any event, that you can connect to Brandt ending up as president?"

He looked at her, and the implication of the question registered on his face. "You mean this goes back to his mother's murder?"

"Now you're getting the hang of this, but think, is there an even earlier event that you are aware of that is tied to his rise?"

Jason concentrated, trying to remember every fact he could about Brandt. "Something about his grandmother, maybe? In that first stop in New Orleans he mentioned something about her conniving to arrange a marriage of his mother to a rich man. As I recall, she ran off with a sailor. Right?" He pondered the implication of that sentence. "This plot goes back that far…generations back? Is that what you're saying?"

Julie corrected him. "I'm not saying anything. I'm just asking questions."

There was a far away, wild look in Jason's eyes. "Please, continue asking questions… if you would."

She winked. "It would be my pleasure. You've already mentioned Brandt's mother's murder, and he brought that up in your first interview. I'll let you draw your own conclusions there."

"It's definitely connected. That's his pipeline to this unseen world, like you are for me."

"Then chronologically speaking, what would be the next fact that's connected to all of this? Take your time."

It took a moment, but it came to him. "Brandt did that movie in Ireland when he was still an unknown actor. It was his big break. He told us about it in the Beach episode." Seconds passed as synapses in his brain fired. "That affair was all about linking him to Nikki even before she was conceived. Is that possible?"

Julie shrugged. "You know the rules. Do you want to continue? It's only going to get weirder."

He sat dazed but intrigued. "In for a dime, in for a dollar. Ask me another."

"Let's see, what do I want to ask next? Since you brought her up, let's talk about Ms. Nicole Broussard, shall we? What do you know for sure about her? Start at the beginning."

Jason rubbed the spot between his eyes, like he often did when his headaches were most severe. While this headache had eased, the habit remained. "From the beginning, hmm. What do I know for sure? Well, I know that her mother was involved with a bishop, and he's her biological father. That man later went on to become the cardinal charged with keeping the Secrets of Fatima safe. That can't be a coincidence, can it? Is the Church behind this?"

She quickly redirected him. "Don't get lost in the weeds speculating about responsibility. Stay focused on what you know."

This topic triggered a question that had been on his mind for a while. "Is this whole thing God's plan? Did He use me?"

"You know I can't answer that question." She looked at him sympathetically. "Let me ask you this. Would it make you feel better if you believe that, whether it's true or not?"

Silently, he pondered her question. "I think so."

"If it helps you, then believe it." Julie shrugged, not seeming to care about his choice one way or another, turning the questioning to the subject they were just discussing. "Let's get back to figuring everything out. What else do you know for sure about the life story of the one and only Nikki Broussard?"

Eyes closed, he reset and again sifted through his memories. "Let's see…she was raised by a nice couple from Boston that she assumed were her parents, I know that. And I know she got a Journalism

Degree from Harvard, but ended up working at the *National Conversation*."

Julie interrupted. "Does that seem odd to you? A degree from Harvard, but working at that rag. How does that make sense?"

Jason had posed the same question to Nikki, so he was ready with a response. "It was because of her drug and alcohol abuse…" He paused as his stomach fell. "That was the plan all along, wasn't it? She was always supposed to end up there, wasn't she? Even the conflicts with her parents were part of the master plan. All of her struggles and addictions literally drove her to that tabloid."

He took another break from the conversation to gather his thoughts. "The plot was always to have a gifted writer on staff at a place like the *National Conversation* so she could write wild and crazy stuff about Brandt. I mean, he's the biggest star of our time, so she was bound to do story after story about him. It built buzz with a segment of voters he would need to reach, even before the campaign began. It really didn't matter if the stories were true of not, it was all about gathering steam and attracting interest, even before he was a candidate. Even the fact that her mother had a romance with Brandt became a headline. Everything combined for years of publicity."

More connections formed in his mind and the truth rang as clear as a musical note. He looked squarely into her black eyes as he voiced an epiphany. "I see now. Her parents were murdered to send her back to the bottle, and your murder did the same to me. That made us both ripe to accept Brandt's offer of joining his campaign. He needed her in the digital tabloid space, and me and Anthony in the more mainstream celebrity space to fuel his unconventional campaign. I'm right, aren't I?"

She looked at him impassively, then her eyebrows arched. "You know a lot more than you thought, don't you? Let's switch topics for a moment, shall we? Tell me why you think we've been fixated on this assassination stuff. Why did we talk so much about Kennedy and Lennon? What was that about?"

"You know that was some crazy shit, right?" He tapped his chin in concentration. "And all those costumes, hilarious. I guess you wanted me to understand the motivations of those who would kill famous people. You wanted me to make an informed decision when the time came. Right? You wanted me to understand the implications of my Sunday night decisions."

"Is that the only reason?" She tilted her head.

Jason sensed the outline of another puzzle piece, so he concentrated harder. "Hmm. Let's see." He closed his eyes and William Brandt's last interview popped into his mind. "Now that I think about it, I think both you and Brandt wanted me to go into those tapings with an edge, unsure if I were dealing with a devil or a saint. Anthony saw the magic from the beginning. Every one of those episodes went more viral than the one before." The implications became clearer. "The more off balance I was off-screen, the more sizzle Brandt and I had on-screen. Me and Nikki didn't just need to be *involved* in the plan, we needed to be *on edge* to give our interactions with William Brandt that little extra spark. Everything mattered, and it was for the sole purpose of getting him elected instead of Seymour Wellington."

Another revelation struck like a bolt of lightning, and this one was much bigger. "And that's why you had to die. You said Brandt didn't *want* you to die but he didn't stop your murder. If he had, I might have done those interviews, but if you weren't dead, they wouldn't have had the pop that Anthony and the rest of America saw and felt. He *had* to let you die to get elected and prevent Wellington from becoming president."

She left him alone in his head as the totality of the puzzle piece came fully in view. He stated it plainly. "Brandt made the kind of decision that Ari Salzman didn't. He traded four lives for millions. He let you, Nikki's parents and Prescott Carver die so the world wouldn't be plunged into nuclear winter. Wow."

She pursed her lips and nodded before speaking. "You're doing so well. Now, we're almost finished. Why don't we talk about what happened at that final debate? Tell me exactly what you remember."

Standing, Jason began pacing in the small cell, replaying the drama from Radio City Music Hall. “A lot went down and I’m having a hard time remembering it clearly. That hasn’t exactly helped me with the FBI either.”

Julie reassured him. “Do your best. Just tell me what you remember.”

Going back and forth on the eight-step trip from one end to the other, he continued. “It was like…like the universe gave me chances for revenge…and I passed. After that, all hell broke loose.”

Sitting silently in her orange jumpsuit, she seemed content to let him figure it out in his own time.

After two more laps, he spoke again. “Okay, there was a gun there and I don’t think it was a coincidence it was the same model I had practiced with in Texas. It evidently hasn’t been found or I’m sure I would have had some difficult to answer questions from the FBI.”

Julie watched him complete a few more laps before posing another question. “Who do you think put it there?”

His hands laced behind his head as he continued walking. “Assuming it was real, and not a figment of my imagination, which is definitely possible, then I would assume it would have to be someone from the secret service. It would have been easy because it’s the same make and model they carry.” He took two more paces and the lightbulb went off. “Shit, Mesa Merino led me right to that seat. He planted that gun…but why?”

He continued walking and talking, trying to answer his own question. “He told me he was nervous about protecting Brandt in that place. Maybe he wanted a little back-up. He saw me at that firing range, so he knew I could handle a gun.” His shoulders rose. “Maybe that’s it?”

She reflected his doubts. “Think that’s it? Really?”

The shoulders now fell. “Nah, Merino was a nice enough guy and was always willing to give his life to protect Brandt, but he never struck me as an outside-the-box thinker. I don't believe he could have concocted a plan like that." Then inspiration struck. "Meredith Merino. His dead wife told him to do it, didn't she? You mentioned you talk to her, and he's still grieving. He would have done anything she asked."

Julie's head tilted and she shrugged. "That's one explanation, but could there be another? Maybe one where someone *wanted* you to take your revenge on Brandt?"

The pacing continued for several long seconds as he thought. "Fraser! He wanted *me* to kill Brandt. Somehow, he knew you were giving me lessons in assassination for your own reasons, and hoped I would take my revenge and gun down Brandt. That was the scenario where I would have been killed and he lived, and would have made Wellington president. When he saw me put the gun away, he knew he had to become the backup plan. He would kill Brandt himself, just as his partner, Powell Moberly had done to Carver."

"You are so close to understanding everything. Can you feel it?"

His hands shook and his stomach quivered. "Would you ask me another question?"

"I'm here for you, Jason." She drew in a deep breath. "You said that Brandt needed you to be on edge in those interviews, right?"

"Yes. And it worked. Everyone's commented on our unique chemistry in front of the camera."

Julie spoke deliberately. "Brandt knew of Fraser's plan to kill me, and didn't stop it." She paused for a moment, squeezing her hands. "But why did *Fraser* want to kill me and Nikki's parents in the first place?"

The question stopped him in his tracks. "Why indeed?" He swayed unsteadily.

Speaking softly, she patted the empty space beside her on the thin mattress. "Have a seat before you fall, dear."

Unsteadily, he did. The harder he pondered the question the worse his head felt, but he was determined. “I have to figure this out.”

“Jason, I believe in you, and deep down, you know the truth. You know the truth about Fraser, and you know the truth about yourself. Take your time and you’ll figure it out.”

He forced his eyes shut as hard as he could, and focused with all of his might. His body rocked forward and back with each word. “Why…would…Fraser…want…you …dead?” His rocking slowed, and he squeezed his eyes even harder, and when he did, he saw flashes of light on the inside of his eyelids. “Why?”

Jason’s whole body tensed as he fought to answer the question, his stomach rolling and on the verge of pushing its contents up. Eyes still closed, he screamed, as if to the universe. “WHY!!” His entire body jerked, as if touching a frayed electric cord, and the answer formed whole, from nothing. “It was a bet!”

With the revelation his chest relaxed and he could breathe again. “Am I right?”

Julie’s lips turned up ever so slightly on the ends. “I can only ask questions, not answer them. Why would you believe there was a bet involved?”

Speaking like it was as obvious as the slightly crooked nose on his face, he replied. “It’s Fraser’s last word to me, right before he tried to shoot Brandt. He called me a ‘loser.’”

“And what do you think he meant by that?”

“Me and the FBI thought he was talking about the campaign, but he wasn’t.” With his heartrate returning to normal, he spelled out his theory. “It’s the only thing that makes sense. There might not have been an actual bet, but Fraser believed I would become so unglued by your murder that I would actually kill Brandt when I learned of his role in your death. Meanwhile Brandt believed I wouldn’t go through with it.” Jason drew in a quick breath. “So, Fraser killed Nikki’s parents because he thought her downward spiral would draw me in, increasing my instability and the chances I would gun down Brandt."

A silence fell as neither said a word. Reflecting on what he had nearly done, a tear formed. "The truth is I was right there on the edge, willing to do it. Fraser's plan nearly worked. I actually aimed the gun at Brandt with my finger on the trigger." He shuddered. "Fraser was almost right about me, because I almost did it. I came within a hair of killing William Brandt. But I didn't. That's why he called me a loser."

Julie's smile widened. "And why didn't you do it? You had the means, motive, and opportunity to take your revenge. Why didn't you pull the trigger?"

Jason's shoulders sagged. "I like to think that deep down I'm a good guy, but I also know that in different circumstances, I could have killed Fraser as revenge for what he did to you." He turned to Julie and grinned. "But someone kept coming to me with lessons, lessons that didn't make sense at the time." His head slowly nodded. "I needed to see the big picture and understand the scope of the decision I ultimately made Sunday night."

Putting a cold hand on his thigh, her voice sounded airy. "I never doubted you. Not for a second."

Before she could react, he kissed her cheek, something surely against the rules. "Thank you for saving my life."

For the first time in all her ghostly visits, Julie blushed, and protested...kind of. "That's enough of that."

Jason spoke with wonder in his voice. "Now it all makes sense. We all played our roles perfectly. Me, Nikki, Merino, and especially you. All of us did exactly what we were supposed to do to thwart an evil plot, and now William Brandt is going to be the president of the Unites States of America and save us from nuclear war." He put his hands on his head. "It's amazing. Four generations of planning, and the execution was flawless. Is the universe in balance now?"

Holding her hands out to each side, her Signal Red lips parted in a huge smile. “All is as it should be. You’ve played your part superbly and your involvement is now over. This phase of the mission is complete and your service has been greatly appreciated. I told you that you knew more than you thought. You figured everything out without me telling you anything.”

A deep sense of relief washed over him. “I’ll keep my mouth shut about this with the FBI. I won’t lie, but what they don’t know won’t hurt anyone, and I would also like to avoid spending the rest of my life in a mental institution.” He laughed aloud. “Who would believe a story like this anyway?”

She stood and gave him a big hug. “I’ve really enjoyed spending so much time with you lately, even with your disturbed sense of fashion.”

His embrace matched hers as he held her. “I’ll still be seeing you, won’t I? I mean, you are still my wife.”

Tears formed in the corners of her eyes and ran down her cheeks. “That’s so sweet. Of course I’ll still come around every now and then, but this phase of the mission is over. You need to get on with the business of living. You don’t need to be dragged down by a high-maintenance dead wife.”

Her words finally sounded an alarm in his mind. “That’s the third time you mentioned ‘This phase.’ I thought the mission was over. Brandt is going to be the president and the world is safe. What’s next?”

She stepped back and sniffed, then used the back of her hand to wipe her cheek. “You already know the answer. What are you going to do as soon as you get out of here?”

Once again, he was reluctant to speak of Nikki with his dead wife, but she stared at him with those black eyes until he confessed; his words barely above a whisper. “I’m going to try and patch things up with her.”

Her stare was unrelenting. “You know she’s on the wagon and won’t want to hang around with a drunk, even if you are a high functioning one, right?”

He laughed as he looked around at the cell. “Like I said, I’ve been clean for two days. It’s a start.”

Julie swallowed hard. “She looks great. The *Times* offered her a job, but she turned them down. Says she likes the freedom at the *National Conversation,* and she’s writing a multi-part explosive exposé on all of this. Clean living seems to agree with her.” She swallowed again, and her black eyes bore into him. “Why do you think she quit drinking like that? I mean she loved those dirty martinis, then just went cold turkey.”

Jason started babbling what he had been telling himself. “It was a rough time for both of us. I mean she found out about her biological father and…” He stopped mid-sentence as he understood what his gut had been telling him all along. When his voice returned, he spoke in a whisper. “She’s pregnant.”

Tears now flowed freely. “I know it’s against the rules to tell you, but this one time, to hell with the rules. I think you should know. You’re going to be a father, like you always wanted, it just wasn’t meant to be with me. And, by the way, your granddaughter will do amazing things in the next phase of this mission.”

Jason stumbled backwards, falling on his ass hard on the concrete bunk. “What…what did you just say?”

Putting a hand on the door, Julie turned to her stunned husband one more time. “Me, you, Nikki, Brandt…it’s all just been the opening act. Seventy-five years from now the *really* important things happen. Now, get some sleep, tell the FBI what they need to hear and get out of here. You’ve got a family to raise. The world depends on it.”

The End

Made in the USA
Coppell, TX
11 December 2021